...And Now Hello

...And Now Hello

To Belinda
This is my second book.
Hope you like it!

Carole L. Kelly

Carole L. Kelly

Dream Catcher Publishing, Inc.

ISBN: 0-9712189-1-9

Library of Congress Catalogue Number: 2005923960

Published by Dream Catcher Publishing, Inc.
3260 Keith Bridge Rd. # 343
Cumming, Georgia 30041

www.DreamCatcherPublishing.net

Email: dcp@DreamCatcherPublishing.net

My thanks to Kim Peters, and don't say "I told you so!"; to my team at Health Check who gave me the time to write; and to my wonderful husband, John, who still loves me even though I deserted him for months while I put my story down on paper.

Dedicated to my daddy, Arthur J. McCreary, who lives in heaven.

I miss you, Dad.

To my mom, Burdetta F. McCreary, who lives in her own world and doesn't really know me anymore. I miss you, Mom.

"Hello, hello
I don't know why you say goodbye
I say hello"

Lennon/McCartney

...And Now Hello

Prologue

New York City, New York

Victorino Nico Salvatore, or Victor, as everyone called him – though most of them felt his name was too much of a mouth full and wondered what in the world his parents were thinking to put this kind of burden on a tiny newborn baby –smiled at the thought of what his full name had brought him when he was a small boy in school. A very small, shy boy, with big eyes and a bright smile - that was who he was as a child. Those traits had given the other larger and tougher boys the excuse they needed to tease, chase, and brutalize him at every opportunity. But the little, shy child had grown up to be a big, muscle-bound, handsome boy by his mid-teens and all of the years of abuse had come to an abrupt stop. Some of those boys, those who had made him freeze in fear when he came upon them on his way home, were some of his best friends today and had been for many years. Of course those friendships were forged much later after he had taught each of them that he was not that little boy anymore. Yes, he was Victorino Nico Salvatore, a big man with a big name, and it suited him. Now everyone called him Victor and that suited him equally well.

Glancing down at the clock on his dash, he grimaced and pushed the Mercedes he was driving to go faster. "Damn," he cursed slapping his hand on the steering wheel. The traffic had held him up and he was running late. Although he had been told that they would hold the plane until he got there, he still worried that they would take off before he arrived.

When he had received the call earlier, telling him he should come and that this would be his only chance, he knew they were asking the

1

impossible, but he had to try. "They better not leave without me," he muttered as he pushed his car a little faster, hoping he wouldn't pick up the police since he was doing over eighty at every opportunity that the traffic afforded him; which wasn't often enough.

As he raced through the Lincoln Tunnel toward Teeterboro Airport in New Jersey, he thought again of how his life was going to change after this meeting.

What he was feeling was a new love. One he never expected, one that had hit him hard and taken his breath away and he'd be damned if anything, or anyone, was going to take it away from him.

Teeterboro Airport was a general aviation facility built to relieve the airport traffic created by small aircraft. The traffic could now be diverted from the larger New York airports, like JFK and LaGuardia, over to Teeterboro. With only two runways, one running northeast to southwest and the other running north to south, the airport only allowed planes weighing less than 100,000 pounds access. Victor knew he was meeting a small jet so this explained Teeterboro as his destination.

Victor had never been so excited and he was feeling blessed beyond anything he had ever dreamed. His heart was soaring. He was in love. He was so in love that he was almost sick from it. He knew the next couple of hours were going to complete his life and give it the purpose he had searched for. He was going to take care of this meeting, get his life in order, make some real changes, and then finish one last piece of business. And, he thought pausing to smile, he was not taking "no" for an answer anymore. Chuckling to himself, he thought about how much fun all of it was going to be. Just thinking of her made his stomach turn flips.

"Whoa buddy," he cautioned himself out loud, "you better get your mind back to the business at hand and take care of this first." Then he laughed with pure joy.

Finally, after what seemed an eternity of freeways and off ramps, with signs that had promised he would be there soon, he left the road and saw the airport tower and the runway where the small planes were allowed to fly out of New Jersey. A small jet, with its engines running, had started to taxi from the far left end of the runway toward the airport tower. There were no other jets in sight, so Victor assumed this was probably the one he had been instructed to meet.

Slamming his car to a stop outside the small gate that led to the private planes and the runway, he spun the car sideways, rocketing gravel up in a violent storm of flying debris. Struggling with his seatbelt, he pulled the keys out of the ignition, jumped out of the car, slammed the door shut, and started racing toward the runway where a small jet was approaching the tower as it gathered speed for take-off.

"Stop," he yelled, as if anyone could hear him. "Come back! Stop, damn you! I'm here like I promised!" Sprinting toward the runway into the path of the moving jet, Victor saw the aircraft pick up speed. Trying to position himself on the runway, where the pilot couldn't miss seeing him, he waved his arms frantically, hoping he wasn't too late and that they would stop their take-off.

At that exact moment, when Victor thought he could have it all if they would only stop the plane, when his whole future hung in the balance, when life was so damned good, a tremendous explosion ripped through the sky, turning the plane into a huge, red-orange ball of fire. The percussion of the blast, like a wall of burning steel, slammed into him and lifted him off his feet, hurtling him through the air where he was tossed and turned like a rag doll in the powerful fury of the plane's destruction. Finally, there was only the sound of crunching, burning metal bounding and scraping across the runway and the smell of burning fuel.

It was an inferno, devastatingly beautiful from the airport tower – devastatingly destructive if you were one of the unlucky passengers on the plane.

Victor knew only the fire and pain and the stench of his burning flesh as he fell his final time and surrendered to the darkness that swept down on him. Then he saw her face, his love, his life, all he had ever wanted and he closed his eyes in peace, and whispered her name one last time…. Julia.

Chapter One

The Airplane

Julia Bertinelli, a.k.a. Elizabeth Grant, sat and tried to concentrate on breathing deeply as she stared out the window of the Delta 767ER jet plane bound from Buenos Aires, Argentina to Atlanta, Georgia. Her knuckles were white and her heart was hammering as the plane lurched and jerked through the turbulence created by a storm raging in the atmosphere over the Windward Islands in the Caribbean.

The pilot had announced, several times, on the intercom that he was going to climb up and out of the storm, but at 35,000 feet the violent jerking had only increased in its intensity.

The nice looking, elderly gentleman sitting next to her, in the first-class section of the plane, kept patting her hand and trying to reassure her, in a soft voice, telling her she shouldn't worry and that he had flown this route many times and that he had made it through far worse storms without a single scratch.

She just wished that he would mind his own business! Surely, they were heading for disaster, destined to crash and to die a horrible death. But, the little man seemed to be unaware of their imminent doom and just continued to murmur and pat, murmur and pat.

How she wished that Victor were here.

Whoa, she thought, where had that wish come from? She was surprised by the thoughts of him that had entered her mind, even though the night they spent together would certainly never be forgotten, at least not by her. Blushing, she told herself to stop thinking about that night when they had made love and how he had given herself totally to Victor, for a few hours. She had work to do and she needed to remain focused. Still... she couldn't help thinking that she could get through this ordeal much more easily if Victor were sitting beside her, instead of the little man who was her seatmate and who obviously couldn't save a flea if he needed to. Victor with his broad shoulders and beautiful eyes... Stop it, she told herself. Just stop it!

Julia was afraid of flying and this storm wasn't helping. Trying to relax she forced herself to take another deep breath and to loosen her hold a little on the armrest between her and "Mr. Murmur". She thought the name she had given him was very appropriate and he had not disappointed her since he continued to pat, murmur and wish her well.

If anyone who knew her could see her now, she mused, trying to relax by taking another deep breath, giving "Mr. Murmur" another reason to start patting her hand more rapidly, they wouldn't recognize her. She looked so damned horrible!

Julia had asked her hairdresser in Argentina to cut her hair very short, and to spike it, glue it, or whatever they did to make it stand straight up; bleaching it as light a shade of blonde as possible since her natural hair was black.   This new "do", as she liked to refer to it, accompanied by a whole gob of make-up, which she never wore, tight toreador pants, a very low cut, skin-tight top, which her seat mate had made a valiant attempt to ignore, blue contact lenses to hide her amber

6

eyes, and high heeled platform shoes, all made her look a little like a hooker or a fifty year old woman with very, very bad taste.

Her friend Annabelle, who owned Julia's favorite dress shop in Buenos Aires, had assured her that no one, not even her best friend, would recognize her. When Julia had looked in the mirror following her transformation, she had almost lost her nerve to carry out her plan. But, Annabelle told her to focus on her objective and to stop whining.

Unfortunately, Annabelle was right; the outfit and hairstyle met her objective in spades. The trouble was that she had a whole suitcase of outfits just like the one she was wearing, with lots of large jewelry, skin-tight/push-up bras, panties that were disgraceful and big purses. Worse still, this is all she had to wear during her trip. It was almost too much to bear, since she favored beautifully tailored suits and pearls, not this look.

Oh, well, she sighed, resigning herself to stick with her original plan. She didn't really know what she was walking into and she didn't want anyone to recognize her until she was ready to unveil her true identity.

A year ago, Julia would have never dreamed she would be leaving Argentina, and that her husband - Julia stopped. What should she call Roberto? Husband? Yes, they had been married before God in a cathedral. The fact that she was already married at the time and had two children, and that Roberto had kidnapped her during a crime of passion, did cloud the issue a little. Her loss of memory during the abduction certainly helped Roberto's cause and thus they were married. Anyway, that man who had taken her away from everything she knew and all those she loved, her abductor, the man she should hate was the man she came to love and cherish; cherish beyond words. But now he was dead and she was alone and although several months had passed, she was still devastated by the loss of him.

The husband she had left behind over twenty years before, David was now remarried. Certainly he and her two children couldn't possibly believe she was still alive after all this time. In other words, Julia's, a.k.a. Elizabeth's, life was just one terrible mess.

Thinking back to her life in Argentina, she admitted that she had loved Roberto. He was all that she had known for twenty years before he told her the truth. She had lived with him day in and day out and her every breath was shared by him. He was the one who taught her how to ride and how to defend herself. Out of the tragedy of her soul and the secrets he kept from her, he taught her that she could still love. He had become the world to her and she had loved him with a manic intensity, believing the sun and the moon rose in his eyes; missing him when he was away even for a few moments. He was the kindest, most gentle, soul, and a fiercely intense lover. And, it hurt her every time she took a breath because she still missed him so much.

Who could, or would, ever understand this kind of love? She knew it made no sense and she hated herself each time she thought about the twenty years she had spent with her captor who had been her husband and in turn, her best friend.

She had gone to a priest who blessed her and told her to forgive herself; that she could not have known about the terrible crime he had committed against her. He told her many times that the sin was all Roberto's, but this did not stop the tears falling from her eyes as she mourned and longed for the man who was dead and gone, the man who had destroyed her and her family's lives. She was torn apart by the guilt she felt for having loved Roberto, and the guilt that was slowly eating her alive.

She knew Roberto's story. She knew the reasons he had decided she was the one that would replace the girl he had loved and lost. She could even feel his pain as he confessed his crime against her, but she would never really understand what drove him to take matters into his hands and take her from Paris, never allowing her to return to the life she had left behind.

Julia sighed and let the tears fall; she knew the words on the tapes that Roberto had left for her following his death, should help to alleviate some of her guilt for loving him, but they didn't.

Roberto had decided to take Elizabeth while he was visiting Paris as part of his revenge and hatred for the Americans. But more importantly, he felt she looked like his lost, murdered love, Julia. After the kidnapping, Roberto had called her "Julia" and continued doing so for the next twenty years, refusing to allow her to use her given name, Elizabeth. In time she "became" Julia and the memories of her life as Elizabeth disappeared, like a dream you can't seem to remember when you wake in the morning.

Now she was Julia. The name Elizabeth was completely foreign to her Roberto had brainwashed her well over the years.

Discovering her true identity and that Roberto was not her husband had almost caused her to lose her sanity. Then she had learned about her children, the ones she had left behind. As the memories flooded her mind with regret, her heart squeezed tight and she thought again that she might go mad from the pain of losing them for all these years.

Now her daughter, Alexandria, was hurt and may be dying. It was so hard to believe that the tiny baby she had left behind was now a grown woman – since her only frame of reference was a photo she had of her baby's tiny hands and face covered carefully by a soft pink blanket.

The phone call Julia had received earlier, delivered another blow to her already fragile state. Her only daughter had been severely injured in a car roll over crash. Could she get to her in time? Would she even be allowed to see Alexandria?

Everyone supposed Julia was dead. No one would believe she was her mother.

Julia's heart ached. She was the one that should have raised her daughter, sharing in her memories of growing up. But that had been denied her and her little girl. Now she had to go to America and find a way to be there for her daughter, if her daughter survived her injuries.

"Why, Roberto?" she cried to herself. "Why, did you bind our bones and our souls together? Why did you do this to me, my children and my husband who I left behind and who were surely destroyed by your act of violence? Why did you leave my husband behind, to raise two babies alone in the dust of his shock and despair that must have become a way of life as time went by and the search for me was abandoned?

"Victor," the voice whispered to her. It was Roberto's voice she knew that. People would think she was crazy if she ever told them that she spoke with Roberto frequently. But lately, each time she cried out, "Why, Roberto?" the voice would whisper Victor's name, and nothing else.

What does it mean, Roberto? Why do you whisper Victor's name to me, she thought to herself.

"Victor," the voice whispered again and Julia's tormented soul calmed as it always did when Roberto spoke to her. Closing her eyes, she drifted off to a troubled sleep; one she needed since she had not rested since she learned the news about her daughter.

"Mr. Murmur" stared in astonishment. He had watched her and seen the tears streaming down her face and had assumed that she was crying out of fear. Then a strange thing had happened. She had started smiling softly and then she closed her eyes and went to sleep. Strange, strange indeed, he thought as he continued to pat her hand.

Chapter Two

Rosita stood in the NBC studio. 8H, home of Saturday Night Live, in the Rockefeller Plaza between Fifth and Sixth Avenues in Manhattan. Lauren Prescott was on camera arguing with her soap opera husband about his flirtation with Gina, his newly hired legal assistant.

They were filming another segment of the daily soap opera, "Another Day". Rosita played the character Gina, and she played her to the hilt. Gina's character was deadly and gorgeous and would try anything to in order to seduce the main character's husband. Rosita had the character nailed down and the fans loved her with a passion that rendered her the star of the show, Lauren was so jealous that she wanted to strangle the newest member of the soap.

Lauren stopped speaking and looked out past the camera lights and noticed her nemesis, Rosita, watching her from the semi-darkness behind the crew. She had a smirk on her face as she watched Lauren's performance. "Damn her," she thought.

Rosita's popularity was killing Lauren on the show; her numbers were way down since Rosita had joined the soap. Lauren hated Rosita but she was also afraid of her. She had to be careful, very careful, in how she handled this little problem. Lauren was worried. She didn't think she was going to be able to run Rosita off the show, like she had successfully done so many times before. This girl was someone to be wary of…this girl was tough.

Lauren had tried all types of sabotage, changing the script and not notifying Rosita, telling her the wrong time for the tapings, or that she would not be needed the next day since she wouldn't have any scenes; hoping that Rosita would appear to be a slacker or better yet incompetent as an actress. Rosita's reaction to these attempts by Lauren had seemed odd. She never complained. She arrived on the set every day whether she had lines or not, she made up her lines, which she did masterfully when Lauren changed the script, and she never missed a taping since she never left the studio until the wee hours of the morning.

Lauren shuddered as she felt Rosita's eyes bore into hers. She could feel the young girl's hatred and contempt. "You are in my way, old woman," she said with her eyes. "Why don't you bow out gracefully? Maybe, we can write a beautiful death scene into one of the episodes? Do us all a favor. You can't win, so why do you even try?" Lauren could hear Rosita words as clearly as if she were standing next to her instead of twenty feet away in the shadows of the set. She trembled with fury.

Lauren had been the star of "Another Day" for over twenty years and had made short work of any and all who had dared to try to usurp her position on the show. She had missed when it came to Rosita though. The young beautiful ingénue had caused a swing in ratings unparalleled in the history of the show. Everyone loved her, or loved to hate her, and her fan mail came daily in huge bags which Rosita felt compelled to empty in full view of Lauren, the entire crew and all the other actors and actresses.

The writers for the show were increasing Rosita's scenes daily, being pushed by a public who wanted more and more of her and who couldn't seem to get enough. Lauren's own role and screen time were dropping exponentially as Rosita's screen time and popularity increased.

Rosita was snapping at her heels and had Lauren on the run. In response Lauren was starting to blow her lines, which is exactly what she did at that exact moment. She could see Rosita's smile as Lauren tried to pull herself back into the scene she was playing and forget about the young girl who was taking her place on the show.

Rosita was smiling and thinking, you old cow. You can't compete with me and I'm going to take you down. It's just a matter of time and you know it.

The owners of the show had told Rosita that they had been subjected to a meeting with Lauren. They had listened to her screeching and caterwauling about Rosita, smiled politely at all the right moments, showed just the right amount of sympathy, nodded their heads in total agreement with everything she said, and then as soon as she left the room, dismissed her as a fearful, aging star, way past her prime, who was completely out of control, and who was definitely dispensable. After all, they all agreed, they had Rosita, didn't they?

The owners then called their team together and told them to get busy writing out Lauren's part, in case Lauren couldn't accept that her future in "Another Day" would consist of the role as a supporting actress and not one as the star of the show.

As they discussed this with Rosita, she had set her face so that it showed just the right amount of surprise and astonishment, coupled with the appropriate amount of humility, of course - she was an actress after all – and then she had told them, in a soft, shy voice, that she felt Lauren was an excellent actress and that surely they realized the enormity of what losing this graceful, elegant woman from the show would mean, and that they must consider how this might affect the future of the show when making their decision– liar, liar, pants on fire.

They were very impressed with Rosita's feelings of charity for Lauren who they knew hated Rosita with every fiber of her being, but they were even more impressed by Rosita's concern over what was best for the show. They knew now that they were surely making the right decisions.

Rosita had left the meeting and had danced with joy up and down the halls leading to her new dressing room. "Ding, Dong, The witch is dead. The witch is dead. The witch is dead. Ding, Dong, The wicked witch is dead," she sang as she skipped down the corridor.

Chapter Three

Private investigator, Joe McGuire, stood up; straightened his slacks and looked at his watch again. He was a good looking, middle aged man; tall with dark hair, graying at the edges, and he looked worried. He had a wide boxer's face with a tiny scar on his chin. His size was imposing and he could be very scary if he ever got really angry with you. Angering Joe was something most people avoided, at all costs.

Julia Bertinelli's plane should have landed over an hour ago. She couldn't get into the country through Miami on such short notice, so they had agreed she would fly into Atlanta instead. The international flights into Atlanta had been arriving all morning, but her flight out of Buenos Aires had been delayed due to bad weather. Joe worried they might miss their flight out of Atlanta, connecting through Salt Lake City, and on to Missoula, Montana, if her plane did not arrive soon.

Alexandria Grant was still alive, based on his latest report, but she was barely clinging to life. He wasn't sure what the Bertinelli interest was in the Grant family, but he had worked for Roberto

Bertinelli keeping tabs on them for years. After Roberto's death, he had contacted Julia to tell her that Alexandria Grant, the youngest child of David Grant, had been injured in a life-threatening accident in Missoula where she attended college. Julia had insisted that she would leave Argentina immediately, meet him in Atlanta, and then fly on to the hospital in Missoula where Alexandria hung to life by a thread after being thrown from a speeding automobile.

Pacing back and forth in front of the gate where her plane was scheduled to arrive, he thought about the plan he had worked out so Julia would be allowed to get into Alexandria's ICU room at St. Patrick hospital in Missoula. Her family would have very limited access to her room that only allowed them a few minutes each hour to visit. Since Julia was not family, Joe had been forced to pull a great many strings in order for her to enter and stay in the ICU room and see the girl.

He hoped Julia approved of his plan and her disguise. He had guessed at her sizes so he hoped everything fit. Joe was getting really anxious to get to the hospital in time. He was paid handsomely so he didn't mind waiting, but he sure hoped Julia's plane arrived soon and her rush to America was not wasted.

He didn't think they had much time to lose.

Chapter Four
Washington, D.C.

Robert Walker, semi-retired, former Director of the CIA, who should be home and not at the office, absently rubbed at his aching, left leg which was impossible.

He didn't have a leg there anymore

Walker was a fit, grey haired man of average height with a face like an aging Jon Voight - who people sometimes mistook him for - who was a decorated World War II hero, who had spent the past forty-five years working for the Federal Government and the CIA.

Damn, he thought, as he rubbed his prosthetic limb more vigorously. They said this feeling of pain - phantom pain as it was known - would go away after a time.

It hadn't and it was a damned nuisance.

The left leg was gone below the knee. They had taken it off after years of infections and several operations to try to repair the damage that he had suffered during the invasion of Anzio, Italy, over 50 years ago, when he was a young lieutenant. They had tried everything to save his limb but, unbeknownst to his doctor, Walker had actually been relieved when it was finally removed. However, that had been 10 years ago and this insufferable pain and itching was driving him crazy. The only relief was that the intense pain came and went. He enjoyed those times, those few hours, when he didn't feel like his leg was still attached to his body. The doctors repeatedly told him that the pain wasn't real, that there couldn't be any pain now and he had to accept that reality, but all the same, he could still feel the damned thing throbbing, throbbing, and throbbing some more.

Picking up his cane, he pulled himself up from his chair, and started walking around the room, hoping that this would help him concentrate on something besides his missing limb. He held a stack of papers in his hand and he wanted to read them again. Something about this guy, something he couldn't quite put his finger on, was bothering him.

"Persons Of Interest," is what the agency called men like him. Roberto Bertinelli, one of those men, was now dead based on the CIA documentation. They had been looking at him for years. To their knowledge he appeared to be an honest man living quietly in his country, who donated huge sums to charity, never calling attention to himself, while enjoying a peaceful life in Argentina. He lived way below the CIA radar, so, for some time, he never attracted more than a moments notice.

However, years after Elizabeth Grant's abduction, they had learned that Bertinelli was one of the many single males in Paris at the exact time she disappeared. It appeared he had checked out of his hotel and left the city the day before the attack, but he was still someone they had listed as a possibility. With nothing else to go on, the agency had kept him as a name in the back of their burgeoning file on one of the biggest unsolved crimes against a United States Diplomat, on foreign soil. It was one of the most baffling he had encountered in his career.

David Grant worked for the FBI and he and Walker, as a member of the CIA, were long time friends and had worked together on many cases over the years. Walker had never told David about

Bertinelli since the CIA had nothing that really tied him to his wife, Elizabeth's, disappearance.

But, something was bothering him about this man, he thought trying to remember what it was that was nagging at him. What had he missed, he thought?

Robert tossed the papers down on his desk. It was probably time for a break; maybe he should go out and have some lunch. Since David did not know anything about Bertinelli, he decided he wouldn't mention any of this to him. It was probably nothing anyway. Elizabeth had been missing for over twenty years. It seemed her recovery was not probable anymore and nothing was going to bring her back. He doubted she had survived, but he would never say that to David. Maybe, he should just forget about whatever it was that was bothering him and let it go. Besides, it was an old, old case and David had enough on his hands right now worrying about his daughter, Alex.

He knew from David that the hospital had her listed as a Jane Doe when she came in from the Life Flight helicopter and it was only later that one of the students involved in the wreck identified the injured girl as Alexandria Grant. David had said that the emergency room department head had called him once his daughter was identified. David had pulled all the strings and connections he had at his disposal and a government jet had whisked him and Lainie, from Washington to Missoula. They were on a plane within one hour of the call.

I'm just getting old, Walker mused, as he stared down at the file on his desk. He had just celebrated his 70th birthday with much fanfare and celebration thanks to his wife, children and grandchildren. He knew he needed to slow down and that there probably wasn't anything in the file that he had missed. It was undoubtedly just the result of years of experience digging through documents just like this one, looking for something he had missed, then dogging the criminals, finally bringing them to justice, that was keeping him re-reading the Bertinelli file time and time again.

Still, he kept wondering, what was it about this man's file that was bothering him? There was something, but what was it?

Chapter Five
Chicago, Illinois

Brian Grant looked through his notes on eMicro, reviewing them more thoroughly this time. He was looking at the evidence of the fraud he had found when performing his due diligence for an IPO that eMicro planned for summer of next year.

The company was located in Milpitas, California, and part of his responsibility was to review the books and records, as well as the manufacturing processes, the inventory records, and the controls in place at the company. He had discovered a problem when he was going over the sales records, shipping documents and the accounts receivables.

Brian knew that one of the ways to increase inventories was to create records for product that didn't exist, to produce false shipping and receiving reports, and to file spurious purchase orders. eMicro was doing all of this and more.

When he had approached his boss, the senior partner of Hart & Newman, Barry Newman, who was heading up the offering for the

IPO, about the fraud he had suspected, Newman had studied him for a minute with no expression on his face. Then he said, "Brian, we're a young firm and you have a wonderful future here at Hart & Newman. This IPO is a big deal for us and it will put us over the top. Believe me, we won't forget how you helped us. But..." he paused, "Brian, we don't want to hear any bad news. Don't go questioning everything, just get the job done! And Brian, don't talk to anyone else, just make sure you have enough to support what you report and don't go digging any deeper than you have to. The market is right, we need to move quickly, so get it done fast, my boy!"

After that he learned that Newman had gone to college with the CEO from eMicro and that they were old and fast friends.

But, Brian did talk to someone about it. He talked to Robert Boland, "Magic Maker", as he was referred to in the firm. He was the right hand man to Newman & Hart and he was the best researcher, fact finder, information gatherer, dealmaker, deal breaker, people finder and all around guru the company had. Everyone loved him and they all thought he was the glue that held the company together. There was nothing Mr. Boland couldn't do and, for some reason, he had taken a strong liking to Brian, spending a great deal of time working with him and teaching him the ropes.

He never flinched when Brian told him the whole story. Something passed across his eyes, just a flicker, as he listened quietly. Brian couldn't tell if it was pain, anger, disappointment, disbelieve or maybe just fear, but other than that brief flicker – for just a tiny moment- Robert made no other sign that he had even heard a word that Brian said

As Robert listened to Brian, even though his face didn't register his emotions, he couldn't help but feel damned proud. Proud that a young man like Brian would stand up against Newman by disobeying and bringing this issue to him. It was probably the death knell for the company, or Brian – depending on how this all worked out - and if he helped in any way, it would also be the end of his personal career at the firm. His very lucrative career, he might add, thinking of his very comfortable lifestyle and the money he had accumulated over the years that he had wisely salted away in case of a rainy day. Yes, it appeared that rainy day was here in the form of this young man bearing very bad news. What to do, what to do, he thought?

Do I help Brian? There was no question in his mind. Newman wouldn't like it, but the die was cast.

Chapter Six
Missoula, Montana

David and Lainie Grant waited in the hospital lobby at Saint Patrick's Trauma Center in Missoula for the doctors to speak to them about their daughter, Alexandria. When they had arrived she was still in surgery and had been for over eight hours at that time. The staff had not given them much hope based on the extent of her injuries.

They had met with a young highway patrol officer who had gone over the police report and then given them a description of what he had seen during the reckless ride that had led to the accident. Alexandria had been in a Suburban when the driver lost control of the vehicle just as they had driven out of the canyon on I-90 outside of Missoula on their way to Bozeman, Montana. As the right front tire dropped off the roadbed onto the shoulder, the speed of the vehicle - which was clocked at over 85 miles per hour - caused it to flip end over end, throwing passengers out the front and back windows with each revolution.

From the extent of her injuries, it seemed that Alexandria was the first, or one of the first passengers, flung out of the speeding vehicle. The force of being thrown at such a high rate of speed had ripped

Alexandria out of her shoes. One of her boots was found in the van and the other along the roadside where the vehicle first left the highway.

She was near death when they found her lying on the darkened highway.

The driver was thrown out next and, when his blood alcohol level was tested, he was at four times the legal level and tested positive for cocaine use. He suffered severe head injuries.

Then, all the other passengers were thrown out, one by one. They left the van at varying times and speeds as the van started to slow in its rotation. One young girl had landed face down on top of Alexandria's body. She only suffered a broken wrist since she was thrown from the van during one of the last rotations. Another girl with long hair was found lying under the right front wheel of the Suburban where it came to rest on her hair. She had a broken pelvis.

The highway patrolman had pursued them for less than a mile, with his lights on and his sirens howling. The driver was weaving erratically, back and forth over the center median, before he left the road. When he told them the scene of the accident reminded him of his time in Vietnam, with the sound of crying and screaming in the darkness, some of the passengers staggering around with blood pouring down their faces, and others lying deathly still on the ground, David and Lainie started to weep.

Alexandria had been airlifted by helicopter to the trauma center where she was placed on life support because she couldn't breathe on her own. The officer didn't know anything more about her condition at this time.

David's left leg was shaking violently and his body quivered and vibrated as if all his nerves were alive under his skin. It was like an electrical shock was being placed on his chest every several minutes, as he sat trying to calm himself while trying to remember to keep breathing in and out, after the trooper finished giving his devastating report.

Sitting in a chair right off the main entrance of the hospital emergency room where he and Lainie were asked to wait, he found he couldn't control his arms or his legs. It was as if they were acting on their own. That, coupled with a strange buzz in his head, made him think he might just be dreaming. Surely this couldn't be real, he thought, as he stared at the busy emergency room filled with a mass of humanity; hospital staff rushing to and fro, babies crying, and people moaning and smells that included everything from vomit to rubbing alcohol assaulting his senses and making it all seem more unreal.

It's like a small war zone in here, he thought, filled with injured, bleeding and desperately ill patients. So what am I doing here, he asked himself?

But, somewhere back in his mind, he knew. He didn't want to face it; his baby couldn't be one of the unlucky little girls whose future might be decided here tonight. But they had told him that she was here and that she was severely injured. He prayed they were wrong and that someone had made a mistake.

Lainie took his hand, jarring him back to reality, back to the questions he had been asking for hours. Where the hell was the doctor? Why didn't someone come? What was going on? Was Alex alive? Why doesn't someone come talk to them?

As David jumped up from his chair and began to pace back and forth, a young doctor with weary eyes, dressed in green scrubs, stepped into the busy room and said, "Mr. and Mrs. Grant?"

"Yes," they both responded, turning to him.

"Hello, I'm Doctor Hunter, the trauma surgeon who operated on your daughter. We completed the surgery several hours ago. I didn't come to get you right away because we have had some real difficulty waking her. We sent her down for an MRI and there is a great deal of blood on her brain. We are going to take her back up to surgery and place a tube in her skull to release some of the pressure. I am going to let you see her for just a few moments before we go back in."

"Is she…, is she going to be okay?" David said with tears in his eyes.

"We don't know," he replied. "She has lost a great deal of blood. The bottom half of her liver was torn off and her spleen was torn in two. There was massive hemorrhaging in her stomach cavity. She doesn't appear to have any broken bones, but we have not had a chance to evaluate any secondary injuries since we had to stop the bleeding first. It was a long and strenuous operation.

We removed a piece of her liver that was separated and only connected by a small piece of tissue, because, at her age, there is a good chance that the liver will regenerate itself. We cauterized the tear and started the work on her spleen. We placed a net bag around the organ, forcing the two halves back together where we hope it will mend. If we can save her spleen it will be far better for her in the long run. That is," he paused looking sadly at both of them, " if she can survive all her other injuries.

There is a long and terrible incision on her body," he continued, "since we had to cut her from her neck to her pubic bone, but it should heal nicely over time, even though she will be left with a large scar. She has tremendous bruising and cuts from the glass that is still imbedded in her back, face and head where she was thrown through the windshield. From the extent and type of injuries it appears that she left the vehicle backwards. These are also wounds that should heal without too much residual damage. The amount of blood lost and the blood surrounding her brain are our big worries now," he finished softly.

"It may be frightening when you see her. She was unable to breathe on her own so we had to perform a tracheotomy and place her on a ventilator.

27

Shall we go up now and see your daughter?" he said gently. "Please keep in mind that she has sustained terrible injuries from the trauma caused by the accident and that her condition is very grave at this time."

***

When Lainie and David reached the surgery suite, Alexandria was lying on a gurney in the hall between the two operating rooms. David was dazed and felt dizzy and disoriented. "Why is her skin so yellow?" he thought, never dreaming he had spoken out loud as he looked at his little girl who was surrounded by machinery; lights beeping and flashing, a tube protruding from her throat, and bags of fluids hanging from a multitude of steel poles that seemed to surround her small body.

"It's from the Betadine," Doctor Hunter responded. "Your daughter was covered with mud and debris when she was brought to surgery. We cut her clothes from her body and scrubbed her with Betadine to try to avoid getting dirt into the incisions we knew we had to make. But wait," he said as he stopped and stared at his patient. "Give me a moment. Something does not look right about your daughter's legs and the way her feet are turned."

The doctor walked back to Alexandria and lifted the sheets that surrounded her hips. David could see massive, blood swollen, black and blue lumps where her waist met her hip joints on each side. It was all it took, the final blow, and David started to cry, taking huge gulps of breath and sobbing out loud. Lainie was almost as hysterical and they clung to each other holding on with all their might.

Trying to control himself, David saw the doctor walk away from Alexandria and back toward them.

"I'm sorry," he said hurriedly, looking back at his patient while he spoke. "We missed it the first time, but both of her hips are dislocated and her legs are pulled completely out of the socket on each side. When we take her back into surgery, we will need to relocate them properly. I need to ask you to go out to the waiting room so we can get started. I don't know how long this will take, but when you see your daughter next she will be in a Trauma Critical Care Unit on the fourth floor. You will only be allowed access once an hour for ten minutes and only one of you may go into the room at a time. I will come to this waiting room to see you as soon as the surgery is completed," he said, already backing away from them. "I'm sorry, I must go. I will do everything in my power to save your little girl," he said turning away and barking orders at his team of assistants who were to take Alexandria back to the surgery suite.

Chapter Seven
Chicago, Illinois

Brian and Mr. Boland had spent a great deal of time strategizing about their game plan. Brian had been surprised that Robert had agreed with him and that they were going to work together toward a possible solution.

The first order of business, they had agreed, was to find a good private investigator; someone they could trust implicitly. As he was wondering where they might find the right person for the job – Robert did not feel they should use his usual contacts - Brian 's phone rang and he heard his father's voice.

"Dad, what a surprise. How are you?"

"Brian," he said, immediately, "you need to get a flight to Missoula. Alex has been hurt. She is at St. Patrick's Hospital in Missoula. Lainie and I just arrived and Alex is in surgery. You need to hurry here as quickly as you can. It's very serious."

At first Brian couldn't believe what his Dad was saying – surely this couldn't be – but then, as his father continued speaking, he knew it was true. He could hear the tears in his Dad's voice, and time stood still as he recounted the accident and the severity of her condition.

"Do they think she will be all right?"

"They haven't told us. We just know that she sustained massive injuries from a car accident and is in surgery. We haven't heard yet what her real condition is. I hate to say this but," he choked, "if you want to see your sister, you should probably come now," and then he started to cry. Saying goodbye, Brian reassured his Dad that he was on his way.

Brian was dazed. He loved Alex and they were very close. She was his baby sister and the thought of losing her, stunned him,

Mom and Dad must be devastated, he thought. Pushing his fear and pain away, he dropped all of the eMicro documents into his brief case, called a cab that would take him to the O'Hare airport for a flight to Missoula, shook hands with Mr. Boland who wished him good luck, and hurried out of the office. He knew he should hurry.

Chapter Eight
Missoula, Montana

Lainie had taken a walk to try to calm her nerves and David was sitting alone in the trauma surgical waiting room with a small group of people, all praying for their individual family members, or loved ones, who were unconscious, on a table of steel, in a cold room, filled with bright, glaring lights, while masked nurses and doctors dressed all in green – making them look a little like Martians - cut, pumped, clipped or stapled their sleeping bodies and tried to save them from the catastrophe that had brought them here tonight.

No one in the room was speaking as they huddled over their cold, oily cups of coffee; sometimes staring and other times weeping silently as they rocked back and forth; a look of sheer exhaustion and panic on their faces.

Patients brought here and placed in the trauma ICU surgery room weren't here unless that person's life was on the edge of being ripped from this world and hurtled into the next, and everyone sitting here, waiting and dreading the outcome, knew that possibility and felt it like a horrible pain in the middle of their chest.

David wondered what had caused these other poor souls to end up here in this room with him, waiting for the words that might crush the wind from their lungs, leaving them gasping for air, shattering their hearts, forcing them to try to go on without someone they loved.

Was it a tragic automobile accident, like Alexandria's, he thought? Did it catch them unawares? Or was it a heart attack caused by overeating, weight, high blood pressure or a lack of exercise? His poor baby had done nothing to deserve this night of pain, other than to get into a car with a drunken, stoned driver. She could not have known the extent the driver was incapacitated and the consequences of what had happened to her was so unfair.

David had already lost her mother; did he have to let his baby go too? The thought was just too unbearable and David felt like he might die from his grief if anything happened to his little girl.

Oh God, he begged to himself, please let her be okay. Please let her live and let her be okay. Then he huddled over his own cup of cold coffee and started to rock back and forth as the tears fell and he sobbed. No one noticed They were doing the same thing and they understood what it took to make a grown man cry.

Chapter Nine

Lainie and David were alone now. Everyone else had gone. Each of the other parents had met their doctor as they came from the surgery suite and the room had been filled; sometimes with screams of joy, thanking God, hugging each other and clasping the doctor to their breast, telling him thank you, thank you, over and over; and other times, with screams of pain as the physician delivered the news on each patient. Every time a family struggled to remain standing as the doctor hit them with the dreaded words, "I'm sorry. We tried, but there was nothing we could do," Lainie and David had begun to cry and wail along with the others in the room.

One patient was a small, young, girl who had been hit by a car while riding her bicycle. Her injuries had claimed her; in spite of the hours the surgeons had spent trying valiantly to hold on to her tiny life. Her mother had needed to be sedated to stop her piercing screams of anger and denial.

David had been shaken to the core and Lainie had jumped up from her seat and had stood staring blankly out of the hospital window as her shoulders shook with pain for the families whose lives had blown apart; while they both tried to imagine what they would do if the doctor walked into the room and told them that Alexandria was dead.

34

As the hours struggled by, David started to lose hope that his daughter would survive her injuries this terrible night. What was taking them so long, he asked himself over and over?

It was then that an elderly, woman came into the room, pushing her broom and picking up the empty and half-filled cups littering all the tables.

Appearing to be startled that there was still someone in the room with her, she said, "Lordy, you pore li'l children. You all still here? I thought everyone was gone or I wouldn't be bringin my ole bones in here and disturbin' you folks. I know you must be sufferin', waitin' on those doctors to come out and tell you how yore baby girl is doing. I can come back later," she finished, as she started to roll her cart out of the room.

"No. That's all right," David said softly. "Someone doing something besides crying and moaning would probably do us both some good right now. Don't go. We don't mind."

"Well, I'm not sure that I might not moan a little. You know these old joints just doan want to git down and do like they used to when I was a youngun," she chuckled, "but if you all are sure you doan mind?" she said, looking from Lainie to David with great big eyes behind large, dark rimmed glasses. When they shook their heads and agreed that it was okay, she set to work, but continued talking as she pushed her cart along the room.

"I heard about yore li'l girl. I'm telling you now that yore li'l girl is gonna be jus fine. I know she will cause I can jus feel it in my old bones. She gonna be puny for a while but she gonna be jus fine. When she gits up in that ole ICU room though, you need to watch over her. You oughta git yoreself a sitter so nothin happen that you doan know about when you not able to be here," she said firmly as she wiped down a table next to Lainie and David.

"What's a sitter?" David asked, reaching for Lainie's hand, and staring up at the old lady.

"Well sir, I'm about to tell you. A sitter is a nurse, that you hire yoreself and you have them stay in that ole ICU room when you cain't be with yore li'l girl.

Yes, sir. You doan want to go and have nobody round to make sure if they's a doin things right or not. Why, my sister's husband almost got the wrong medicine give him. Might jus have killed him, if that lady they hired doan have her ole eyeballs peeled and stopped it right there.

Yes, sir. I doan let nobody, who be really sick, get in that ole intensive care without someone to watch over them. All these ole hospitals make a mistake now and again and it ain't gonna be happenin with my folks. No sir, and that's a fact!

You need to git you one of those sitters for yore li'l baby when she goes up there. Uh huh! Now, I'm not tryin to mind yore bizness and you can tell this ole lady to just shut her mouf, but I just got this feelin that I should talk to you folks and now I done did it," she finished with her chest stuck way out and her head tilted back as if daring anyone to deny anything she had just said.

"Where are you from?" David asked wondering about her accent."

"Why Louisiana when I was born, but now I mostly live here."

Lainie and David looked at each other, then David spoke. "Where would we find a sitter? You know, someone like you mentioned that we could hire to do this for us?"

"Well, oh my, let's me see, I just might have that ole card right here in my wallet. This company here done did a fine job for my sister and it ain't cost that much. The lady they sent us was real nice and she took real good care of my brother-in-law, doan you know. We all just fell in love wit her," she said smiling as she pulled out a crumpled card and handed it to David.

"You all call them. They'll set you up real good and then you doan have to worry about yore baby when you have to sleep or need somethin to eat. Our lady stayed most nights when we all needed to git on home and git some rest and it worked out, yes it did. We was there durin the day and she was there at night. Saved that boy's life; she shore did!"

David thanked her as she finished the room, gathered her supplies, wished them well and headed out the door, while he studied the card.

Mildred Avery stepped into the hall, pushed the cart and supplies into a closet, stepped out of the uniform she had on over her clothes, stuffed it in all in the trash can, pulled off her glasses, closed the door, walked past Joe McGuire, winked, and took the money he handed her.

Mildred was a part-time actress and one that Joe hired from time to time when he needed some extra help on a case. The card she had given David had Joe's service on it and he would be the one responding to David's call for a sitter.

"You did good Mildred. I'll call you next time I need some help," Joe said smiling at his friend's back as she continued walking. "Your flight back will leave in about two hours."

"Thanks, Joe," she said, losing her stooped over demeanor, her slow-stepping gait, and her southern mammy voice. "Call me anytime."

Chapter Ten

David and Lainie were waiting outside room 402C on the fourth floor, of the Trauma ICU Critical Care Unit. Alex had made it through the surgery and was in a bed across from the central nurses station. The surgery to place the tube in her skull had released some of the pressure and the swelling on her brain. In addition, both legs had been put back into their hip sockets. They had been told that if she lived, this injury could have the greatest long-term implications.

She was on complete life support, not breathing on her own, and she was still unconscious, possibly in a coma. She had received four pints of blood and might need more if her count continued to go down.

Vicky, a girlfriend of Alex's dropped by to see how she was doing. They had been in the same automobile together when the accident happened. Vicky had been thrown out right before the Suburban came to a stop after flipping over more than five times.

Sitting quietly in the waiting room, she told them what she knew about the accident.

"We were driving to the Grizzly/Montana State game. It was the final game of the season. The game was in Bozeman so we had to drive I-90 to get there. We really didn't know the guy who was driving, his name was Tom and he was older than all of us. I think he graduated a couple of years before us. It's a long story about how we ended up in his vehicle. I'll try to tell you about it another time if you want to know.

I was sitting next to the window with Alex and Beth sitting in a seat beside me. Alex was in the middle. The seat was the one directly behind the front seat. There were four kids in the front seat, the three of us in the second and five kids sitting on the floor in the back. We looked for seat belts but there weren't any. It was sort of an old car, I think.

Tom was driving really fast and weaving all over the road, and we were really scared. I kept saying "Our Father's" and "Hail Mary's" hoping God would keep us from dying. We held hands real tight and talked about rolling up into a ball if the car hit anything, plus, we thought we would be in the safest position in the car if that happened.

Alex acted really funny on the way there. She was staring out the window and when she turned to look over at us, about half way to the game, it was like she wasn't really seeing us. She said, 'We're going to die tonight. All of us are going to die tonight.' Then she turned back and stared out the window.

God, Beth and I started screaming after she said that, so Alex started begging Tom to let us out, screaming at him that we didn't want to die. He kept screaming back at her, beating on the steering wheel with his fists, that we better shut up and that we were a just a bunch of babies and that he wasn't stopping.

It happened right after that. I don't remember much, just waking up and finding myself lying on top of Eric. My wrist was broken, but, other than that, I'm fine," she said glancing at her plaster cast.

"I found Beth," she paused and took a deep breath trying to hold back her tears, "lying next to the right front wheel. I thought she was dead." It was only then that Vicky started to shake and weep. Lainie tried to hold back her own tears and be brave while she tried to imagine what this young girl must have gone through and the courage it took to come here and speak with them.

"She's going to be okay, I think. Her hair was real long and it was stuck up under the tire. The paramedics had to cut it off real close to her head so they could move her. She's in another hospital and she looks kinda funny with real long hair on one side and none on the other," she smiled slightly. "She has a broken pelvis, but all she talks about is her hair," she grinned openly. Then she grew somber once more and said more softly, "We weren't drinking or doing any other drugs," she exclaimed, wanting them to know that they were innocent of any of those charges she had heard spoken in whispers.

"We know," Lainie replied. "The hospital told us that they took some blood tests. Alex's results showed that she only had a diet coke in her system and there was no evidence of drugs or alcohol."

"Yes, that's no surprise. Alex was so straight. All she ever drank was Diet Coke. We teased her all the time to loosen up. I guess it's a good thing she never listened."

No one spoke, so Vicky continued, "After I knew Beth was going to be okay, I tried to find Alex. It was real dark and the police had some lights set up, and then the helicopter came. That's when I saw her. She was bleeding and not moving. They told me she wasn't breathing and I freaked out. I mean, like she is my best friend and all she tried to do was protect us and I didn't want her to be dead."

Lainie and David moved over to hug Vicky, who had survived an accident that should have killed them all.

Chapter Eleven

Julia Bertinelli was shaky, but the love she felt for her daughter was keeping her on her feet. She was going to do this.

She had met Joe McGuire in Atlanta after stepping off the flight from Buenos Aires. He was holding a placard with her name on it and was looking right past her, busily checking all the other passengers while holding a picture of Julia that he referred to from time to time, when she had smiled and walked up to him. She laughed as she remembered his shock and how his eyes had swept over her, examining her from head to toe, looking back at the picture he held in his hand.

"Mrs. Bertinelli?" he had asked, obviously puzzled by the strange creature standing in front of him.

"Yes, it's me. I just had a makeover. They said it would make me a new woman. I think it did. How do you like it?" she had asked, turning in a circle and smiling more brightly.

Joe had been dumbstruck. There was no way he could have answered her question. The look on his face said that Julia looked like an aging prostitute, not the beautifully dressed, graceful woman in the picture he was holding. But, Julia guessed he wasn't about to say that to the woman who was paying his bills. He was probably wondering

41

what she had been thinking when she decided on this particular makeover. He had just stared at her, silent and still, with a startled look on his face like a deer in the headlights.

Since Joe made no move to leave, Julia took his arm, forcing him to walk. "It's okay. I know how I look. For personal reasons, I don't want anyone to recognize me right now, so this is my disguise."

Getting no response from Joe, who was still staring at her with disbelief, she said, "Don't we have a plane to catch?"

That was then though, but she wasn't laughing now. Following several more flights, then baggage claim where the airline agent confessed they could not find her bag but promised to send it right over as soon as it arrived, and the ride through Missoula at rush hour, she was so burned out she could hardly stand.

Now, she was at St. Patrick's Hospital, minutes away from meeting her family that she had not seen for over twenty years, looking like a rapper chick dressed up in a Halloween costume. Besides all that, if that wasn't enough to bring her to her knees, she was feeling really bad about the plan Joe had put together.

She was all in white, wearing a nurse's uniform, full blown with white nylons and white shoes. Per Joe's instructions, she had removed most of her make-up; the red lipstick had to go he said adamantly, removed her nail polish and tried to subdue her hair a little. Her nurse's hat helped some. Well, she hoped it did.

The uniform was too tight and showed her figure a little more than she would have preferred for a first time meeting with her family. Of course, they didn't know she was anyone they knew, much less a member of their family, but she still wished her uniform were a little bigger, particularly in the hips and chest.

She thought Joe liked it, based on the way he had looked at her when she walked out of her hotel room to meet him, and the way his eyes kept drifting over to look at her during their ride to the hospital.

He was a nice guy Julia thought. Cute too. Too bad she was married, although it was to someone who didn't know she was still alive and would never recognize her because she looked like a freak. All of sudden Julia started to giggle and before she knew it, she was laughing so hard that tears were running down her cheeks and she was doubled over holding her stomach, trying to get her breath.

Joe waited, staring straight ahead at the traffic.

Once she got herself under control, Joe explained to her, while she tried to hold back her giggles, that she would be a sitter, or a private duty nurse, who would stay in the ICU room with the patient, to make sure that the correct drugs were administered, that the patient was comfortable, and to report any irregularities in the patient's care.

Then he explained that David Grant had called his agency and made a request to hire someone to perform these functions for his daughter. Julia would be the answer to that request. Julia sobered as she listened to his words. She didn't want to know how Joe had pulled this off, giving her a way into her daughter's room, but she was grateful.

However, Julia was also terrified. She didn't know anything about nursing or about the care of a critically ill patient. Joe told her to read the charts and ask the nurses on duty lots of questions about what drugs her patient would be getting and how often they would check her vitals, or blood pressure, etc. He reassured her that the staff at St. Patrick's was excellent and that, since Alex was in ICU, she would receive round-the-clock care. Julia was really only there to help the parents feel more comfortable, and less guilty, when they left the hospital for a few hours. Her shift would begin an 8:00 P.M and would end at 8:00 A.M.

Julia didn't know enough and she was filled with fear that she would do something wrong and everyone would see through her disguise. And, she was afraid to see David. It had been so long. She didn't know how she was going to be able to handle being there side by side with him and not tell him who she was.

Joe knew Julia was exhausted, so he chalked up her unusual behavior to all the hours she had spent on her feet, and tried to move past the niggling suspicion that all was not what he thought, as it related to the Grant's and Julia Bertinelli

"Would you like to wait until you've had some rest?"

"No, I want to go up now. I need to see her." Julia knew Joe was very curious about her interest in this patient, who, unbeknownst to Joe, was her daughter, but she told him nothing.

Not her daughter, she had to remind herself. She had to stay focused and remember that Alex would be her patient, not her little girl, and that was going to be the hardest part for her. She could not let anyone know her relationship to Alex. Not yet.

Julia stood outside the hospital with Joe, while she tried to get up her nerve to go in and meet with her family. They were her family, she told herself, and she had every right to be there, didn't she? Even with these thoughts running rampant through her head, she wondered why she felt like such an outsider. Then she took her hands and smoothed her uniform, straightened her hat, shook off Joe's arm and walked into the hospital where her daughter was waiting.

***

Julia, was just turning the corner approaching the ICU ward, on the fourth floor, after forcing herself off the elevator, when she saw David and Lainie, standing outside Alex's room, speaking to a nurse and a doctor.

Julia paused and pretended to read the fake chart Joe had provided, peeking over the top, while she secretly watched her husband. David was older, tiny lines surrounded his eyes, his mouth was set in a grim line, and his face was pale, strained with grief. Julia's heart was in her mouth as she studied him, wondering what he would do if he knew she was alive. Turning away, she looked at Lainie. She was also pale as a ghost and appeared to be crying while listening to the doctor. She was stunningly beautiful, even with her hair tousled, no make-up and her faced streaked with tears. No wonder David loved her, she thought, as the serpent, named jealously, slipped quietly into her blood stream and curled around her heart.

"Are you Julia, the private duty nurse hired to attend to Alexandria Grant?" a small compact nurse asked her, ripping her back into the present.

"Yes, yes I am," she replied trying to control her shaking hands by pushing them behind her back, hiding the chart.

"Well, come on then. I'm Lucy Tyler, the head nurse on this shift. Nice to meet you," she continued obviously not interested in anything Julia had to say. "Let's get you introduced so the poor parents can take some time to get a shower and maybe rest for a few hours. They've been here for about eighteen hours straight and Lord knows they must be dead on their feet. We tried to tell them that we would watch Alexandria very carefully, but they insisted they weren't leaving until they met with you and had you situated," she said with a tight mouth signifying that she wasn't too pleased with the arrangement. "We're not sure why they felt they had to hire you, but here you are, so let's get this over with."

Julia had to walk quickly to keep up with nurse Tyler who was practically running down the hall. This is not the way she wanted to meet someone she had not seen for twenty years, and with each footstep that brought her closer and closer to David, she felt as if she were going to faint.

"Excuse me, Mr. And Mrs. Grant, here is the private nurse you hired. Her name is Julia Bertinelli," she said, interrupting both the nurse and the doctor who were discussing Alex's treatment. "I need to

45

get back to the desk, if you'll excuse me," she finished abruptly as she spun on her heels and walked away.

"I'm sorry," Julia said quietly with her head down, averting her eyes.

"No problem," the doctor said, "we were just finishing. Mr. and Mrs. Grant, I will speak to you again tomorrow morning. Why don't you try to get some rest? Your daughter's condition is stable for now."

David and Lainie watched the doctor walk away before turning back to Julia who was standing nervously behind them.

"Julia. Is that your name?" David asked.

"Yes," she murmured softly.

"Do I know you," David asked looking at her closely.

"No, sir."

David gasped as he looked at her more intently, then his face blanched of color and he swayed on his feet. Lainie grabbed his arm.

"David, what is it? Are you okay?" she asked alarmed.

"I'm sorry," he said taking his wife's hand, "I don't know why, Julia, but you reminded me of someone I used to know. You look nothing like her, and your accent is very different, I mean there's no resemblance whatsoever," he said looking at Julia's bleached hair and blue eyes. "But, I swear I just saw the ghost of my dead wife when I turned to you. It was a real shock, I'll tell you," he babbled on. "I thought you were her for a moment and my heart nearly stopped. I guess it must be the stress over Alex," he finished lamely.

Julia had stopped breathing and stood paralyzed before him.

"I didn't mean to frighten you," he continued. "I guess it makes some sort of sense. You know that Elizabeth would probably be hovering around here somewhere if she knew Alex was hurt like this. She loved her children very much," he continued almost as if talking to himself. "That must be it, please forgive me."

Julia just shook her head, to indicate she understood, and waited because she couldn't speak.

"Let's go meet Alex. She is very ill and we are happy to have someone like you to watch over her."

Julia turned to follow David into the room, nodding once at Lainie, who had not said a word and was watching Julia intently. Walking on trembling legs, Julia walked behind David, while her heart broke in two.

Chapter Twelve

Julia was alone with Alex now.

David had taken Lainie back to the hotel. He would check in with her, during the night, to see if there was any change in Alex's condition, and she should call him, immediately, if she thought he needed to come back to the hospital.

Julia had heard his words as if they came from a far distance. Her eyes were fixed on the bed where her daughter was lying with what looked like the cockpit of a small airplane surrounding her unconscious body.

After David had left, Nurse Tyler had returned and listed Alex's multiple injuries and what Julia should be watching for during the night. When Julia asked if Alex had ever spoken, the harried nurse replied that, "No, the patient hasn't regained consciousness since the accident. She might never speak depending on the extent of the injury to her brain." Then she went on to reassure Julia that the nursing station was just across from Alex's door and that they would be in and out of her room on a continual basis, throughout the night.

Julia nodded all her replies and never took her eyes off her daughter.

After they were all gone, she approached the bed and sat in a chair beside her unconscious daughter. Taking Alex's hand into hers, Julia began to weep.

Chapter Thirteen

Lainie Grant unpacked her small suitcase while David showered. She was so tired but she didn't know if she would be able to sleep once she could lie down. A hot shower would probably help, she mused.

They had heard from Brian and he was on his way. That was such a relief. Once he was here, then whatever was going to befall their daughter could go on and happen. Fate would decide; it always did. But, they needed to be together, as a unit, so that they would have the strength to face whatever Fate handed them and Alex. David and Lainie couldn't do this alone.

They were a tight knit family. Alex and Brian had never caused a single day of pain or heartache for their parents. They were good, decent, well- mannered children, who played hard and worked even harder, made excellent grades and cherished their family one and all.

Maybe losing their Mom so early had forged the bond between their father and his children. She didn't know. All she knew was that when she officially became a member of the Grant family, the bond between them all had tightened into a find golden chain that no one could break; each link forged tightly against the next.

She smiled. They were all wonderful and she was blessed to be their Mom.

But Lainie Grant was worried about the nurse they had hired. David's reaction to her was a shock and she wasn't sure if she was buying his explanation of why he was so taken by her. As she was pondering his reaction, Lainie heard the shower water turn off, so she pushed the thoughts aside. It was probably nothing and right now she wanted a shower and a bed, in that order.

Chapter Fourteen

Julia had stopped crying and was looking at the terrible bruises and swelling on Alex's face. Her hair had been shaved and an enormous white bandage wrapped her head. They said there was a tube inserted into her skull to help with the pressure built up by the blow she received when thrown from the car. Julia shivered.

Holding her daughters hand, she started speaking, "Alex, you have been hurt and you have been hurt badly. You must fight. You can't give up. Listen to me. You can do this. You're stronger than you think. Fight for me baby. Fight for me and keep thinking positive thoughts. Hold on for me. I'm here for you.

I'm your Mom and I am here with you. I don't know much about your life, since I lost you, but let me tell you about what I do remember when you were just a baby, before I went away."

Then Julia slowly recounted the memories of the time she had with her daughter. How her pregnancy had caught her and David off-guard, how excited they both were when Alex was born, what a good baby she was, how she slept through the night right away, about her cute smile and the way she would take her little hands and place them on your mouth when you spoke to her, and how very much they loved her. On and on she went speaking softly, about the short time she had spent with her daughter, crying sometimes, while constantly begging her daughter not to die.

It was exactly 2:45 A.M., as Julia was speaking, when Alex opened her eyes and looked at her.

"Are you an angel?" Alex asked softly.

Stunned, Julia held her breath.

"Am I in heaven?" she asked, a small frown puckering her forehead.

"No, I'm not an angel. I'm your …nurse," Julia stammered. "My name is Julia," she managed to squeak out. "You're in a hospital, you've been hurt, but you're going to be okay. We are very happy that you are awake," she smiled.

"Are the others dead?"

"No, they all survived and all of them are going to be okay, based on what we have been told. You were all very lucky."

"Good. I'm glad," she whispered. " My friends are real nice and I didn't want them to die, like me."

Pausing, she looked straight into Julia's eyes. " I know you're an angel, cause my Mom is dead. So, I must be dead too."

Julia couldn't speak.

"It's nice that you didn't want to tell me that I died," she whispered very softly.

"Thanks, Mom," she sighed. Then her eyes closed.

Julia started to speak.

Then the alarms went off.

At first Julia didn't know what they meant, then she glanced up at the monitors. One showed a flat line, where a green line had been pulsing along, just minutes before.

"Oh no. Oh no," she said, jumping up, wondering what she should do, wringing her hands and turning in a crazy circle.

Then a loud speaker blared, "Code Blue!"

" Room 4C!"

"Code Blue!"

Almost instantly, a team of white uniforms, several hundred it seemed to Julia's reeling senses, came rushing into her daughter's room, pushing a series of carts; screaming directions, all at once, as they flowed, seamlessly, into the room like a wave of water.

It was complete pandemonium.

Julia was pushed from the room, and the door to Alex's room was slammed shut as everyone inside continued to yell out instructions to one another.

Julia bent and pressed her forehead against the closed door, and started praying that they could save her daughter and that she would not die.

***

Julia was sitting in the waiting room when Nurse Tyler walked in.

"She's going to be okay. They were able to revive her and her heart is beating again. Scared the hell out of all of us, but we did it."

Julia looked up and smiled as her heart filled with joy and as peace spread throughout her body. Her baby had made it!

"Your first time?" Nurse Tyler said.

"Yes, I've never seen anybody..." Julia tried to speak.

"It's okay. I understand. I remember my first time. I actually fainted. At least you didn't do that. It was damned embarrassing when it happened to me. The Senior Nurse gave me such a tongue-lashing I almost quit nursing," she laughed as she remembered.

"Is she going to be okay?"

"Well, it's not good that this happened, it doesn't really bode well for her recovery. We're not sure yet what happened. Did you notice anything before it happened? Did she move? Anything happen at all?"

Julia, started to tell her what happened but she wanted to tell David first, so she sat quietly with her head down.

"Well, okay, you're probably still shook up. Take your time. If you can think of anything, please put it in writing for me. I need to go now. Take care. You did real good for a first timer."

As she left the room, Julia said a prayer of thanks that her little girl was still alive.

***

Lainie and David found Julia in the waiting room after they finished meeting with the Trauma team doctor.

"Oh, there you are, Julia," David said. "We wanted to speak with you since you were in the room when Alex..." he couldn't continue.

Overcome, David started to choke and he couldn't speak. Lainie was crying, so they held each other while David tried to gain control of his emotions.

Julia looked away. The scene was too unbearable. The pain they were sharing and the love they felt for each other made her feel as lonely as she had ever felt. She stared out the window as their gentle murmurings faded in the distance as she tried to give them a tiny bit of privacy.

It's very dark outside and probably awfully cold, she thought. I should have brought some warmer clothing. Joe had given her a white sweater to cover her uniform, but it wouldn't be much once she left the hospital. She didn't have a car yet, since they didn't want to take the time to find a rental for her to use while in Missoula before coming to the hospital. She wasn't sure how she would get back to her hotel…. Lainie spoke interrupting her scattered thoughts.

"Julia, do you know anything about what caused Alex to stop breathing? Did anything unusual happen? The doctors gave us a bunch of mumbo, jumbo that we didn't understand. You know, how the cranial pressure, blah, blah, blah. We thought she was holding her own…" Then she stopped and said through clenched teeth. "My little girl, I can't lose my little girl. God, I hate this!"

David pulled her closer to him. "Ssh, Ssshh," he said, holding her more tightly. "It's going to be okay. It's going to be okay."

"She spoke," Julia said softly

"What?"

"She spoke."

Stunned, David released Lainie and jumped up from his chair, turning to Julia. "What do you mean? Who spoke? What? Did Alex speak? Is that what you're saying? That Alex spoke?"

"Yes, she spoke and then all the alarms went off, and then they were all running around screaming something, and I was praying, and it was real loud, and I thought she was dead, and that little line that was moving before wasn't moving anymore, and they said 'Get out' and they said her heart had stopped, then they pushed me out, and," Julia stopped when David grabbed the hands she was waving frantically in the air as she spoke.

"Stop, Julia."

Then David kneeled down in front of her, and took her hands into his. All at once, Julia felt such a surge of love for him that she almost screamed out into the room, "It's me. I can't do this, David. I can't pretend. Alex is my baby. Mine! And she could die and I need you." But she stopped before the words left her mouth, took a deep breath and told herself that this was not the time to be thinking of making a scene when her daughter was possibly dying, so she clamped down on her despair and pushed all that she wanted to say back inside where no one could see it.

"Julia, it's okay. It must have been very frightening for you," David said. "Take a moment, then tell us what Alex said."

"She opened her eyes and she wanted to know if I was an angel. I told her no, that I was her nurse and that she had been hurt, but that she was going to be okay."

"She asked you if you were an angel?"

"Yes."

"Do you know why, or what she could have meant?"

"No."

"Is that all she said?"

"No. She asked about her friends and if they were dead. I told her no, that all her friends had survived. She seemed to be happy about that because she said 'Good, I didn't want them to be dead like me."

"Dead like her?" Lainie asked shocked.

"Yes, that is what she said. I remember her words very clearly."

David swallowed hard, squeezing Julia's hands, unable to speak. Then Lainie said, "Was that all."

Julia started to cry, "No. Then she said, 'That was nice that you didn't want to tell me that I'm dead'. Then she said, 'Thank you', and closed her eyes.

I started to tell her, you know that she really wasn't dead, but then the alarms went off and I never got the chance."

"She thought she was dead and she was thanking you for not telling her?"

"I guess so. I'm not sure."

Then David stood up and went over to Lainie while trying to digest what Julia had just told them.

"This is good, I think. Lainie, don't you think this is good? I mean that she talked. That she was awake and could speak. I think it's good."

"Did you tell the doctor, yet?" Lainie asked.

"No. I haven't told anyone but you. I work for you and I thought I should tell you first. Besides, I wasn't sure exactly what I should do."

"We'll tell them for you," David said excitedly. "I think this is really good news. The indication is that her heart stopped and that's probably not great, but she's okay right now and I think the fact that she can talk somewhat coherently is a really good sign. I wonder why she thought she was dead? Do you have any idea?" David said turning back to Julia.

Deciding not to tell them the rest of the story, she held her breath, crossed her fingers behind her back and said, "No. I don't know."

Chapter Fifteen

Julia was safely ensconced in her hotel room. Joe was in the adjoining room of the suite and he had told her to knock on the door that joined the two if she needed anything. Other than a long bath, Julia didn't want anything except to be left alone.

David and Lainie had asked her to go to the hotel for the remainder of the night. They would stay with their daughter and she should return to work at 8:00 P.M. tomorrow night. She had left at 6:30 in the morning and she could barely wait to lie down.

She should be with her daughter right now, but she was confused about how to handle David. He loved Lainie, that was very obvious, and he thought Julia, or Elizabeth, was dead. Lainie and David had raised her daughter and, like it or not, Julia was an outsider. It just made her head ache when she thought about it.

She scrubbed at her face and head. She couldn't do anything about her hair but she wanted the contacts out and her make-up off.

The bath was running and Julia was just stepping into the tub when the phone rang.

"Hello."

"Well, you are one hard woman to track down. I've called every hotel and motel in Missoula trying to find you. How are you doing? I've been worried about you."

"Victor?"

"In the flesh."

"Victor, how did you know I was here?"

"I called Argentina and wormed it out of Carmen. Then I got on the phone and checked every flight that might take you out there and every hotel you could possibly book on such short notice. I thought you might go to the hospital, but it sure was tough finding you and I was starting to get worried that the information I received was wrong."

He didn't ask her why Joe McGuire was staying right next-door, in an adjoining bedroom in the suite, but he would know soon enough. He had a man working on it.

"Oh, Victor, I'm glad you called. I need someone to talk to. I'm having a very rough time handling seeing my family again and not being able to tell them who I am. Plus, Alex is still in danger, and I'm worn out because I can't sleep and I didn't realize how tough this was going to be," she sighed tiredly.

"Okay, so spill it. Tell me everything. I'm a real good listener, as you know, and I'm here for you as long as you need to talk. By the way, are you in the tub? I thought I heard water running." If she was in the tub, Victor hoped Joe McGuire was somewhere far away, or he was not going to be happy about it.

"Yes, but they have this little phone right here on the wall so we can still talk. Isn't that great?"

Great, Victor thought. Then he sighed. He had to push the picture of Julia sitting naked in a tub full of warm water, while another man shared the two-bedroom suite with her, out of his mind. He had to push it way back there, or he wasn't going to be able to focus on what Julia was telling him.

"Yeah, that's really great," he lied.

Julia was unaware of the picture she was sending Victor, so she just settled back into the warm water and started talking.

Chapter Sixteen

Julia found her son, Brian, sitting in Alex's room when she arrived for her shift the next day. He was so focused on Alex that he didn't notice Julia as she stepped into the room.

"Alex, I'm here. It's going to be all right now. I told you that I would always come when you needed me and even if you haven't asked, I'm here to help you get through this. You need to be strong and fight so that you can get well and come back to us. Listen Alex. Do you hear what I'm saying? It's Brian and I'm not leaving until you're better."

Turning away from his sister, Brian noticed Julia and spoke. "Are you her nurse? The one that Dad said he hired to watch over Alex?" he asked stroking his sister's forehead.

"Yes, my name is Julia."

"That's a pretty name. Alex would like your name."

"Thank you."

As he turned back and began speaking to his wounded sister, explaining to her that he was going to leave for only a few hours, and that he would be right back, Julia tried to control her heartbeat.

Her son was tall, over six feet, with black hair and dark eyes. He was handsome, somewhere between a movie star and a famous male model and he was all grown up. She could see the shadow of his beard and the strong muscles in his shoulders and arms that pulled and stretched his shirt each time he moved. Her little boy was a man now and Julia could not stop staring at him.

"Mom says that Alex spoke to you. Is that right?"

"Yes."

"That's pretty amazing. They say she hasn't spoken since. I wonder why she chose to speak to you?"

"I don't know. I've wondered myself since it happened."

"Well, I guess it doesn't matter," he said standing and stretching out his back. "The doctors say it's probably a good thing.

If you don't mind," he continued, "I'm going to go to my hotel for a few hours and try to get some rest. It was a very long flight and I'm pretty bushed. I'm going to leave the number for my hotel. If there is any real change, I want you to call me first. Mom and Dad are down for the count and need some time to decompress a little. I want to try to take some of the burden off of them for the next few days, if I can."

Julia took the number without saying a word. She just nodded her head as he left the room.

Outside, Brian stopped and looked back at her. Wow, he thought. Where did they get her? She's beautiful. Then he turned and made his way to the elevator.

Chapter Seventeen

It would be ten days before Alex opened her eyes again and the family would be in a panic by then, worried that she wasn't going to get well. She would not know any of them and would be confused by their presence. When removed from the tubes, after they proved to themselves that she could breathe on her own, and offered something to drink, Alex would not know what a drink was or what she was supposed to do when they held a straw to her lips.

Lainie was in the ICU room, sitting with her daughter, when the miracle happened. Julia had left them alone, while she went to speak to the nurse about Alex's IV bag that was nearly empty. Lainie had been in the room about five of her allotted ten minutes, when Alex opened her eyes and looked over at her.

"Alex, oh Alex," Lainie whispered after noticing that her eyes were open. "You're awake. I'm so glad. Can you talk to me, sweetie? Can you say anything?" Lainie asked.

"Who are you?" Alex croaked.

"I'm your mom, don't you remember me?"

Lainie could see Alex struggle to reach back into her memory and try to find something about Lainie that would help identify the woman seated by her bed. As she focused, her forehead pinched together and her face filled with confusion.

Lainie tried to be calm as she continued to try to jog her daughter's memory.

"Alex is your name," she said softly. "Lainie is my name and I'm your Mom. David is your Dad and Brian is your brother. Can you remember anything?"

After a long moment, Alex said, "I don't know you. I don't know who you are," then she closed her eyes and appeared to go back to sleep.

Lainie turned and left Alex's bed, trying to stay as calm as possible so she wouldn't alarm her daughter. She walked quickly from the room to find David. She stopped and asked Julia, who was sitting quietly in a chair outside the room, to please stay with Alex while they paged one of her doctors. Then she walked quickly away, wearing an anxious expression on her face.

After entering her daughter's room, Julia moved to a chair beside her bed and sat down, taking Alex's hand into her own, while wondering what had happened that had caused Lainie to leave so abruptly.

Looking at her daughter, who appeared to be sleeping, Julia bent down to her daughter's face and kissed her gently on the cheek. Then, she placed her cheek against Alex's hand and whispered, "Oh Alex, if I could only tell you the truth. Oh baby, please get well."

Alex opened her eyes, turned her head, and looked at Julia. "What's a Mom?" she asked.

Julia looked up. Alex's lips were trembling and tears were pooled in her dark eyes. Julia was so surprised she didn't know what to say.

"There was a lady here and she wanted me to remember her, but I don't, and I'm afraid cause I don't know what a mom is; and I tried to think, and I don't know who she is either," she continued as the tears spilled down her face.

"That's okay," Julia said trying to comfort her. "You don't have to remember. Can I ask you something?"

"I guess."

"Okay, Alex," Julia smiled softly, "that's your name, you know. Do you remember speaking to me the other night when you woke up the first time?"

"No."

"Do you remember an accident that happened when you were riding in a car on the way to a football game and that you were hurt when that car crashed?"

Alex thought about that then she said, "Vicky?"

"Yes, that's very good. Vicky is your friend and she was with you when you had the accident. She's fine by the way."

"Friend?"

"Yes, but that doesn't matter. You are not to worry if you can't remember something. I'll help you to learn what you have forgotten. The injuries to your head have caused you to lose some of your memory. You have a very large bandage right here," she smiled, taking her hand and touching her daughter's forehead. "Don't be afraid. It's going to be okay, I promise."

Alex tried to smile. "I like you. You're nice. Will you stay with me? I'm afraid that lady might come back and ask me something and I won't know the answer and I'll get scared again. Besides, it hurts my head when I try to think," she said squeezing her eyes shut.

"I won't leave you. You don't have to think right now. I want you to try to rest. You have to regain your strength. I'll be right here."

But Alex wasn't listening she was already asleep.

Chapter Eighteen

The next time Julia saw Brian was several days after Alex woke up. She was getting a cup of coffee in the cafeteria. He was sitting at a table, near the back, and he was studying some papers.

"Hi, Brian, can I join you?" she asked, looking down at her son.

"Sure, Julia. I'm sorry. Let me move some of these papers out of your way," he said, starting to shuffle papers. "Sit down. I need to take a break from all of this anyway." Pulling all the papers back to his side of the table, he seemed to be lost in thought.

Julia sat down and looked carefully at her son. Clearly something was bothering him. "What are you doing? Working?"

"Yeah, I have a problem with one of my clients and I'm trying to figure it out."

"What sort of work do you do Brian?"

"I work for a firm in Chicago that handles clients, money, and their initial public offerings. All that sort of thing."

"Really. Maybe we could talk about that sometime. I have a rather large trust fund I inherited and I need a little investment advice. If that's not the kind of work you do, if you could even point me in the right direction, it would be helpful."

"Really," he said but thinking she did not look like any of the wealthy women he had ever met. "It's not what I do, but we have a great guy in our firm who does handle investment portfolios. When you're ready just let me know."

"Great. It will probably be after this assignment. Would it be okay if I come to Chicago and see you?"

"Sure. Just call me first. I'll leave you a card when I head back to the Midwest."

Julia sipped her coffee and studied her very handsome son.

"She's taken a special liking to you," he said.

"Excuse me?"

"Alex. She seems to really like you," Brian repeated.

"Yes, I guess she does."

"She hardly speaks to Mom and Dad or me," he said, looking down, moving a saltshaker that was sitting on the table around in small, tight circles.

"I'm sorry."

"Just seems sort of strange, you know."

"Yes, it must be hard for all of you."

"Do you ever wonder, why? You know, why you?"

Julia reddened and then she spoke without thinking, "Maybe it's because I'm a stranger and she doesn't have to struggle to remember all the things all of you keep asking her. It hurts her head, you know, when she tries to remember all of you," Julia blurted out.

"Really, I didn't know that," Brian said thoughtfully, not in the least disturbed by her outburst. That's a really good point. One I hadn't considered."

Julia was obviously upset and embarrassed that she had spoken so harshly to him, because he could see the color high in her cheeks and the way she refused to look at him.

Not wanting her to think he was upset, he reached over and patted her hand. Some electrical connection seemed to pulse for a moment when he touched her and it surprised him, but it didn't last, so Brian ignored it. "It's okay, Julia. No one is blaming you. I'm just thinking out loud. That's all."

They spoke a while longer about the weather and other safe topics, then Julia excused herself and left the table.

Brian watched her go. There was something about her that was very disturbing. She was stunningly beautiful even with that God awful hair stuck every which direction, and way too much make-up. But, it was something else. He just couldn't put his finger on it. He better keep an eye on his Dad too, he decided. He noticed that David didn't seem to be immune to this pretty lady's charms either, based on the way he had seen his Dad staring at her when he thought no one was watching him.

Chapter Nineteen

Alex was moved out of ICU seven days after she woke and spoke for the first time. She was started on a plan to rehabilitate her injuries, mainly her hips and legs. She was unable to walk and every effort she made to try, left her shaking and sweating with pain. Her incision was still healing and very painful. That, coupled with her other injuries and her blood loss, had sapped her strength.

The rehab unit, where they hoped to start the healing process, was filled with every type of machinery; walkers, striders and bikes - to help patients learn to walk again, or to strengthen their muscles that had been damaged or atrophied by their illnesses - weights, and mats, along with whirlpool baths and hot pools. It was all there to help the patient attempt a return to a normal life, after lots of hard work and painful exercise.

Of course the machines and work alone would not be enough. Everyone knew this. So, there would be plenty of prayers, sent up to heaven, by those who loved each of them. Because, one and all, they shared a common hope that all of their loved-one's hard work, along with copious amounts of prayer, would be enough to give them back the person they had lost during whatever tragedy had befallen their families.

They placed Alex on a schedule for a workout twice a day. She would start on an exercise bike and move to a walker when she grew stronger.

Alex refused to go unless Julia went with her. She wouldn't budge from her position, no matter how many times David tried to explain that she didn't need Julia to be with her.

So, the family changed Julia's hours so that she could remain at the hospital with their daughter during her difficult and painful rehabilitation.

In addition, Alex was to participate in a brain injury clinic. The head of the clinic had explained that, while a part of Alex's brain had been damaged and could never be repaired, this damaged portion only represented a small portion of the total brain. Through the clinic, they would hope to teach Alex how to use another part of her brain so she could resume at least some portion of the life that she had known before. The doctors told the family that they had had wonderful results with young adults who had similar injuries as Alex. They did caution them all, however, that Alex might never remember anything before the accident, that her past and all the memories attached to her previous life might be completely erased. They did feel that she could learn what she needed to learn to go forward and to be an active, productive member of society. Alex would either remember her parents and family over time, or they would be forced to accept that she would have to be taught who they were and what their individual roles meant to her. They should never push her to try to remember, since everything at the moment was colliding around in her head, memories, sadness, pain, despair, and confusion, as she tried to recover. They should accept her, as she was, each day and make no demands on her memory.

Julia went to rehab with Alex twice a day. The nurses took her in a wheelchair and placed her on the electric bike, tying both of her feet to the pedals. The rule was that she would pump the pedals for five minutes at the lowest speed.

Alex soon learned, though, that if you turned the timer ahead, she could get away with only a couple of minutes. Even with the reduced time on the bike, Alex would pour sweat, tremble all over and her heart would pound like a runaway train. Julia suffered with her as Alex endured her body's response to this new trauma she was forcing upon it, and as it tried to heal and strengthen from the wounds she had suffered.

A few days later, after watching Alex push the timer forward each session, Julia walked over and stood directly in front of Alex's bike, holding on to the handlebars.

"I know."

Alex smiled a tiny smile. "Know what?" she asked innocently.

"That you're moving the timer ahead."

"Oh."

"You're not fooling me, and you need to start pedaling the entire five minutes, young lady."

"It's hard. I can't do it," Alex said softly. "It hurts so bad."

Watching a tear, as it moved down Alex's cheek, Julia's heart went out to her.

"Alex, yes you can. It's hard now but it will get easier. Listen to me. If I could do this for you, I would, but you're the one who is injured and you have to do this, or you will never walk again."

Alex looked up at her, and after considering her words, she said, "Okay. I'll try. It's going to kill me and it will be on your hands, but I'll try."

"That's my girl. Now, don't even try any more funny business with that timer. I'm watching you every minute."

Alex laughed, but Julia could see the tremendous amount of courage it took for her to keep pedaling, as the pain etched her face, her sweat poured, and her limbs trembled violently.

David stood just inside the door of the rehabilitation room where he could see his daughter working with Julia. He hurt so badly for his little girl, as she struggled to get through her five minutes on the bike. He was also burning with jealousy.

Alex had never smiled at him or Lainie. In fact, she barely spoke to them. Screwing her eyes shut, she would turn away from them and start to cry. They were both so devastated they could hardly handle their visits with her anymore. Watching her talking to Julia made him miss his daughter. They had given him back her body, but where was his little girl? She just wasn't the same person anymore.

The doctor had tried to explain that over time, Alex would automatically remember her individual personality traits that made her who she was, and the ways that she responded to those around her would also come back. It was all back there inside her head, he had said, somewhere still hardwired into her brain, and that she would either remember them or learn to accept who they were. David had heard the words, but it didn't help the pain. When he saw the difference between the way Alex reacted to Julia and the way she reacted to him, it broke his heart.

Julia was yelling. "Come on Alex! You can do it! Keep pumping, sweetie! Pump harder! Come on, you're almost there! Ten, nine, eight; come on just a few more seconds, Alex!"

As the timer rang, Julia bellowed, "You did it! Whoooee! You did it! See, I knew you could! Look at you!" Julia roared loudly, as David watched her erupt into a dance - round and round in circles, jumping up and down, pumping her fists into the air.

Alex clapped her hands and laughed excitedly, as she watched her nurse doing a strange and wonderful dance of joy.

Julia was beautiful, David realized, as he reveled in his daughter's victory. In that flash of time, for just a moment, something held him perfectly still as he embraced that knowledge. She reminded him so much of Elizabeth and he wondered again if that was why he was feeling this connection to her.

Alex smiled radiantly, "I did it. Did you see that? All five minutes! I did all five minutes!"

"Yes, you did my brave little girl. Yes, you did."

Then Julia hugged her tightly while she murmured soft words of praise for her efforts. Alex hugged her back and smiled so brightly that she beamed from head to toe.

David turned away and walked from the room, never letting them know that he was there.

Chapter Twenty

What David, Lainie and Brian did not know was that Julia and Alex were secretly working on a surprise for them. Each day, for the next several weeks, as Alex was regaining her strength, during the time when Alex wasn't in one form of rehab or another, Julia worked with her.

"Now tell me again, what each of these things are."

"This is my left shoe," Alex said, holding up her left shoe. "It goes on my left foot, right here see?" she said lifting her left leg. "But first this thing, that is called a sock, has to go on my foot, before I put on my shoe. My foot is right here," she smiled happily pointing down at her foot.

"Good, go on."

"This is my right shoe and it goes on my right foot," she continued lifting her right leg. "But first this sock thing has to go on before I put on my shoe."

"Great. That's just great, Alex."

"Do you think, I can show Mom and Dad and Brian, today? Do you think I'm ready?" she asked excitedly.

"I do. I will get them right now and then you can put on your wonderful performance for them. You did just great, Alex. I'm very proud of you."

"Do you think I can do it? Do you think they'll be surprised?" Alex said, clapping her hands with glee.

"Oh, yes. They will be very surprised and proud of you for all the work you've done. I'll be right back." Then Julia walked out of the room.

Julia pondered her daughter's improvement as she walked down the hall to the waiting room, situated at the end of the hall. The words, "Mom and Dad", had gone right through her, when Alex had said them.

She had spent many hours going over a diagram with Alex, explaining who the people were, what a Dad and Mom meant, whom Brian was, and what all their names were. It had killed her each time she had had to tell Alex that Lainie was her Mom.

She sighed as she approached the door to the room where Lainie, David and Brian were waiting. She pasted a bright smile on her face, pushed open the door and said, "Hello, everyone. We have a surprise for you. Alex would like to see you in her room."

"Alex asked for us?" David said, surprised

"Yes. She would like to see all of you."

***

After everyone entered the hospital room, Julia asked Alex to go ahead and show her parents and Brian what she could do.

Alex was so nervous her hands were shaking. "I'm not sure, Julia. I think I'd better wait. Maybe I should practice a little more," she trailed off to a whisper.

Julia went to the bedside and placed her hands on both sides of Alex's face. "You can do this Alex. Remember that day on the bike? You know, the day you did all five minutes?"

"Yes," she said smiling a little.

"Well, this is another day just like that one. A day when you know you can do something you haven't been able to do before. Nothing can take this victory away from you, except you. If you decide not to do this today, the next time will be much harder. Alex, you can do this. I wouldn't have told you that you were ready, if you weren't."

The others in the room stood motionless, not understanding what Julia was saying, not knowing all the hours of work it had taken to get to this point in Alex's recovery.

"Okay. You're right. I can do this. Okay, Mom and Dad and Brian watch this. Julia and I have worked and worked. Gosh, I hope I do this right."

Then she began. The fact that she called them 'Mom, Dad and Brian', had left them all breathless, but as they watched her stumble through the simple process of a shoe and a sock and how it related to a leg and a foot, they couldn't stop the tears of sorrow that fell when they saw how badly she had been injured, or, those of joy that followed because they knew now that she was going to recover. They were also beginning to realize how hard that recovery would be.

"I don't know how to tie my shoes yet, but it's okay, cause Julia said I don't need to know that until I can reach down and put them on my feet by myself," Alex said excitedly, beaming with pride that she had been able to do it and pleased by the expressions on everyone's face.

"I don't exactly remember all of you, but Julia gave me this paper," she held it in the air, "and I sneak a look at it after you come into the room. Now I think I can figure out who each of you are. Now, I have memorized your names and it's getting easier for me," she said smiling at each of them. Pointing at David she said, "Your name is David but you're also called Dad. And your name is Lainie and you're also called Mom," she said smiling proudly at Lainie. "And you're

Brian and you're something called a brother," she finished triumphantly.

Alex's family was stunned. One by one though, they finally found their feet and started to move over to Alex. When they were all there at the side of her bed, they each wrapped her in their arms. Then, they were all talking at the same time, slapping each other on the back in their excitement. Alex smiled at Julia who was left standing alone on the other side of the room.

Julia looked at her little girl who had worked so hard. She had deep blue circles under her eyes, she had lost an enormous amount of weight, she still couldn't lift herself up, but she was determined to get well. And, Julia was determined to help her. Alex still didn't know her family, but she now knew that she should call this person Mom, that person Dad, and that person Brian. It was a start.

As she was watching them all, David turned and walked up to her, his face flushed and his eyes full of tears. "Thank you, thank you Julia. We will never be able to repay you for this gift." Then, without any warning, he pulled Julia into his arms in a tight embrace. "Thank you, thank you."

Julia was lost in time as she was wrapped in his arms, as the world shifted and she stood once more on the steps leading down to the sidewalk of their Paris apartment, on the last day she had seen David as he embraced her and they said goodbye, before she left for the park with her children, never to return. She wanted to hold him and never let him go, but she stood frozen by the memories of a time long ago.

Then, David was gone and Brian was standing in front of her. "Julia, you are a miracle," he said smiling. "Where did you come from? Maybe you really are an angel, like Alex said," he teased her. When she didn't respond, he took her hand then reconsidered. "Oh hell, I'm not going to shake your hand. I'm going to hug you too. This is too damned wonderful to do anything but hug the hell out of you. Thank you so much."

As Brian hugged her, Julia whirled away from the room. She was in a cellar now, lost and alone, so scared she couldn't eat or sleep, thinking maybe, after all this time, there was no one coming to save her - clinging to a worn picture of a little boy who was standing by her side, a baby girl, lying sleeping in her arms, and a handsome man who was smiling brightly for the camera. The man was standing beside a beautiful young woman, with his hand on her shoulder – a woman who couldn't have been her, surely not, she bore no resemblance to the emaciated woman she had become – a woman who was really gone now, one of the lost ones, a sliver of a dying memory, someone people used to know and love, a woman who was being destroyed, day by day, when no one came to rescue her, and who, she now knew, was never going home. As the memories flooded over her, Julia's heart cracked in another place - there were so many cracks now, she thought – and she wondered how many more she could endure. The pain of it all was so unbearable that it left her shattered and broken as she stood in her little boy's embrace.

After Lainie came over and hugged her too, telling her thank you, over and over again, Julia excused herself and left them all together, laughing and talking, asking Alex to do it again, one more time, so they could marvel at all she had learned. As Julia drifted away she realized that she was just the ghost of someone they used to know. She was a dead woman walking.

Chapter Twenty-One

Julia paced the floor in her suite, back and forth, wringing her hands and crying. Joe had tried to comfort her, but she had screamed at him to leave her alone. So he did.

She couldn't stand it anymore. Being "Miss Goodie Two Shoes", dressing in a way she would never have considered in her entire life – so much make-up it took her a half hour to scrape it off – her hair that looked like dead straw; while standing back and watching her children and her husband as they bonded, cried and laughed together – oh, let's not forget, Lainie; little, ole, beautiful Lainie that they all loved and adored - while she, the real wife and Mom, was ignored because she was nothing more than just a hired nurse. "NOBODY!" she screamed, wrapping her arms around her body and bending over at the waist as she wailed out her anger and frustration.

Storming around the room, howling, she heard the phone ringing in the background. "Damn it. Leave me alone. I don't want to talk to anyone," she growled.

"Julia," Joe said. "It's Victor. "I'm sorry, I couldn't let it ring one more time, so I picked it up for you. Victor has a message for you.

His exact words were, 'Tell her to shut up and get on the phone and to do it now."

"I don't want to talk."

"Take the phone, Julia."

So she did. She cried and wailed and felt sorry for herself, and cursed everyone and everything and finally she started to talk rationally about her family and how it hurt that she had to keep her true identity a secret and how it was just too much to bear. Joe heard it all.

"Julia, can you hear me?" Victor asked.

"Yes," she said hiccupping and blowing her nose at the same time.

"Julia, I have a cabin in Montana, tucked up into the trees, on the side of a mountain near Seeley Lake that I hardly ever use. How about if we go up there, this weekend, for a few days? I'll fly out and you can walk in the snow, lay around in front of a fire, read and just regroup from what you have been through the past couple of weeks. I'll feed you, stay out of your way, and you can sleep as much as you want."

"You would do that for me? Aren't you too busy?" she sniffed.

"Yes, I would do that for you. No, I'm not too busy. Let me put something together and I'll get back to you with the details."

"Victor, wait. I'll need to make arrangements with David, before I can commit."

"That's okay. I'm sure he won't mind after all that you've done for Alex."

"Okay, assuming that David agrees, I think I'd like to go away for a few days. Also, it would be nice to see you again. At least you know who I am, for God's sake," she moaned and started to cry again.

"Julia, stop. Don't keep beating yourself up over this. It is not your fault that you have been placed into this position. We'll talk and then you can decide what you want to do next. Okay?"

"Okay," she said hiccupping into the phone.

"Are you going to be all right if I hang up?"

"Yes."

"You sure?"

"Yes, and thank you Victor. Thanks for everything."

"Anytime, sweetie."

***

As Victor hung up the phone, he wished that there were something that he could really do for Julia. He couldn't help her with what she was trying to do now. She would have to face all of the problems with her family alone, while he stood on the sidelines and watched. It tore at him because he wanted to protect her.

He hated it when she cried. Roberto had hurt her, made her cry, and almost made her lose herself. And, this scheme she had concocted, by coming back to America, was hurting her even worse. In time, Julia would probably learn the truth. It was a sad and unforgiving truth. Her life and her dreams of reuniting with David and her children had been destroyed long ago by time passing and the tragedy they suffered. Once her family's hopes of finding her had been shattered by the passing of the years, they had been forced to accept the finality that she was gone and that she was never coming back. Now, nothing was ever going to be able to put the pieces of her past life back together again.

Victor didn't know if she was strong enough to make it through this next sad passage that life had placed in front of her and was forcing her to walk through.

He was madly in love with her, but he knew that she didn't love him in return. The night - it seemed so long ago now - the one and only night, he thought sadly, that he had made love to her, he had thought then that he could, and would, make her acknowledge him – who he was and how he felt - and that he could make her feel for him what he felt for her. But it didn't happen. Instead, she had left him behind, drowning in his love, and she had left Argentina. She had responded to

82

him and made him feel that maybe there was a chance for them. A short note said, "I'm sorry, Victor". That's all, and then she was gone. His hopes and dreams had been crushed.

After she left for America, Julia never called. She didn't tell him where she was or what she was doing. She hadn't reached out to him and she seemed oblivious to how this might hurt him.

He would never leave her. No, it was impossible, now that he had known her physically, now that he had been joined to her. A large ceremony with a priest would not have made him more committed or in love. He was as tied to her as the tides were tied to the moon that caused them to move back and forth on a ceaseless journey, eternally forever moving. There was no one else for him. No woman could touch him now. She had made him immune to them all.

He would always be there for her, if she wanted him. He knew he was just a friend and it killed him to admit it, but if that were all he could have, then it would have to be enough.

Victor sipped his drink and stared out the window of his penthouse apartment and dreamed the impossible dream, as he longed for his perfect fantasy to come true. The fantasy that Julia would someday come to him and tell him that she loved him too.

That was when the phone rang.

"Julia," he said, grabbing the phone.

"No, it's not Julia," a female voice answered, as if insulted.

"I'm sorry. Who is this?" Victor asked confused.

"Victor, it's Rosita."

Victor was surprised. "Rosita Juarez?"

"Yes. How many Rosita's do you know?"

Victor had not heard from Rosita since May, almost seven months before. He had heard that she had left Argentina to go to the States where she was playing a role in a national soap opera. The reason she had left Argentina still haunted him.

"Rosita, what a surprise? How are you?"

"Well, I was doing great until you called me Julia," she spat into the phone.

"Oh, I'm sorry. I was just talking to her and I thought that she was calling me back."

"So, you're with her now?" she accused.

"I don't know what you mean by 'with her', but no, we are nothing more than good friends."

"Really."

"Yes, really. Now, why did you call?" Victor said, perturbed by her questions about Julia.

"Well," she replied softly, changing her tone, "I'm working in New York now and I wondered if we could get together some night for dinner."

"Rosita that would be great. I would love to see you and Luke. By the way, congratulations on your marriage."

"Thank you, but I wasn't going to invite Luke. I thought it could be just you and me so we could catch up."

Victor paused. This was not a good idea. The last thing he wanted was to revive the old rivalry between him and Luke. "Rosita, I'm not sure that is appropriate. You're a married woman, now. I think Luke might be upset if he found we were seeing each other and we weren't including him."

"Well if I don't care what he thinks, why do you?"

Embarrassed, Victor answered, "Rosita, the circumstances that surrounded our relationship before you married Luke would make him uncomfortable. I know that when he found out we were seeing each other, he was not happy about it. Now, that you're married, I think he would be even unhappier. It might lead him to think we are still involved."

"Involved, well that's one word for what we were. You always were the master of the understatement. But, we are not in Argentina, where you have to get my parents permission to take me out anymore. I'm a grown woman now and I want to see you."

"I know that Rosita. But, you are another man's wife now. I would love to see you," he continued, "but only if you invite Luke to join us for dinner."

"God!" she exploded. "You are such a pain in the ass!"

Victor said nothing.

"There are some things I need to talk to you about and I don't want Luke to know," she wheedled.

"I'm not sure what you would want to talk to me about that you would want to keep a secret from Luke. Is it a legal matter? Can we discuss it over the phone?"

"No, it's not a legal matter. It's personal and we can't discuss it over the phone. We need to do it face to face."

"I really would love to see you, Rosita."

"Then let's just do it. Don't make this so hard and don't make me beg you. I've missed you so badly. You know there was a time that you wanted to marry me," she said coyly.

"Rosita," Victor sighed, rubbing his hair with his hand and starting to pace the room, "let's set the record straight. Whatever future you and I might or might not have had, is in the past. When you married Luke, our future ended. I cannot have any relationship with you that doesn't include your husband. I'm sorry."

"Well, damn you to hell and damn your bitch girlfriend Julia too," she yelled into the phone. "Don't think I don't know what's going on. I heard you that time when she was sick. You know, after the funeral when the poor, little thing might be dying. I was there, hiding in the hall, and I heard you tell her that you loved her. It was disgusting! Your best friend was hardly cold in the ground and you were all over his wife. And, when you made love to me, before Roberto died, you called me Julia! Do you know how that made me feel? You were screwing his wife and you tell me that I'm married.

When did that start to matter? Do you know how much I hated you and your little bitch, after I learned your dirty little secret?" she said raising her voice.

"You heard me? I don't understand. I called you Julia? When?" he asked, trying to register all that she was saying.

"Yes, I heard you and yes, you called me Julia. I'll never forget the way you betrayed me. Never! I spit on you both. I damn you both to hell, for what you have done to me."

"But, I don't understand. What have we done to you?"

But Rosita had hung up.

Victor stood staring at the dead receiver in his hand.

Chapter Twenty-Two

Rosita was fuming.

She was so mad that she was talking to herself.

"How dare you Victor Salvatore," she hissed out loud. "I hate you and Julia. What is this 'Holier Than Thou' attitude? I mean you're the one that lusted after another man's wife for years. I loved you so much and you crushed me. I will get even with you. Don't worry. I have the perfect weapon and you are not going to know what hit you."

Pacing the floor Rosita came to the conclusion that Julia would have to go.

"Julia, you are in the way and you will have to go," she said out loud. "If Victor and I are to have any future, you have to go."

Someone stood in the hall, listening through the paper-thin walls of Rosita's dressing room, as she continued her one-sided conversation.

Chapter Twenty-Three

Julia was reading by her daughter's bed when David entered her room. Motioning for Julia to follow him outside into the hall, he held the door for her while she walked past him.

"What are you doing here Julia, you must be exhausted after today and all the excitement."

"Well, I don't know. I just wanted to be here in case she woke up and needed me for something."

"Julia, they gave her something to help her pain and to help her sleep. Alex has had a rough day and she won't wake up until tomorrow morning, now."

"You're right. What are you doing here, yourself," she teased him, looking up into his face.

"Well, actually, I hoped I would find you here. I wanted to speak to you about Alex. Have you had dinner?"

"No, but I'm not sure I'm hungry."

"Oh, come on. You have to eat sometime, besides I'd like to get to know you better."

Julia was surprised and pleased. David wanted to have dinner with her. Maybe all was not lost.

"Sure, that would be nice. Besides, I'd like to talk to you about Alex and her care going forward."

"Good. Get your coat and we can go over to 'Kemo Sabe'. They were still open when I drove by just now and I hear they make a mean steak and a great martini."

Brian, who had come back to the hospital to see if Alex was comfortable, stepped back in the shadows of the hallway, and watched as his Dad helped Julia into her coat and then walked with her to the elevator.

"Uh oh," he thought.

***

David and Julia were finishing their meals and laughing at some story David was telling about a case he worked in Washington, when the waiter approached and told them that the restaurant would be closing in about a half hour since it would be 11:00 P.M.

They were startled. They had been having such a good time they hadn't noticed how late it had become.

"David, before we get pushed out of here, I need to talk to about Alex."

"Sure, what is it?"

"You know that Alex will soon be discharged and sent to a rehabilitation facility that is affiliated with the hospital."

"Yes, what's the problem. You do think she should continue her rehab therapy, don't you?"

"Absolutely. But, what I am thinking is that maybe she should go somewhere else – somewhere outside of Missoula."

"Really," David said looking closely at Julia. As he was listening to her throughout dinner, he had felt a bond growing between him and this woman who was a virtual stranger, who was sitting across from him sharing a meal. He found himself drifting in a magical haze

89

of lust – she was beautiful and when he looked at her tight body, his knees felt weak - and something else too, something that he had not felt since he had met Lainie. Thinking of his wife, he reminded himself that he wasn't doing anything wrong. He wasn't acting on anything, he was just having dinner with his daughter's nurse and there was nothing wrong with that, he thought, assuaging any guilt that might have tried to rear it's ugly head.

"There's a hospital in Washington, named Georgetown University Hospital."

"Yes, I'm very familiar with it."

"They are affiliated with the National Rehabilitation Hospital and it is one of the foremost leaders in traumatic brain injury and multiple orthopedic trauma recovery in the country. They have an in-patient program that she would need initially. Later she could move to an outpatient schedule and she could live at home with you and Lainie while she continued her rehab. It would put her closer to home now, so you and Lainie could go back to work and still visit her, and Brian could go back to Chicago."

David said nothing.

Julia continued, "If you wanted me to, I would be happy to change my nursing schedule, in order to make sure she gets the appropriate care and that her care proceeds the way it should. I think Alex would be happier being closer to home, knowing that she is not keeping you from getting back to a normal life. I know that her grandparents are too old to travel, but they could call her from time to time once she regains some of her memory and maybe later she could visit them," she finished after spilling out her entire story basically in one breath.

"How did you find out about this facility?" David questioned.

"I've been researching in the library and I have a friend who lives in Washington who checked around for me. He says Georgetown University is world renowned for their recovery rate and new methods they use to help stimulate memory loss. They also have a wonderful program to help the patients recover their strength and to learn to walk again."

"It sounds wonderful. But, do you really want to leave your home here and relocate to Washington?"

"My home isn't really here, not in my heart anyway, so I think maybe I would like to visit the nation's capital for a while," she said smiling up at him. "Also, I think I can really help Alex in her recovery, so if you would allow me to, I would love to see her through all of this."

David contemplated what she had told him. "You're amazing, you know that. I don't know what we did to deserve you and I don't know why we were so lucky to have you drop into our lives out of the clear blue, but we sure are glad. I will have to call your agency and tell them how wonderful you are," he said smiling.

Julia didn't speak, so David continued.

"I'll talk to Lainie and I think we can probably come to agreement that it's the right thing to do. If you will bring your research to me tomorrow, we'll look at the facility you have in mind. Thank you for taking the time to look into this for us. We have been so out of our minds with worry that we haven't even focused on the next step in her treatment."

"Great. I want to help Alex make a full recovery. Let me know if you like the place, so I can get the proper transfer papers put in the works. We will have to transport her on a special medical flight, so there will be lots of red tape to work through."

"Okay."

"David, there's something else."

"Yes?"

"Alex is doing better right now, so I was wondering if it would be okay if I took a three-day weekend, beginning Friday? I would still come in tomorrow and make sure everything is scheduled for the next few days.

I have a friend who has a cabin at Seeley Lake, and I would like a couple of days to get my personal life together and recharge my battery a little."

"Julia," he smiled, "of course you should go. I hear that area of Montana is truly beautiful. There will be lots of snow, burning logs in fireplaces; deep comforters on all the beds, along with snowshoeing, skiing and hot cider after you leave the slopes. Well, actually, I don't know anything about it, but based on the brochures at my hotel, it looks pretty wonderful," he laughed.

"Yes, my friend said the lodge is very lovely. But we will be using a private home."

"Do you ski?"

Julia paused, "I don't know."

"You don't know?"

Realizing her mistake, she said, "Well, what I meant to say is that it has been a very long time and I'll probably be pretty rusty, so I'm not sure if anyone will be able to call it skiing when they see me doing whatever it is I'll be doing."

David laughed. "Well, I wish I was going with you. I'm going to be very jealous of your time away. You will come back, won't you," he said softly, looking into her eyes.

"Oh, yes. You can't get rid of me. I'll definitely be back," she said, embarrassed, but pleased.

Looking down at her watch, she said, "David, thank you so much for dinner, but it's late and we'd better get going, before they throw us out on our ears." Standing up and moving away from the table, she was thinking about how handsome her husband was, and how easy it might be to get him to love her again, based on the way he had been staring at her all through dinner.

After David flagged a taxi for Julia - she had refused his offer for a lift to her hotel - he embraced her and kissed her on the cheek as he helped her get arranged in the back seat of the cab. "Thanks for everything, Julia. I'll see you tomorrow." Then he walked back to his car.

Julia felt tingly all over. Twice today he had held her, then he had flirted with her and now he had kissed her. Not a bad start, she thought.

***

Lainie was awake, but feigning sleep, when David unlocked the door and slipped quietly into their hotel room, silently stepping into the bedroom. Julia's perfume, she would know it anywhere, drifted in the air as he moved noiselessly toward the bathroom and closed the door.

"Oh, David," she whispered. "What are you doing to us?" Squeezing her eyes shut, her warm tears dripped down her cheeks onto her pillow as she swallowed her fear.

Chapter Twenty-Four

Joe rapped gently on Julia's door that stood ajar between their two suites.

"Julia?"

"Good Morning, Joe," Julia said placing the paper she had been reading down on the table beside her. She was dressed in her nurses uniform, minus the hat, and looked absolutely serene. Compared to her manic, crazed appearance last night the difference was startling.

When he hesitated, Julia prompted him. "It's okay, please come in. I promise I won't scream or bite you," she said laughing. "Besides, I've ordered both of us some breakfast."

"Julia," he said, with a tightened jaw, "we need to talk."

"Yes, I know we do. You probably have lots of questions after my tirade last evening. I assume you heard it all?" she questioned.

"Yes. I'm sorry, but it was hard not to."

A knock on the door interrupted them. Julia stood and opened the door to a young man, dressed in a very starched white shirt and black pants, pushing a cart full of coffee, orange juice, water, eggs, bacon, scones, pastries, fruit and other breakfast items.

"Please place everything on the table next to the desk," she instructed the waiter.

He smiled and carefully placed the various dishes on the table. Before he left, he couldn't avoid giving Julia the once-over, from head to toe. Grinning at her, he turned and left the room.

Julia blanched. "It never stops," she said with a grimace. "No matter what, they just can't seem to help staring at me in amazement whenever they see me in this get-up. He's probably out in the hall doubled over in laughter."

Joe didn't respond, but he disagreed. The reason the young man was staring was that she was absolutely beautiful and the form fitting uniform she was wearing made her easy, oh so easy, to look at.

Julia poured each of them a cup of coffee. "Please help yourself."

"This is a great deal of food, are we expecting someone else?"

"No, just you and me. I thought I should fortify you for this meeting," she smiled.

"Is it going to be that bad? I mean are you in trouble? Are you wanted by the FBI, or something?" Joe asked teasing her.

"No, I'm not, but Roberto was."

Joe laughed.

"I'm not kidding. He was a wanted criminal."

Joe choked on his coffee. "Roberto, your husband? He was wanted by the FBI?" he asked clearly astonished.

"Yes, my husband Roberto. He was wanted by the FBI," she said strongly.

Joe didn't speak; he was clearly stunned.

"I know you're not an attorney, Joe, but before I explain, I would like you to treat this conversation as if it were an attorney/client privileged conversation; in other words, I want you to treat it with complete confidentiality. You will understand why, after I tell you my story."

Joe took another sip of his coffee and studied her. She seemed calm and clear eyed, without the visible anxiety that had seemed to plague her this past few weeks. His curiosity was clearly on high, revving out of control. He couldn't wait to hear her explanation for some of the things she was screaming last night.

"You might want to set your cup down, before I start," Julia explained.

Joe did.

"My name is Elizabeth Grant. It is not Julia Bertinelli. I am David Grant's wife."

"I don't understand," Joe sputtered. "You mean ex-wife?"

"No. I mean wife," she insisted. "David and I were married twenty-five years ago and we never divorced, although I was probably declared dead, now that I think about it," she mused as an after thought.

"Wait. You mean to tell me that David Grant is a bigamist? That can't be. I know he's married to Lainie since I had the wedding photographed for Roberto, and by your own admission you were married to Roberto, so how could you still be David's wife, if you ever were? And, what do you mean when you say you were probably declared dead?"

Julia sighed, "It is a very long story. Let me give you the shortened version of what happened." Settling back into her chair she began to tell the story.

"A little more than twenty-five years ago, I was married to David Grant. I had two children; Alex, my daughter and Brian, my son."

Joe interrupted. "Alexandria Grant is your daughter?"

"Yes, she is." Then she continued. "David was assigned to Paris and during our visit there, I was kidnapped by Roberto Bertinelli. During the abduction, I received a head injury that left me with no memory of my previous life; much like my daughter is experiencing today. I married Roberto, unaware that he was my captor and I was eventually taken to Argentina to live with him. I spent twenty years with him, learning to love him and finally was left to grieve over his death. During that time, I learned of his crime against my family and me. I was not going to come back to America. I felt too much time had passed, my children were all grown up and David had remarried. They all thought I was dead and I made the decision to leave it that way. However, Alex was injured and I knew that I could not let her die without me at her side. So, I changed my appearance and came to Montana to help my daughter and to see if I should tell them the truth about me."

Joe said nothing.

Julia continued, "Last night, it all came out of me. All my grief, my anger that no one knows who I am, my fear that my daughter might have died and that she has a horrendous recovery in front of her, the fact that I have to do this alone and that they have each other, flew at me like a room full of banshees tearing at my heart. It caused me to break all my resolve to be patient, to just stand by while my whole world was sliding out of control. Unfortunately for you, my friend, you had to witness that terrible scene and by witnessing it you were forced into a minor role as a participant in my emotional breakdown. I'm sorry for that."

The room was quiet for several minutes. Finally, Joe spoke.

"Let me see if I have this straight. You were David Grant's wife and you were kidnapped by Roberto, you lost your memory and you were taken to Argentina where you spent the next twenty years married to your abductor?" he said incredulously.

"Yes."

"Your daughter, Alex, is injured and is in the hospital here, but no one knows who you are since they think you are dead?"

"Yes."

"Roberto was a criminal and wanted by the FBI, but he got away with it and now he is dead."

"Yes."

"You are here, pretending to be a nurse, hoping you can get your husband and children back."

"That's right."

Sitting quietly for a few moments, Joe leaned over toward where Julia was seated. "Wow, Julia. That's quite a story. It's not that I don't want to believe you, but it's really hard to swallow. First of all, Roberto didn't seem like the kind of guy that would do something like this and second, I just can't see him as some sort of criminal. I'm sorry."

Julia didn't speak at first. After a short time she said, "I understand perfectly. It does sound like a bad movie script," she smiled looking at him for a long moment. Making what seemed to be a difficult decision, she stood up. "Let me get something for you that might help you understand what happened to me. I'm sure all of this is very confusing, and disturbing and this might help. I'll only be a moment."

Joe watched Julia leave the room. She was certainly a beautiful woman. He could see why Roberto wanted her, maybe even how he might become obsessed; she could probably do that to a man. But, could Roberto want her enough to kidnap her? He didn't buy it. No way.

He himself had desired a few women with a great intensity, he had actually been completely obsessed about one of them a long time ago, but he never would have resorted to violence – he never would have kidnapped them, for God's sake.

But, why would, Julia, or Elizabeth, or whatever the hell her name was, make up such an outlandish story? Reminiscing, he looked back on all the years he had known Roberto, but he couldn't find anything that the man had ever done that would lead him to believe that he would commit this kind of crime. However, it still was odd, he thought, that Roberto had asked him to watch the Grant family, to send him reports of their lives, and to take pictures of them for his files. Why would he do that?

As he was asking himself these questions, Julia re-entered the room carrying a small box in her hands.

"Here are a series of tapes that Roberto dictated prior to his death," she said handing them to him, "they will explain everything for you. I'm asking that you listen to them with an open mind. Then we should talk again. Maybe tonight at dinner, if you would like."

Joe looked at the tapes in the box and the tape player. Taking them from her hands, he said reluctantly, "Okay, I'll listen, but I can't promise you anything, Julia."

"That's all I ask. That you just listen."

"Okay, I'll try to finish them before dinner so we can talk. Would you like me to make a reservation for this evening?" he asked.

"Yes, that would be nice. Thank you. I need to go now," she said glancing at her watch. "I have to get to work. By the way, I'm going away this weekend, and we should probably discuss my plans."

"What? Did you say you were going away? Where are you going?"

Turning back to him, Julia patted him on the arm. "We'll talk, Joe." Then she leaned over and kissed him on the cheek. "We'll talk."

As Julia grabbed her coat, Joe scrambled up to get his.

"That's okay, Joe. Don't get up. I called a cab and I'll get one back to the hotel this evening. Relax. Eat your breakfast."

Joe started to protest, but decided against it, watching her as she went out the door and closed it behind her. Then he sat back in his chair, grabbed a croissant and took a bite, touched his cheek where she had kissed him, put in a tape, plugged in the recorder and pressed start.

***

"Click"

It was 1974 and it was a beautiful, glorious morning in Paris, full of wonder and light - the morning I decided to take you.

I had parked the van close to the area where you and your son played most of the time. It was near a large pond and your little boy was always mesmerized by the antics of the frogs so both of you spent a great deal of time sitting very still, close to the edge of the bank, watching the frogs leap back and forth among the lily pads. The spot was hidden out of the direct site of your nanny and usually it was deserted by the other early morning Parisian's, those individuals usually preferring the jogging paths and the strolling carriage lanes. I did not know exactly what I was going to do or how I would manage to get you to the van, but as it turned out, it was easier than I expected.

I had just found a place on the grass and was sitting sipping my coffee and pretending to read my paper, when you arrived with your son's hand clutched firmly in yours. You were dressed in a simple white cotton dress with white sneakers, with no socks, and you hair was unbound so that it swirled and swayed as you walked. There was a white soccer ball in your hands and you and your son were having a lively, animated conversation. There was a large grassy area to the left of the pond where I supposed you intended to play ball. I was dismayed since I did not know how this change of events would affect my overall plan.

When you looked up and saw me sitting on the grass, I could see you hesitate and start to walk away. I almost jumped up to run after you, but instead, I calmly waved, said good morning in French and indicated with a flourish of my hands that you would not bother me if you played with your son. These gestures somehow reassured you, so you began the game by kicking the ball softly to him while he chased after it with his little legs and attempted to kick it back. His kicks were rather erratic and you were sent running this way and that, back and forth across the grass.

You never looked more beautiful than you did that morning when you yelled your encouragement to your little boy each time he kicked the ball straight. Or, when you held your hands up to your face, to cover your smile, when he missed the ball entirely, lost his balance and tumbled to the ground. I watched you secretly, by peeking over the top edge of my paper, afraid to breathe too hard, afraid I might miss my opportunity. Thankfully, it was not very long before that opportunity presented itself to me in the form of a ball that flew past me when you kicked it a little too hard.

Your son raced after it as it headed toward the street and you started to run after him screaming his name and begging him not to go out into the street. When he was close to me, he stumbled and fell and I pushed myself up from the ground and scooped him up into my arms. He was frightened and surprised by my grabbing him and he began to struggle, pounding me with his little hands and crying for his mommy. When you ran up to where we were standing you held out your arms and said, "Shush ,Brian, it's okay. Mommy is here, hush now." You were looking at me strangely as if you sensed danger. Speaking to me in French, you said, "Thank you very much but please put my son down." When I did not do as you asked, I saw a flash of fear in your eyes. "Please," you repeated as you stepped closer to me. When you approached another step closer I said, "Certainly, I'm sorry," and I placed him on the ground at my feet.

As you stooped down to take him in your arms, I grabbed you from behind and placed the chloroform over your mouth and nose. As you struggled - you were much stronger than I had anticipated - you pulled your face away from me and moaned, "Run, Brian! Go to Nanny! Hurry, baby..."

But, by this time, I had you again and the chloroform was stronger than your will to get away and your body went limp. I ran to the van with you in my arms, opened the door, placed you inside, slammed the door and then jumped in and drove away as quickly as I could, trying not to draw too much attention to myself. As I looked in the rear view mirror, I saw your little boy standing there with a stricken look on his face and I could see him mouth the words, "Mommy! Mommy!" Then he turned and ran away as fast as his little legs would carry him back toward your nanny, who had just come around the grove of trees that protected me from view."

"Click"

Chapter Twenty-Five

Joe McGuire sat quietly looking out the window of his suite. The traffic was moving slowly along the streets with their headlights burning. The streetlights were on early since the days were growing shorter and shorter as Christmas approached. It had been snowing steadily most of the day and the snowplows had been moving up and down the streets trying to stay in front of the drifts building on the roads.

Joe was troubled by the story of Roberto and Julia Bertinelli. He hadn't listened to all the tapes yet, so he wasn't sure why Roberto did what he did, but he knew now that he had kidnapped a woman from Paris, France and that Elizabeth Grant was that woman. It had shaken him to his core when he heard Roberto tell the story of the crime. Why, he thought? Why would Roberto do this?

Inserting another tape, he settled back to listen.

"Click"

"She was fifteen and tall for her age, Roberto said. We had been promised to each other from birth, as was the custom among families in Italy. My family and hers owned vast vineyards and this marriage

would consummate the joining of our lands and fortunes. It was a long awaited union and one that greatly pleased both our families.

She was beautiful and had long black hair that looked like silk. Fortunately for us, we were both very happy about the arrangement between our families and longed for the day when we would finally become man and wife. It was another custom in our village to marry early so when she became sixteen we would be wed.

"Less than four weeks later," he continued, "the Allied forces sent over two hundred planes to bomb the Abbey of Monte Cassino, which stood on the massif above our town. Saint Benedict had built the monastery in the sixth century and it was considered a most holy shrine. The Allied forces believed that the Nazi's had set up outposts in the Abbey so they dropped leaflets from the plane, like thousands of large snowflakes, saying "Against our will we are now obliged to direct our weapons against the Monastery itself. We warn you so that you may now save yourselves. Leave the Monastery at once." We were not at the Monastery but it didn't help, the people in our town had nowhere to go. The Allies learned later that there were no Nazi outposts in the Abbey but the damage was done.

As the Abbey was destroyed, only the cell and tomb of Saint Benedict survived, our town was hit again and again by the shelling. We were being obliterated in a cloud of flame, smoke and shattered stone. Every day we faced a landscape that resembled hell.

My mother had always been a small woman with a fragile constitution. The trauma of the bombing and the constant reports of another neighbor dead or a friend losing a limb had finally taken its toll. About two weeks after the ferocious bombing of the Abbey, she fell ill. Our water supply was low and we were almost completely out of food. My father was bereft and would not leave my mother's side, so it was left to me to try to remedy our desperate situation.

I knew that each day American fighter-bombers dropped brightly colored parachutes with canisters of ammunition, food and water to the Allied soldiers who were isolated on the slopes surrounding our town and leading up to the Abbey. I had determined if I waited for a very windy day, that I might be able to watch for the landing and secure at least one of the canisters for my family

The day the conditions were right, I set out alone. I had walked only about a mile when I heard someone behind me. I ducked behind a small outcrop of rocks and waited. I saw my love as she came creeping up from the last tree she had attempted to hide behind. She had followed me!

Cursing silently, I waited until she was along side the place where I lay in the snow; then I jumped up and grabbed her from behind placing my hand across her mouth so that she could not scream. She fought me with a strength I never knew she had and it was all I could do to hold her.

"Stop! It is only me, Roberto. Stop fighting me," I hissed holding my mouth close to her ear. "If I let you go do you promise not to make a sound?"

When she nodded her head, I released her and dragged her to the ground behind the rock. "What the hell are you doing here," I demanded trying to speak softly but strongly enough so that she would understand how unhappy I was to find her here, especially since we had agreed that I would do this alone.

It was then I hear a voice.

A voice speaking in English.

"Damn," the voice said.

Dragging her behind me, we ducked down. My heart was pounding in my throat. It appeared that someone had found my tiny shack. Fear rushed through me. Could we turn around and get back? Did they hear us?

Pressing my finger against my lips, I instructed her to be quiet as we started to back away from where the sound of the voice appeared to be coming from.

"Well, well, well," a voice boomed right behind us. "What do we have here? Come over here Walt and look at what I found!"

As we turned in fright, we saw an American soldier with a gun aimed at us. He was big in the way that men whose ancestors come from Norway are big. He had blond hair that was cut very close to his head and massive shoulders and legs.

Another man approached us from the side, also carrying a weapon. This man was even bigger than the first. He stood at least six and one half feet tall, a giant of a man. Where the first man was blond, the man named Walt was swarthy looking and had piercing blue eyes. With his coal black hair and coloring he could have easily been mistaken for a southern Italian if it weren't for his size.

"Aieeeee... Chi...hua...hua!" he shouted. "What do you have here? No stinkin' Krauts... no sireee. No couple of Heinies, no way. You found us a couple of Eye...talians! Whoooeee!... and one of those Eye..talians is real pretty too," he said as he jerked her out from behind my back.

"Let her go," I yelled as I pushed him away from her.

"Private Broderick, get a grip on him, will you," commanded the man named Walt who still held her by her arm. The blond man pushed me back with his rifle and left it pointed against my chest.

"Back up! Don't be stupid! We are not going to hurt you. Capisce?" he said as I staggered back.

The dark man jerked her scarf off of her head and all her beautiful hair spilled out in waves across her face and down her shoulders.

"Mama Mia," he whispered stroking her cheek, "you sure are beautiful, little one."

"Don't touch me, you pig!" she spat knocking his hand away.

"Click"

Chapter Twenty-Six
Seeley Lake, Montana

Julia was seated in Victor's rental car, a white Lexus sedan, with leather seats and a sunroof. They were in route to a cabin that Victor owned on Seeley Lake in Montana.

The roads were clear, but it was very cold, and snow covered the sides of the road. All the trees and the tops of the mountains were covered in a velvety white blanket. It was a winter wonderland stretched out as far as the eye could see. Everything glistened in the sun, like thousands of tiny shards of glass, creating a prism, whenever the sun touched them. The change, as they drove beneath canopies of trees laden with snow, only to burst back into the sunlight a moment later, caused Julia to squint her eyes and sigh with contentment.

When they had loaded the trunk of the car, you could see your breath as you spoke, so Julia spent a great deal of time, speaking randomly about this and that, so that she could watch the condensation as it formed in the air. The breeze that blew that morning draped them in biting cold, and was as pure and clean tasting as water from a mountain stream.

Julia was dazzled by the whiteness that surrounded them in every direction.

The drive took them further and further into what appeared to be a fantasy world, created by a fairy's wand, and the ice and the wind. She was lost in the wonder of it and didn't speak.

"Julia?" Victor asked interrupting her thoughts.

"Yes?" she replied not turning away from her window.

"Are you going to leave your hair that color and keep it cut that short?"

Julia laughed out loud. Although the beauty of the landscape had mesmerized her as they traveled on the road through the mountains, Victor had obviously not shared her feelings. He had stared hard at her whenever the opportunity rose where he could remove his gaze from the road and still not get them both killed.

She had noticed him, noticing her.

"It's my new make-over, Victor," she explained. "At first, I didn't like it. I thought I might look sort of cheap and trashy. But, now I'm starting to appreciate all the stares and now I'm considering the possibilities of entering a wilder side of life. I'm adjusting to it and I kind of like it," she finished.

"You've got to be kidding, Julia!" he exclaimed.

Julia laughed again, smiling into his face. "Don't worry, Victor. I'm only teasing. As soon as I can, I'll be back to the old Julia. I hate this look."

Victor didn't answer as Julia turned back to continue her look out the window. She still looked beautiful with her blond hair and blue eyes. There wasn't much she could do that would take that away from her. And, truth be told, she looked pretty sexy in her red lipstick, tight pants and her sweater, which outlined her every curve. Yes, he admitted, there were some real positives to her new disguise, he thought glancing over at her again.

But, Victor thought, even though she looked great, he wanted the old Julia back. The Julia he knew. The Julia with the simple, tailored clothes, honey brown eyes, long black hair, shining and swinging down her back touching her waist, and a smile that could stop you in your tracks with it's shear brilliance.

She had lost that smile after Roberto died, he thought – that smile, along with her hair, her clothes and the sparkle that used to be in her eyes. And, damn it. He wanted it back. He wanted his beautiful, lost, angel back.

***

Julia stood in the foyer of one of the most beautiful homes she had ever seen. It was made of logs and glass, soaring up for two stories into the forest of trees that surrounded it. And, it was immense. When she asked Victor how large it was; he had responded that it had about three thousand square feet of living space, if you included the decks.

They had arrived at Seeley Lake about mid-day, after crossing over Holland Creek and the Swan River. Julia had not spoken a word for most of the trip. She was so overcome by the mountains and all the snow draped on every available square inch of land surrounding them; sometimes in huge, billowing waves that crowded out the side of homes up to their roof tops, leaving only the track of smoke curling up from the chimneys. It looked like a Courier and Ives post card.

After unloading the trunk and carrying the bags inside, Victor said, "I have to make a couple of phone calls, Julia. Make yourself at home. I won't be long. Please feel free to explore the house if you want," he said walking away to a room on the left of the entrance that was obviously a study or library, based on the books that lined the shelves of the room.

Julia decided she would look around.

The floors were wide plank fir with gorgeous American Indian rugs scattered about. They appeared to be Navajo in origin, if she remembered her art classes in college correctly. They added bright spots of color, in different areas, here and there, as you looked around the room.

Soaring to the ceiling, against the front wall, in the middle of a great room was a twenty-foot tall rock fireplace, which was surrounded by plump, soft, dark leather couches, with lots of throw pillows of western motif, and side tables that appeared to be made of rock and wood. The floor to ceiling windows gave incredible views of the Swan and Mission mountains. The cedar, fir and pine trees were bent over from the weight of the snow on their boughs and some of the trees were sporting long icicles that hung from their branches to the ground. The view appeared to be part of the room. The windows disappeared and it was almost like being outside in the middle of a forest. It was beautiful and breathtaking in its simplicity, while maintaining a gentle air of manly elegance.

Leaving the room, she entered the kitchen.

Julia stared. Who would ever use the endless array of appliances, cabinets, and the dual stoves and refrigerators that circled the room, she wondered. There was a large island of granite in the center of the kitchen with a myriad of stools surrounding it. A beautiful, old, oak planked dining table was nestled into a nook that was filled with windows and large benches and chairs with comfortable cushions. Looking around her, Julia knew she would be afraid to cook in any part of this kitchen, since she was not neat when she cooked and always made a terrible mess. Then she thought of Carmen, her wonderful housekeeper back in Argentina, who could create the chaos resembling a small tornado strike when she baked, and she laughed. You wouldn't want her touch anything in this kitchen; it was too shiny and immaculate.

"I need to ask Victor if he cooks and who cleans this place for him," she mused aloud. Wondering, not for the first time, if there were any women currently in his life.

As she wandered back to front of the house, she heard Victor still speaking with someone on the phone. She decided to continue her exploration upstairs.

Climbing a wide, log staircase, she turned to the left off the landing and entered what appeared to be the master bedroom and private bath. The bed was made of logs. Very masculine, she thought. It was enormous - filled with giant pillows and a gorgeous silk duvet of pale, muted green. The center of the bed was filled with a huge, plump of rounded softness that led her to peek under the duvet. There she found a glorious, thick, featherbed; so soft and inviting that Julia wanted to jump onto the bed and sink down into the middle of it.

Standing back and studying the room, she thought about how masculine it all was, with just a touch of softness, but when you put it all together it somehow worked in the room. The silk fabric set against the tree logs, reminded her of Victor – tough but gentle.

Ooops, she thought. Better not to dwell on that thought, she cautioned herself.

There were French doors directly across from the bed that opened onto a snow swept balcony. It overlooked the trees and the lake, and had a breathtaking view of the mountains, that appeared to be so close that you could touch them if you reached out your hand. Julia stared in amazement as she walked out the doors onto the balcony. The sun was slanting down, streaming light through the branches of the pine trees, which were laden with snow. The wind was whispering through the branches, rustling them gently; causing small avalanches of snow to drop from the branches, which made gentle plopping sounds as they hit the ground. The frozen lake, to the right of the woods, glistened like a thousand diamonds that had been placed side by side in the snow.

When the sun struck them, a brilliant rainbow of light dazzled your eyes. It was magical.

Julia was overcome and swayed dizzily on her feet for a moment. She was suddenly filled with an overwhelming sense of peace and joy. A feeling that all was well with the world, and that she shouldn't worry anymore, swept over her. God was in everything around her - in the hills, the misty mountains, the lake and the dying glow of the sun – his creations, every one – that lay spread out in the vista before her, and she was comforted and struck still at the same time.

"Victor," the voice whispered after a time.

"Be still, Roberto," she whispered out loud, as she stood wrapped in the embrace of the trees, the mounds of snow and the majesty of the mountains that surrounded her.

***

The sun was just a glimmer on the horizon when Victor found Julia still standing, looking at the golden edges of light playing on the lake.

"Oh, there you are Julia," he said softly, not wanting to break the spell. "I was wondering where you were hiding. I'm sorry I took so long."

Julia said nothing.

"You should come in now; you're trembling from the cold."

Julia smiled and turned away from the mountains and stepped back into the room.

"Victor," she said breathlessly, "this place is really very beautiful. How did you ever find it when you live so far away in New York?"

"A buddy of mine used to own it," he answered, "and we used to come up here to get away from New York and to go skiing a couple of times over the winter months. Sometimes in the early spring we would come up and do some fishing. He was transferred to Japan, met a

Japanese maiden, fell madly in love and decided to stay. He called and asked if I was interested. I was. And, here I am."

"Well, I'd never leave here, if I owned this piece of paradise."

"You like it, huh?"

"Oh, yes. It's like heaven," she breathed, turning back and looking out the window where the light was almost gone.

"Well, young lady, you are welcome to use it anytime you want. Feel free to come and go, as you like. I can have a key made for you, if you want."

"What about girlfriends? I wouldn't want to surprise one of them when I showed up uninvited," she said, hoping to extract information about his love life.

Victor wasn't biting. "How about something to eat? Are you hungry?" he said easily sidestepping her question.

Julia cursed herself for being so transparent.

Victor smiled.

Looking back at the bed, her face grew hot and she looked around the room nervously, thinking about the possible sleeping arrangements.

Victor noticed.

"Look, Julia. This will be your room. My room, has a very uncomfortable, lumpy bed, that's too short, with no pillows, and is way, way, way... down this long, dark, lonely, cold hall," he pointed, sniffing as if he was crying.

Julia laughed.

"Seriously, you don't have to worry," he reassured her. "I'll behave. Although, I have to admit, you are pretty fetching with that wild hair and that outfit that leaves nothing to the imagination," indicating her ski pants and tight sweater. "It will be a struggle for me, I'll admit it. But, I won't stray from that dark, cold, lonely room, way down there, up here to your warm, beautiful, comfortable bed."

Julia laughed again.

"Listen, Julia, I promise you that I won't do anything you don't want me to do. How's that?"

"Deal," she said grinning broadly, hooking her arm through his. "Besides, I'm not worried, cowboy. I think I can handle you."

Oh, Victor thought, how he wished she would.

***

Julia and Victor had just finished a meal of shrimp scampi, rice and a spinach salad. He was washing and she was drying the plates and utensils while they talked.

"Where did you learn to cook like that?"

"Well, being a bachelor for so long has forced all kinds of terrible, and burdensome things upon me. Not having a 'little woman' around to wait on me hand and foot - you know you 'little women" all are supposed to cook, feed and keep us manly men satisfied in all ways - I was forced to take action. It was either go out every night to a restaurant, or, damn it all, learn to cook. Being on the road so much didn't help either, since I was forced to eat out all the time, usually for the duration of most of my trips. When I got home, the last thing I wanted to do was to go out anywhere to eat, thus, out of necessity, my skill as a cook was born."

Julia laughed happily. "Little women and manly men?" she asked still chuckling.

"Yes, that's the way we new age bachelors, otherwise known as manly men, speak down to you 'women folk'," he grinned.

"Really? "Well, you're a good cook. I'll give you that. The meal was excellent. You are going to make some 'little woman' really happy one of these days."

"So you think, 'I Can Cook!' will look good on my 'little woman' dating resume?" Victor laughed.

"Yeah, Mr. 'Manly Man', it would certainly impress me if I were out looking for someone to hook up with."

Hmmmm, he thought, starting to work on the pots and pans with more vigor.

* * *

Victor had started a fire in the fireplace, and it was roaring away as they sat on the floor, leaning back on soft cushions eating popcorn.

"I can't believe I'm eating anything else after the dinner we just had," Julia said crunching down on a popcorn kernel.

"Well, you can't sit down in front of a fire, out here in the wild, wild, west, that is, without some popcorn or some beans, and I thought you might like popcorn a little better."

"Good choice," Julia said laughing, as she picked up another kernel and tossed it into her mouth.

As they sat quietly, enjoying the fire and each other's company, Victor noticed that Julia's mood had suddenly changed. One minute she had been smiling and, the next minute, she was so down, it was as if someone had poured a cold bucket of water on her head.

Finally, after some time had passed he said, "Julia."

"Yes," she answered, never lifting her eyes from the fire.

"What's wrong? Would you like to talk about it?"

Julia didn't answer for so long a time, that he thought she hadn't heard him.

Then she said, "I feel like this was a mistake."

Victor paused before saying, "Coming here with me?"

"No. This is great. I meant my coming back here to the States to try to see my family."

Victor said nothing.

"Now that Alex is better, maybe I should go back home."

115

Victor noted that Julia had used the word "home" as a reference to her life in Argentina. Interesting he thought, but he said nothing.

"They don't know who I am and they seem to be very happy with each other. And..." she paused, "I hate sharing David with Lainie. I mean, after all, he is my husband. And, I guess it just hurts," she finished lamely.

Victor was afraid of her answer, afraid of what she might say, but he had to know, so he asked. "Julia, do you still love him?"

Julia stared at the fire, listening to it as it sizzled and popped; it's warmth spreading out through the corners of the room. Turning back to Victor, she noticed the light from the fire as it played across his face. He was handsome. No, more than handsome, he was gorgeous. Tall, dark, broad shouldered, slim hipped, a great cook, sweet, kind, and a real romantic, every little girl's fantasy man. Furthermore, when he made love to you, it felt like he was stripping the skin from your body. But even after you were all his, when he had removed any boundaries that might be left, when you could hardly breathe you were so overcome with wanting, he took your soul and led it through the motions of an ageless, mind-bending dance. La Petite Morte', the little death, they called it and it was truly just like dying when Victor made love to you. He was a heart-numbing lover and he had a beautiful body to do it with.

Blushing, Julia turned away from him. These were not good thoughts to be having when you were talking about your children and your lost husband, she reminded herself.

What Julia didn't know was that Victor had been holding his breath, the entire time, waiting for her response.

"I don't know Victor. I don't know how I feel about him anymore. It's been so long and he's changed and I've changed. I just don't know how I feel or what it all means. He seems like a stranger to me now."

Victor released his breath. Well, he supposed that this was better than her blurting out, "Yes, I love David madly and I want him back". Only slightly better, he admitted, but better.

They changed the subject, after that and continued to talk about other things until after the clock struck midnight.

"Julia, I think I'm going to go up now. I'm tired. Do you want to stay here a while longer?"

"No. I'm ready."

Outside the door to her bedroom, Victor leaned down and kissed her gently on the cheek. Then he moved over to her mouth and kissed her again. A spark of fire bolted through him.

"Good night, Julia," he said, moving away down the hall to his room.

***

Julia was awake.

She couldn't sleep.

It was sometime after two a.m., when Victor came.

Julia couldn't move.

As Victor approached the bed, she bundled the sheets into her fists in anticipation, her body starting to tingle with want and need. She knew she should ask him to leave, but she also knew she wouldn't.

Victor was naked and he was aroused when he knelt down beside her bed and pulled her hand up to his lips. His breath was like a hot wind blowing on her palm. He whispered her name, "Julia," so softly it was like a sigh. Then he kissed her palm, placing his tongue in the center of her hand and licking her very gently.

Julia started to speak, but Victor lifted his fingers and placed them gently against her lips. Her body flared into a burning flame, when he groaned out her name as his lips moved against her mouth.

Then he placed his hands on her face and started to feel her cheekbones, her eyes, her mouth, slowly touching each of the contours of her face, as if he were a blind man and could only use his fingers, in the darkness, as a way to identify her.

As he moved his hands down to her throat, he pulled the covers from her naked body. He stared at her with eyes burning with desire as he drank in her beauty.

Slowly, very slowly, moving a heartbeat at a time, he touched her, as if she were a sacred chalice. Then his hands found her breasts and he fondled them while he kissed and licked at her ears. Then he moved away, slowly kissing her face, until he reached her mouth. There he spent long moments, still kneading her breasts, while he licked her parted lips, ever so gently, like a kitten might lick at its milk.

She was trembling now, but she didn't speak and she didn't move. She was weightless and she was flying high above the bed.

Pulling her nipples gently until they were rock hard, he moved his hands down her sides counting each one of her ribs. Then he spanned the flat of her stomach with one hand, holding her with his eyes. As he smoothed his palms over her hips, he seemed to contemplate how small she was in his hands.

Stopping, he picked up Julia's hand, pressed it to his mouth, and then licked the webs between her fingers.

Julia's mind was spinning.

Slowly he placed each of her fingers, one at a time, into his mouth and sucked them.

Julia was on fire. Her heart was pounding and she wondered at the desire she was feeling. She wanted him to stop, it hurt her to want him like this, but she couldn't move a muscle to push him away. She wanted him to take her, but she couldn't speak and ask him to. She was like a desperate addict and he had the drug to relieve her pain, but for some reason he withheld the potion from her burning body.

118

Victor moved his mouth back to her lips and spoke her name as he licked and bit down gently, never putting his tongue into her waiting mouth.

He stroked her legs, her feet, touching each bone and sinew, kissing and licking her body, slowly, slowly moving over her, a little at a time.

Julia had melted. Her bones had liquefied and she was drifting in a haze of burning lust as he continued to move over her body.

Finally, he touched her sex. She was hot and wet.

"Julia, oh Julia," he whispered reverently.

Taking her legs, he pulled them apart so that she was completely open to him. Then he climbed onto the bed and entered her, moving very, very slowly until he filled her up.

Julia climaxed as soon as he entered her, but Victor only continued to move slowly, back and forth, into her waiting body, taking his time, driving her deeper and deeper into ecstasy.

Julia didn't want it to ever stop.

Then her passion flared again, Victor knew it, he could feel her tighten around him, but he would not be rushed. He kissed and sucked at her mouth, driving her higher and higher. Pulling her up into his arms, he pumped her gently, in and out, whispering her name, until they both soared into the heavens and the world exploded into a thousand, blinding, rockets of light. As she fell back to earth, she drifted away on a sea of bliss.

Julia thought she must have fainted, because the next thing she saw when she opened her eyes, was a beautiful sunny morning and Victor sitting on the edge of her bed fully dressed.

"Wake up sleepy head. I brought you some hot coffee."

Julia stared at him. He was acting like nothing had happened the night before.

"I made some breakfast, if you're hungry," he said, smiling and handing her the steaming cup of coffee.

Julia sipped the coffee that was clearly from Argentina, based on its strong aroma, and contemplated him through sleepy eyes. Apparently, he was not going to mention last night. Well, okay, she thought. Two can play this game.

"Sure, I'll be right down. Thanks for the coffee."

***

Victor sipped his third cup of coffee as he stood in great room watching Julia through the window as she played in the snow. She was bundled up from head to toe in a hat, muffler, gloves, jacket, boots, and ski pants. She looked adorable.

She was attempting to make what must have been her very first snowman, since it did not resemble any snowman he had ever seen. The body was made of two large globs of snow that were oblong and not rounded into balls, plus they were sitting off-center from each other. It was extremely tall and thin, not jolly and round like most. The pitiful creation looked like a lop-sided, headless, monster, weaving drunkenly through the snow. Victor loved it.

A small ball of snow, way too small for any snowman head, was lying at her feet. She was winded. You could see the puffs of condensation, as she panted. Her cheeks and nose were red and she was grinning from ear to ear, obviously delighted with what she had sculpted with her own hands. She was truly delusional, he thought. She had probably been out in the elements too long and it had affected her brain.

He laughed, as she stood with her hands on her hips, surveying her work moving around the snowman, looking at it from every angle, clearly pleased with the results.

God, he was crazy about her. He thought about the night before when he had gone crazy. He wanted to be sorry for what had happened, but he couldn't muster up the feeling. It had been as if he

120

were in a drug-induced trance. He couldn't have stopped his feet from moving down the hall to her bedroom and taking her, if he had wanted to, which he hadn't. He had been like a man dying in the desert, burning with fever, struggling with delirium, and Julia had been a cool, wet drink of water, that he had to have or he would perish.

He loved her. He wanted her with his entire being. Now the question was, could he make her love him too? Did he have enough time? He had to try.

As he watched, Julia picked up the ball of snow at her feet – it must have been heavy, because she appeared to be straining under its weight – and heaved it up with all her might, aimed her pitch at the top of the snowman, missed her target, staggered backwards and fell into a huge bank of snow.

Grabbing his jacket, Victor pushed his arms into the sleeves, opened the front door and leisurely walked up to where Julia was lying deep in the snow, struggling to get her breath.

"Need some help, little lady?"

"Damn, Victor. I was trying to surprise you, but I can't get the stupid head on the silly thing," she said standing up and brushing snow from her clothes.

Victor's breath caught in his throat, as she looked him in the eyes. He had the irresistible urge to throw her down in the snow and kiss her until she begged him for more.

Instead, he picked up the lump of snow, and walked back to her snowman, or whatever it was that she had made.

"And, just what is it that you were going to surprise me with?" he said surveying the strange creation in front of him.

"Why, my snowman, of course. I've been working on it all morning," she said proudly.

"Oh, so that's what you call this thing? A snowman?" he teased her, placing the small lump on top of the other two larger lumps that were her masterpiece.

"Oooh!" she said. "You're so mean!"

Then she started pelting him with snowballs. He didn't know it, but she had made quite a stash of them while waiting for him to come outside. That was going to be the second part of her surprise.

"Why you…you…. little sneak," he said as she hit him square in the chest. "I come out here to help you save this eyesore you've been building in my front yard – I'll be the laughing stock of my neighbors for years, by the way – and this is the thanks I get?"

Julia laughed. "Well, I might not make the best snowman, but I can throw a mean, fast ball. I was champion pitcher of the girl's softball league in high school, I want you to know," she bragged, throwing another perfect pitch and hitting him in the back.

Just a few more seconds, he thought, bending down with his back to her, as he made his fourth snowball.

"Oh, really, Miss Smarty Pants," he taunted her, still turned away from her. "Well, I was the champion pitcher on our college team and we won the college world series, two years in a row – thanks to Moi'," he said as she hit him in the back with two more throws.

Turning around to face her, she could see that he was armed with snowballs and that he looked dangerous.

"Uh oh," she said as she spun around and attempted to run. But, the snow was so deep that she ended up shuffling away instead, which left her at a distinct disadvantage since Victor was closing in.

Catching Julia in the shoulder with his first throw, he hit her in the back with his next.

"Where are you going, Julia?" he chided. "Don't want to play anymore?" he said whipping the next snowball into her legs as she stomped through the snow.

Then he was on her. He tackled her and they rolled down the embankment. They were both out of breath and laughing when they stopped.

Victor was on top of Julia, and she felt good beneath him. Placing his fingers on her cheeks, his heart emptied out, as he looked into her beautiful, laughing eyes.

"Do you always come to your games so unprepared, Mr. Star Pitcher for the College Team?" she teased, smiling up at him.

"What do you mean?" he said, still stroking her cheek.

"Your hands are like ice."

Looking down, Victor noticed that he had never put his gloves on, and now that she had mentioned it, his fingers were starting to sting and burn.

Her words broke the spell. Kissing her on the forehead, he jumped up and helped her to her feet.

"Don't you really like it?" she said pouting.

"Like what?" he said brushing snow from his face and off his neck.

"My snowman!" she demanded, placing both hands on her hips.

"Yeah. I like it. It kind of reminds me of you."

"Really? How?"

"Well," he said stopping and studying it one more time. "He's just a 'wild and crazzzzzy guy', and you're just a wild and crazzzzzy girl," he said imitating Steve Martin from Saturday Night Live.

"Come on 'wild thing'. Let's get out of these wet clothes and I'll make you something warm to drink."

Julia tromped after him, mumbling something under her breath. Victor threw back his head and laughed.

***

Their wet jackets, hats and mufflers had been hung to dry, so Julia went upstairs to remove her remaining wet clothes.

Victor was wearing a terry cloth robe and soft slippers as he finished the hot cider he was making. He was standing with his back to

Julia when she re-entered the room. Turning to look at her, Victor erupted in laughter.

"What in the hell are you wearing?" he said smiling down at her.

"My pajamas," she said insulted, "and I happen to like them. I think they're cute."

Julia was standing in front of him in flannel, turquoise colored pajama tops and pajama bottoms with feet in them. They were covered entirely with florescent, pink flamingos. She looked so cute, that he wanted to crush her to him and kiss her until she was dizzy.

Handing her a cup of hot cider, he said, "Well, I especially like your little 'feety things'," he said, pointing down to her feet.

Julia just sipped and didn't say anything.

"And, they're real appropriate for a mountain cabin out in the wild, wild, west."

"They're warm and I like them, so there," she said swinging away from him and moving into the great room, taking a seat in front of the fireplace.

Victor was still chuckling, when he walked into the room and joined her on the couch.

"Julia, I left you a robe, outside your room, on the banister, if you would like to use it. I know it will be hard for you to tear yourself away from the 'haute couture' you are currently wearing, but it's there for you, if you want it," he teased.

Julia threw a pillow at him; he threw one back, and the next thing she knew they were in an all out pillow fight.

When she moved a little too close, during one of her attacks, he reached out and grabbed her by the front of her pajamas and hauled her over onto his lap. Then he went crazy kissing her. She kissed him back, lost in his lips and how they felt. He ripped her top open, sending buttons flying everywhere, and then he plunged his face down and took her breast into his mouth. Then Julia regained her senses.

Pulling back, and turning away from him, she covered her nakedness with what was left of her shirt and stood up. Her eyes were wild with desire and she was trembling.

Victor yanked her back to him.

"You're mine, Julia," he growled. "You can run from it but you're not going to be able to hide from it. You belong to me and no one else. See these hands?" Yes, Julia thought. She remembered those hands very well. Actually, very, very well, she thought blushing profusely.

Julia said nothing.

"My fingerprints are all over your body. They won't wash off, so don't try. I left them there so you won't forget, that you're mine now."

Julia shivered and didn't speak.

Releasing her shirt, Victor put his face in his hands and scrubbed at his hair in frustration.

"Not," she whispered.

"Not what?" he asked through clenched teeth.

"I'm not yours."

He looked up and saw the small smile curving her lips.

"Are," he said.

"Not."

"Are."

"No, I'm not!"

"Yes, you are!"

And then they were laughing like little children, rolling over, holding their stomachs; laughing until tears fell from their eyes.

After a while she smiled and said, "I think I'll go get that robe now."

"Might be best," he said regretfully.

"I'll be right back," she said scurrying from the room.

***

The rest of the evening, they spent sharing a light dinner, a quiet drink, the beauty of the dying fire, and carefully avoiding each other's eyes.

Julia spoke to him in quiet tones as she told him everything he needed to know that was troubling her. She spoke about the years before Roberto, her childhood, college, then her marriage to David; the tragedy that took her away from everyone she loved, about the years that Roberto and she had spent together, much of which he already knew; about what had happened since she returned to America, and finally about her fears regarding her future. Whenever she spoke about David, there was wistfulness in her voice that left Victor feeling all hollowed out inside.

When he spoke he tried to reason with her about all the time that had passed, and how time changes people's feelings and the way they view those they loved before. She had been out of their lives for over twenty years. Her family had made new lives, coping the best they could with the loss of her. Maybe, the fact that they were all happy should be enough for her now.

But, Julia was angry. She felt that his point of view was totally unfair. Why should she be the one that was left out? Why should she have to give them up? It wasn't her fault she had been taken from them. Should she be punished for this all over again? Why couldn't she just tell them the truth and go back to being a wife and a mother?

Victor was heartsick. Sure, he thought, part of what he was feeling, as she spoke, was selfish. But, the other part was that he knew that Julia was going to be hurt. There were no guarantees that, even if she told her family who she was, they would welcome her back into their open arms. There was also Lainie to think about. She would be wounded terribly if Julia succeeded in her mission to take back her family. But, Julia couldn't see it. She would not listen.

***

Later that night, after they went to their respective room, after the world was fast asleep, he came to her again. She was waiting this time.

They made love with a manic intensity. She fought to hold something of herself back, but he worked her until she cried out and begged him to take her and to make her agony go away.

He did.

Several times.

When Julia could no longer move her body, or lift her arms to hold him; she was so drained; he gathered her up and held her close to his chest.

"You are mine, little one," he whispered. Then he didn't speak again for a long moment.

"Can't you feel it when we are together?" he asked, speaking in a soft voice. "We are like wolves, my love. I will never leave you. I will mate with you for life. There will be no one else for me, or for you," he added. Julia fell asleep as he continued to whisper. She fell asleep listening to his heartbeat.

***

The next day, Victor closed himself up in the study after breakfast and left Julia alone. It was their last day together - they would head back tomorrow - and they were both trying to deal with what that meant to the both of them.

Julia took a long walk in the snow and tried to tell herself that her leaving and going back to David and her children was the right thing to do. Her family had to be her first priority now and she could not allow herself to be side tracked by the sexual feelings she had for Victor. Just thinking about him made her legs weak.

He had told her over and over that she belonged to him, but it wasn't true. She really didn't belong to anyone now, but she was going to work hard to get David and her children back. Victor was a wonderful lover, and she couldn't deny him anything whenever he touched her, but she was a mom and she needed to be with her children. She couldn't get sidetracked. Victor would have to understand that the two of them could never be.

When she arrived back at the house Victor was seated in the great room, staring out the windows at the snow.

"David called," Victor said, over his shoulder. "He asked that you call him back."

She noticed that he wouldn't look at her.

"Did he leave a number?"

"It's on my desk by the phone."

Chapter Twenty-Seven

Julia dialed the number and David picked up on the third ring.
"Hello."

"David, it's Julia. Is Alex okay?"

"Yes, yes, she's fine. That's not why I'm calling."

"What is it?"

"Julia, I've spoken to Lainie about the hospital in Washington and she agreed it was a really good idea. We wanted to thank you for finding this treatment program for us."

"You're welcome. That's just great. When I get back, I'll start the process of having Alex moved."

"Well, that's what I wanted to talk to you about. We're back in Washington. We moved Alex on Saturday."

Julia said nothing. She was speechless

They were back in Washington? They had moved Alex and they were back in Washington? How could that be, she wondered. Why would they do that?

"And, we decided that we want to start a new regimen now that Alex has been admitted to the hospital here in Washington and that we won't need your services anymore."

"I don't understand," Julia said feeling her world shifting under her feet.

"Well, Alex doesn't really need a sitter now. Obviously, you will be paid extra for your dedication to our daughter and we will never be able to thank you for all that you have done for us. But, Lainie and I feel that we want to be in control of her recovery now. You may certainly use us for a reference at any time, your help was excellent."

Julia said nothing.

"Julia, I'm sorry. I wish you luck and happiness. I truly appreciate what you have done for our family."

Julia hung up on him.

***

David set the phone down in its cradle. What he hadn't said to Julia was that he and Lainie had fought over whether Julia should come to Washington to help with Alex's recovery. He thought she should, but Lainie was adamant that they didn't need her.

"Julia isn't even a hospital nurse. She has been wonderful, but we don't need her anymore. Alex needs to bond with us and Julia is in the way of that."

Lainie had never been so stubborn. Finally, David had given in when Lainie had said, "David, is there another reason you want her to move to Washington?" Obviously, he had no real answer that wouldn't have put him and his marriage in a bad place.

He would miss Julia very much, but it was probably the best thing since he was feeling things for her that he really couldn't afford.

***

Victor found her crying at his desk.

"Julia," he said, leaning over to her.

130

"Is Alex okay?"

Julia shook her head yes, but continued to cry.

"Do you want to tell me what is wrong?"

Julia sniffed and wiped her nose. "They fired me. They fired me from being with my own daughter! They don't need a sitter anymore and after all I'm just a sitter! Aaaaggghhh!" she cried out in agony.

Then she stood up and ran from the room.

***

Victor found her sitting naked on the floor of her shower with the hot water beating down on her. He walked into the steamy stall, fully clothed and sat down beside her.

"I'm here, Julia. Let me hold you."

Julia climbed into his arms and cried until she couldn't cry anymore. Victor wanted to speak, but he didn't. He just held her naked body as the water poured over him, drenching his clothes.

***

Later that night, Julia refused dinner and shut herself up in her room. Victor walked through the snow, stared at the fire, drank several shots of whiskey, paced the floor and finally went up to bed. He did not go to Julia's room during the night.

But, she came to his.

Victor was awake when she climbed into bed with him.

She kissed him on the lips and said, "We need to talk. I'm leaving tomorrow."

He was silent for a long moment. "I know."

"I'm going to Washington and I'm going to get my husband back," she said moving down his chest to his nipples.

Victor sighed, "I know."

131

Julia moved over him and did all the things he had done to her and more and he didn't try to stop her.

"I don't belong to you and I'm going back to David," she said taking him into her mouth.

"I know," he said when he could speak again.

Tears squeezed out of his eyes, down his cheeks, onto the pillow as he cried for the loss of her. Then she mounted him.

"I'm sorry, Victor I really am," she murmured as she rocked back and forth. "You're very special to me, but I have to do this. I'm going back to them. I can't stay with you."

"I know," he groaned, reaching out to her.

***

Three days later, Julia called him.

"They've asked me to come to Washington," she started as soon as he answered. "Alex refused to go to rehab, to eat or to do anything unless they agreed to hire me back. They were frantic, so Lainie called me this time, hat in hand, basically, and asked me to come and work with Alex until she gets back on her feet. I am so excited. I'm leaving tomorrow and I wanted to let you know that I'll be near you and maybe we can have dinner some time."

That was the last thing Victor wanted. He didn't want to see her. He couldn't, not anymore.

"That's great, Julia, but I'm going to be really busy. Why don't you call me after you arrive and I'll see."

Julia never noticed his hesitation, or the coolness in his voice. "Great, I'll call when I get settled."

Chapter Twenty-Eight
Nine Months Later

Lauren Prescott watched Rosita and her entourage. Her head was thrown back and she was laughing at something someone had said. She was hanging onto a very good-looking actor from a competing soap and she was incredibly drunk.

She's sleeping with him, she laughed, watching the way Rosita rubbed her breasts against her companion each time she moved.

They were all at "21" celebrating the various Emmy awards each show had received earlier that evening at the award ceremony. Rosita was the star of the hour having taken two of the prize statues for their show "Another Day". Lauren had won nothing for the first time in five years and she was pissed.

Rosita noticed Lauren watching her and winked, giving her a little finger wave. Lauren choked on her drink. God, how I hate her, she thought, smiling back at her enemy, while she tried to catch her breath.

Luke, Rosita's husband, looked almost as unhappy as Lauren. He was staring at his wife as she threw herself at another man and rubbed her body all over him. Standing at the end of the bar, nursing a beer, he was scowling in anger.

Nice, Lauren thought, as she wondered at the blatant disregard Rosita showed for her husband's feelings. Rosita laughed just then, sending a shiver down Lauren's spine.

But, all in all, things were going well, she had to admit. It was only a matter of time before Rosita self-destructed. She was drinking and drugging, which was getting to be more obvious from the way Rosita constantly wiped at her nose. She had missed her lines a couple of times during rehearsals and had arrived late at the studio, more than once. Everything was working and Rosita was falling deep into the trap.

"Oh, please keep partying, honey," she whispered. "I'll keep supplying the men and the drugs. You see I have lots of money and lots of friends. Just keep cooperating."

Rosita smiled at Lauren as she staggered past her to the restroom. Lauren followed her.

"Lauren, you're looking lovely tonight," Rosita smirked when Lauren entered the room. "Wherever did you get that dress?"

Rosita was at the mirror freshening her lipstick. She was breathtakingly beautiful and it killed Lauren to her very soul to admit it. Her floor length dress was skin-tight, low cut, with almost no back, and it floated down her body, clinging to every curve. She appeared to be naked since the fabric was lined in flesh colored material. The dress was covered with small, diamond-like stones that glittered and glowed as she walked. It was stunning and it was dropping the men in their tracks, leaving them speechless as she moved about the room.

Lauren was past the age of being able to wear anything that even closely resembled the creation Rosita was wearing. So her simple Dolce & Gabbana, black evening gown paled in comparison.

"Rosita, you're drunk and you're making a spectacle of yourself," she said ignoring her jab about her dress, as she passed her on the way to one of the stalls that lined the walls behind the powder room.

"Lauren, what's the matter?" she said stopping her with her eyes, as she continued to primp in the mirror. "Can't keep up? How many awards did you win tonight? Oh, I'm sorry. You didn't win any, did you?" she said with a snicker. "But, I see you are still the belle of the ball anyway aren't you? I noticed all the men draped all over you tonight," she finished, blotting her lipstick on a paper towel.

Lauren paused, "Well, Rosita, what I noticed, in case you hadn't, is that your very handsome husband seems to be enjoying himself tonight. I think he particularly liked watching his wife rub herself all over another man." she snapped back.

"Well, "Rosita smiled wickedly, hands on her hips, turning to face Lauren, "at least I have a husband. What I do outside my marriage is something you wouldn't understand. Of course, how could you? You've never been married. You've probably never been in love. Besides, no man would ever want to marry you. They couldn't stand to touch you. You're such a cold, ugly bitch."

Lauren was stunned by Rosita's hatred. "Rosita, honey," she paused drawing in on her cigarette, "you're just a piece of meat to those men right now, and as soon as they're through gnawing on your bones, they'll throw you back in the garbage heap you came from," she hissed, blowing the smoke into Rosita's face.

Rosita laughed and waved the smoke away. "Yeah, but I'm fresh prime cut, grade-A beef and you're just old meat, honey. You're way past your prime." Snapping her purse shut she smiled brightly and said, "Have a great night." Then she left the room

Lauren's face blanched of all color. She fell back against the wall and began to cry.

Chapter Twenty-Nine
Washington, D.C.

Julia was working with Alex on the walking ramp with parallel bars. She gripped them on each side as she tried to regain her strength. She wanted to walk again. Her legs were in braces and she could now manage a walker fairly well.

Julia watched her and thought about how far her daughter's recovery had come.

The first six weeks after she had flown to Washington to supervise her daughter's care had been hell. Alex had started to run a high fever and slowly over a period of a few days, she had slipped back into a coma. Finally, she had been placed on a ventilator, since she could no longer breathe on her own.

Julia, David and Lainie had been frantic. When they asked the doctor what was happening, he said that Alex had pneumonia, which was not unusual with patients who had suffered the type of injuries that Alex had sustained and who had been bed-ridden for so long a time. They had her on a heavy course of antibiotics to fight the infection that was raging through her body.

Lainie disagreed vehemently with the doctor's diagnosis and expressed it in a very loud voice.

"My daughter does not have pneumonia! She has suffered with asthma since she was a small child and when she has a bad cold she wheezes so badly it sounds like a train is in the room! She does not have pneumonia! You need to look further!"

The doctor's had smiled politely; they obviously knew more than this poor distraught mom screaming at them, and then completely ignored her.

Alex continued her decline daily. Lainie would not leave her side.

Julia was the one who finally instigated the mutiny.

She believed Lainie and she was not going to sit back and watch her daughter die. She begged two of the nurses who were caring for Alex to look at her chart, to listen to her chest sounds and to talk to her mother who was adamant that the girl did not have pneumonia. They did, and finally they agreed that they felt Alex had been misdiagnosed.

When the doctor came for his evening rounds, the two nurses, Lainie and Julia blocked the doorway and refused to allow him to leave the room. As they stood in the doorway, they started speaking at the same time. "She's dying. We don't believe she has pneumonia. You have to do something. She's not wheezing. She has asthma. You need to look again."

"Ladies, please. You're making a scene. Please stand aside," he demanded.

"No. We won't," Lainie said calmly. "You are not leaving this room until you prove to me that my daughter has pneumonia. Where is the x-ray? There is nothing in her chart. Show me the x-ray and I will believe you," she begged.

The doctor studied her for a moment. "We never took x-rays. It was obvious that she had pneumonia," he said defensively.

"Well, if you ever want to leave this room again, you had better order the x-ray right now, because we are not budging until you do," Lainie said harshly.

Looking from one to the other, he realized that they were serious. "Oh, all right," her said. "We are wasting our time, but I'll do it."

That had been how it all started. He had ordered a portable x-ray brought to the room. When he read it, his face had drained of all color. He had barked at everyone to leave the room, and called a squad of nurses and medical assistants to Alex's bedside and slammed the door.

Julia and Lainie had both been crying, pacing back and forth in the hallway, when the door had opened and the team walked out carrying pans and instruments in their hands. They would not meet the two women's eyes as they passed.

Alex had gangrene in her wound! The incision was so infected that the doctor had to perform surgery on Alex while she lay in her hospital bed. He was white faced when he tried to explain how this could have happened. Dirt had gotten into the wound during surgery as they worked on her muddy body after the accident

No one cared. They just wanted Alex to get better.

And she did. Within twenty-four hours, her fever dropped. Every few hours, night and day, she was taken to a whirlpool where she was submerged and her wounds were flushed out. The stitches in her incision had been removed and now the incision was open from her neck to her groin and it left a wide gaping wound. But, slowly very slowly, it started to heal from the inside out.

The infection and the twenty-four hour a day regimen took its toll and set Alex's recovery back by months.

When Julia had the time to consider all that happened, she had been devastated by the knowledge that if it weren't for Lainie's intervention, her daughter might have died. Julia had not known that her daughter had asthma or that she wheezed badly when she had the slightest cold. She was not the one who had raised Alex and she knew absolutely nothing about her daughter's health or anything else for that matter. That truth had hurt her terribly. At the time, she had cried, and the years she had missed with her two children had curled around her and wrapped her in misery.

Finally, she had pulled herself together. She forgave herself for something that she had no control over, and started working harder on Alex's recovery. Now, months later, Alex was within reach of walking on her own and, throwing away the walker that she hated with a vengeance – she said it made her feel like an old woman. Alex would still need a cane and her braces for some indefinite period of time, but she would walk, if she or Alex had anything to do with it. They were that determined.

"I think I'm ready, Julia," Alex said, smiling at her beloved nurse.

"Well, okay sweetie. You've sure worked hard enough for this. So, if you think you're ready, then show me what you can do, young lady."

"I accept your challenge, Mademoiselle," she said raising her fist in the air. "So," she continued, "stand back. Make room for 'Speedy Gonzales'. I will thrill and amaze you with my speed and agility."

Julia laughed at her exuberance. But, as Alex stepped away from her walker and stood holding herself up with her cane, Julia's heartbeat increased.

"I can do it, Julia. Don't worry. I can do it," she gasped with her tongue pinched between her front teeth, pushing one foot in front of the other. She was holding her cane with both hands, one arm crossed over her body, as she shuffled slowly forward.

Julia stood with her hands pressed against her lips, praying Alex wouldn't fall; she was too far away to catch her. Right then David slipped into the room, stepped up next to her and stood watching Alex's progress.

"Daddy. Daddy. Look, I'm doing it. I'm walking!" Alex squealed.

Her right leg and foot still didn't obey the commands that originated from her damaged brain, so it was jerking out to the right from her body and back, crookedly, as she walked. But, she did walk, and it was glorious to behold.

David threw his arms around Julia, hugged her and then walked over to meet his daughter who was trembling from her efforts and appeared to be ready to collapse. He wrapped his arms around her and helped her back to a seat, while she leaned heavily on him for support.

Julia was so happy she could burst. All their hard work had brought about this miracle and she was elated. Alex's smiling face sent shivers of pleasure down her body. "Thank you God. Thank you," she whispered.

It had been almost a year since the accident and Alex was nearly back on her feet. The journey had been hard and painful, but Alex had persevered. Oh, she still had major memory loss and her injuries would probably leave her with a lifetime of pain and potential health problems as she grew older, but Julia knew Alex could face whatever came her way. She was strong.

Julia sighed. She would not worry. Her mother used to say, "Don't go and borrow trouble," so she wouldn't. Suddenly, the memory of her mother caused her to miss her parents so badly that she was flooded with an intense longing to see them again. I will go to Hilton Head before I go to Chicago, she thought, making a decision that had been haunting her for several days.

Julia had sent Joe McGuire to Chicago to meet with Brian. Brian had told Julia that he was looking for a good private investigator, so she had given him Joe's number. When Joe called to report back to her, he told her the entire story about eMicro, the fraud, the cover-up, the mess Brian was in since he had discovered it all during his audit, how his boss wanted him to bury it, and that the IPO had been delayed for another month, which gave them some time. Joe had investigated the case thoroughly, and he agreed with everything that Brian had uncovered. Getting the hard proof to support the documents was going to be difficult, but the bigger problem would be how they would protect Brian and his reputation. That was going to be the real challenge. She was worried for Brian but she knew Joe could handle it. She would have time to travel to Hilton Head to see her parents before she went on to Chicago.

David was laughing with Alex. He looked up and winked at Julia and she blushed. They had been seeing each other, two, sometimes three times a week, and things were really heating up between them.

Lainie was about to become a casualty of their clandestine relationship and that bothered her but not enough to let David go.

Their affair had not reached a physical stage yet, but she could tell that David was ready for it. After her trip to visit her parents, and then Brian, she was going to tell David the truth.

"Hello, everyone," a voice boomed. "Uncle Robert is here!"

A distinguished older man with a very bad limp, holding a cane, entered the room. He was carrying a large bouquet of yellow roses.

"Uncle Robert," Alex said happily. "Don't come over here. Wait there. Watch me. Watch what I can do."

Robert Walker was not Alex's uncle, but since she was a little girl, Alex had called him "Uncle". He loved her as if she were his very own. Alex's recovery had been hard for her and he had tried to visit her whenever he could to give his support. But, today, he was not here to see Alex; that was just a pretense for his visit. He was here to see Julia. He knew that David had been seeing her romantically, he had said so much when Robert had asked, and he was worried. Robert wanted to get a good look at the woman for whom David was preparing to throw everything away.

Alex stood and took a few steps toward Robert, her face flushed in triumph.

"Bravo, my little one. Bravo!" he exclaimed, truly impressed. Walking over he hugged her to him.

After a few moments he released Alex.

"And who is this?" he said waving his arm indicating Julia.

David stepped forward. "Robert, this is Julia Bertinelli."

Robert couldn't speak as a roar filled his head. Automatically, he took the hand she extended to him into his own.

"Julia Bertinelli?" he asked.

"Yes."

"You have a beautiful accent, Julia. Where are you from?" he questioned her, still holding her hand.

"Argentina. I'm from Argentina," she stammered, suddenly afraid.

Argentina he thought. It all fit!

"Ah, Argentina, a beautiful place. Of course, I should have known."

"Yes. Yes, it is," she said, trying to remove her hand from his grip.

"Why, I believe I might have known your husband, Roberto," he said looking hard into her eyes.

Julia was frozen into place. How would this man have known Roberto, she asked herself. If he knew Roberto, did he know about her?

"He died last year," she said softly, fear surging through her causing her hands to shake.

He knew. There was no doubt in her mind.

Please don't let him blurt out my true identity in front of my family, she prayed silently.

"I heard about his death. I'm so sorry for your loss," he murmured.

"Thank you," she managed.

"Julia, maybe we could have dinner one evening. I haven't been back to Argentina in years and it would be lovely to speak to you further about your country," he suggested.

"Well, I'm going to be leaving for a few weeks, now that Alex is better," she said trying to refuse gracefully. "Maybe, but I'm.."

Robert interrupted her, "We must get together. I insist," he said squeezing her hand in a way that let her know he was not taking no for an answer.

Oh God, she thought. What am I going to do? But, she said, "Of course. I'd like that, very much. I'll call you, if you will leave me your number," she said managing a smile.

"Good, I look forward to it," he replied, smiling warmly at her and then releasing her hands.

"David, let's you and me get some lunch. Alex, would you like to join us?" he asked.

"No Uncle Robert. I have a little more work to do before I'm finished for the day. My slave driver," she laughed, pointing at Julia, "won't let me off the hook for anything. But thanks for the invite and thank you for the flowers. They're beautiful."

"Okay, sweetie. I'm real proud of you. Now, that you're up walking, we will be twins when we go out," he teased, indicating her leg braces and cane. "Give me a kiss and I'll go."

After David and Robert left, Julia kneeled down to help remove Alex's braces. It was time for her whirlpool, which she would need in order to relax the overtaxed muscles she had used today for the first time.

"What's going on with you and my Dad, Julia?" Alex asked hesitantly.

"What do you mean? There's nothing going on," Julia said but thinking at the same time, uh, oh. "What in the world are you talking about?"

"Julia, I love you but I'm not stupid, so don't you dare treat me like I am. I see the way you two are looking at each other. I'm not blind. Besides, Lainie told me that you and Dad are seeing each other," she said surprising Julia. "And don't even think about getting mad at her. She was crying and I made her tell me. Now, what the hell is going on? I want to know," she demanded.

Julia sat down on the floor in front of her daughter, pulled her legs up into a lotus position, and thought about how she should answer.

"Sometimes Alex, a man and a woman can be physically attracted to each other. I promise you that your dad and I have not acted on this attraction. We've had a few harmless dinners, that all. I promise."

"Harmless? You're kidding! You and Dad have hurt Lainie. She's my Mom and I won't sit by and let you hurt her. If you try to come between my Mom and my Dad and, their relationship, our friendship will be over!" she said firmly with fire in her eyes.

Julia held her breath then she spoke.

"What if I were your Mom?"

Alex didn't even hesitate. "Then I would feel the same way. I wouldn't let any woman hurt you if you were my Mom, but you're not! Lainie is the only Mom I have ever known and I love her with my whole being. Without her, I couldn't go on. You need to stop whatever it is you're doing and you need to stop now."

Julia said nothing. The pain in her chest, and the shame she felt left her unable to speak.

"I love you very much Julia and you are one of my best friends. But, I would hate you if you broke up my family," she finished.

Julia hoped she could control her voice so she could answer.

"Okay, Alex. I get it," she said softly. Then she added, "I'm going away for a few weeks, that should cool down the situation between me and your Dad. I'm sorry. I never meant to hurt you. I love you very much and I want you to be happy. I would never hurt you."

"I know that Julia. I wasn't going to bring this up and just hope that you two would come to your senses, but I saw the way Dad acted today, how he hugged you, and I knew it was time and that I couldn't wait. I'll miss you, but I think you should go away for a while."

"So that's settled then. And young lady, I think you're trying to get out of the rest of your workout. Aren't you? That's what this is really about, isn't it?"

Alex smiled down at her.

"Well, that was part of it, I have to admit. Okay, so you got me," she giggled.

Julia took Alex's hands into hers, "You don't need to worry, honey. Promise me you won't. We'll just drop it and pretend this never happened. Okay?"

"Okay, but you know what? If I didn't already have a mom, I'd want you."

"And, I'd want you too, Alex," she smiled sadly, helping her daughter to her feet.

***

Later that night, while Julia was packing for her trip to North Carolina, she thought about her promise. Alex was just a child, and if she had known that Julia was her real Mom, she wouldn't have asked her to make the promises she had demanded she make earlier today. She would have understood and supported Julia's actions. Wouldn't she? Surely she would.

So it went, over the next few hours, as Julia tried to make her case that her actions to get her family back were completely honorable. But, in the back of her mind, a small niggling of doubt continued to torment her.

145

Chapter Thirty
Hilton Head, South Carolina

Julia sat on a bench facing the paintings that her mother, Nancy D'Amato had placed on display. The gallery was on Main Street in a small section of Hilton Head. It was a beautiful area filled with coffee shops, ice cream parlors and antique stores. Julia would have enjoyed strolling through the avenues and peeking into each of the little shops if she didn't have to face the task at hand.

She had to see her mother's paintings.

Coming here was so difficult, but she felt like she needed to at least see her mother once more, and looking at her exhibit would give her an excuse to do both before she left the island.

She was staying in a home immediately next door to her mother's and father's home that she had rented for the month. She had been living there for almost the full month and she had never gotten up her nerve to approach them. Instead she had watched them both, secretly from her back deck, always wearing her sunglasses so they wouldn't get a good look at her and be able to make any possible connection as to who she might be. Only once, in that month, had her mother approached her; but she did not realize, at the time, that she was speaking to her daughter. It had happened when she came to Julia's front door and welcomed her to the neighborhood with a glass dish of warm lasagna.

Julia had answered the door and kept her dark glasses on when she did so. She was sure her mother probably thought a middle-aged streetwalker had rented the home, but she was warm and friendly, and seemed to completely ignore Julia's platform heels and bleached blond hair. Julia could only mumble a few unintelligible remarks as she stared at the woman she loved with all her heart, who had stood in her foyer, smiling and doing her best to ignore the fact that Julia was so quiet that she was downright rude. This is exactly what she told her husband, Frank later.

Somehow, Julia had gotten her mother out of the house and safely headed back to her own before she broke into a fit of weeping so intense that it had actually frightened her at the time.

Her mother was old and it made her afraid. Her beautiful face was wrinkled. You could see the lines that her grief had placed forever on her countenance when her only daughter had been taken, never to return. The sparkle she remembered as a child was dimmed in her mother's eyes, and Julia was devastated by her mother's grief and her own; and the intense longing to tell her Mom the truth and to grab her and hold her in her arms once more. She wanted to yell, "Mom, it's me. I didn't die. Mom. I'm alive." But, of course she didn't. She held it all in.

Later when she was able to eat, she had sampled some of her mother's famous lasagna and the smell and the taste created a feeling of homesickness and longing so deep that it sent a trail of fire straight to her heart, like a burning arrow, and set her off into another fit of weeping.

She would leave tomorrow. This would be her last stop before getting on her flight back to Washington. No good would come of telling them the truth. She would let it be.

When she had walked into the gallery – taking a chance and not wearing her dark glasses this time - her mother had been busy with a group of people asking her questions about her work, so Julia was able to slip by without notice. Her intent was to take a quick walk through, see the paintings, and then slip out again.

But, when she had seen the first painting, the room had reeled and she had been forced to sit on a bench, provided to patrons for longer viewings, in order to gain back her equilibrium and to keep from falling. She had her face in her hands and was weeping when she felt the touch of someone's hands on her shoulders.

"Are you all right?" her mother asked softly, sitting down next to her.

"Yes," Julia whispered, wiping her eyes, "the painting is just so powerful and terrible and I… I don't know what happened, but for a moment I felt like I might faint."

"I'm sorry. They are brutal. But I had to paint them. All my friends and my agent are stunned and somewhat upset with my collection. Most of them think I made a big mistake by painting these horrors, much less putting them on exhibit. But," she sighed, "I had to try to free myself of the lifetime of pain that I've had to face. This seemed to be the best way to accomplish that for me."

Julia couldn't answer.

"They're of my daughter, you know," she continued with a hitch in her voice. "She was kidnapped a long time ago and my only grandson witnessed the whole thing. It has haunted him for years, poor little boy. They never found her and they never caught the man," she finished dropping her head. "She left behind a little girl too, my granddaughter. She had a bad accident about a year ago and she is just now recovering. Elizabeth, that's my daughter's name, would have wanted to be here to help her little girl, but the fates decided otherwise," she said with a sigh.

Julia looked back at the painting; a painting of her exact likeness, twenty years earlier, and that of her baby boy, Brian. A dark man had her from behind, Julia's mouth was open in a silent scream and Brian was running away with a look of terror on his face, screaming some unknown words into the canvas. The colors were dark, with deep streaks of red, like blood, splashed and dripping across the canvas.

She looked down and said, "Oh my. How did you stand it? What gave you the strength to paint these scenes from what must have been a terrible time in your life?"

"Yes," her mother replied. "It was terrible. It just about killed me, but it absolutely devastated my husband, Frank. But to answer you, I'm not sure why I painted them, but something was driving me. I painted night and day. I couldn't sleep until the last one was done. I felt a huge weight lift off of my heart when I finished. Then I slept for three days. Those were the best three days of sleep I have had since my girl was taken from me

About a year ago, I was at a dinner with Frank. We were attending some sort of function; I can't remember which one. I left the table, to go to the powder room, when an old man, who appeared to be Chinese, approached me, as I was about to enter the lavatory. He stood in front of me and placed his hand gently on my arm. The he said, 'I have a message for you.' For some reason, I could not speak or move. Then he spoke again, 'There are many lessons in life to learn. One is pain and sorrow. You have learned those lessons well. It is time to move on to your next lesson.' Then he walked away.

I started painting the next morning.

The reviews for my work, this time, have been very mixed, but I don't care anymore. It was something I felt I had to do. And I'm not about to apologize to anyone," she finished looking back at Julia.

"I'm sorry. I don't believe I have ever told anyone that story or said as much as I just told you about my life."

"I'm glad you did. I don't mind," she said smiling at her mother. "I'm glad you painted them. You are a wonderful and talented painter. It was just a shock when I saw this one and the subject matter," she said trying to smooth over her reaction.

"You might want to skip the others then, " her mother smiled. Then she looked harder at her, "Aren't you my neighbor, the one living next door?" she asked changing the subject and looking more closely at Julia.

"Yes, I'm getting ready to leave town but I had heard you had an exhibit and I wanted to see it before I went home."

"Well, I am so glad you came. I want you to promise me that you will come by the house to say goodbye before you go. You seem to be such a nice young lady and I would like you to meet my husband. He's blind and in a wheel chair now, so he doesn't get out much. Maybe next time you come to visit, we can spend more time together. We're both a little lonely, with our grandchildren living in other parts of the country, and we would enjoy visiting with you very much. Promise me you will come to visit. When are you leaving?" she asked looking directly into her daughter's eyes.

Something moved in her mother's face, maybe a flicker of recognition, and for a moment Julia started to wonder if her disguise wasn't working, but then the look was gone.

Julia held her breath. Could she promise to visit her parent's home? Could she take a chance that they wouldn't recognize her? Was she strong enough to pull it off without breaking her promise to herself that she would never let them know she was still alive?

"I'm leaving the day after tomorrow, but I promise I will come over and say goodbye, she said, deciding that her mother looked so hopeful that she couldn't say no. "Would tomorrow evening work for you?

"Yes, that would be wonderful," her mother replied. "But, I must leave you now, if you are better. I need to speak to some other friends who have just arrived."

"I'm fine now. Thank you," Julia responded as her mother walked away.

But, she wasn't fine. Julia was trembling and shaking when she left the gallery.

The next painting she had approached, after her mother left her, had stopped her dead in her tracks. It showed David, Brian and baby Alex standing at a lonely gravesite on a barren hill with their heads bent in dismal sorrow. It portrayed a dark, windy, incredibly miserable, gray day, with heavy black clouds. Her husband and her children's clothes and hair were whipping about as if a great wind was tearing at them. Their faces were wet and their eyes were haunted. The sense of pain and despair, emanating from the painting, almost caused her to collapse.

Turning away, she knew she wasn't strong enough to look at anymore of her mother's work. Her heart had filled with grief as she looked at her family that she had left behind and the paintings that clearly depicted the crime they all had endured. How that crime had affected the people she loved the most in the world was soul wrenching. But, worst of all, the memories of the day of her capture, the fear that had paralyzed her body for months, crushed down on her as she looked at the vivid portrayal depicted in her mother's anguished paintings, leaving her terrified and desperate to get out of the gallery. She was almost running when she left and made her way to her car

***

Julia stood in front of her mothers and father's home straightening her clothes and talking to herself. "You can do this. It's okay. They don't know who you are, so it's going to be okay."

The day was coming to an end, but the sky was still clear, with sea gulls calling, boats moving slowly on the horizon, and children playing and splashing in the surf along the water's edge. Her parent's home was a beautiful Cape Cod styled structure with a gabled roof, cedar shingle siding and long sweeping lawns that led to the shoreline. There were palm and oak trees that framed the front on the street side, and floor to ceiling, wall length, French doors on the back of the house that probably gave panoramic ocean views all the way to Tybee Island.

She had seen the heated pool with a small bathhouse, sitting toward the back of their property, when she had hid on her balcony trying to catch a glimpse of her mom or dad. She wondered if they ever used it anymore since she had never seen anyone swimming.

Gathering her courage, she knocked.

Nancy D'Amato opened the door, welcomed Julia with a beautiful smile and then led her inside to a large foyer, filled with a beautiful, crystal chandelier and some of the most gorgeous paintings Julia had ever seen.

"Oh, this is lovely," she said to her mother, turning in a circle staring at all the beauty hanging on every wall that surrounded her

"Well," her mother said, "they're mine and they are far different than those that upset you so much yesterday at the gallery."

Julia was surprised, "These are yours?" she gasped. "Why they're incredibly lovely. And so is your home."

"Yes. Well, I'm glad you like it. It's become a real comfort for us after all these years. Come into the living room with me. I have made some tea, my husband Frank's favorite, for us to drink while we talk. He will join us in a minute."

Julia followed her mother into another room, more beautiful than the first. Large open windows revealed a view of the beach, the water and the approaching sunset that left her speechless. Large, overstuffed couches and chairs in a beautiful muted pattern of roses surrounded by soft green, pink and light gold color were situated in the room in a way to best take advantage of the beautiful panorama outside the windows. It looked so comfortable and homey that Julia was filled with a wonderful sense of peace. Her anxiety faded into the background, as she stood entranced by the room.

Julia turned back to her mother, and, just as she was about to tell her how incredibly peaceful and lovely it all was, she saw the large oil painting over the fireplace and was so surprised that she froze in motion.

Placing her hands up to her mouth she stared, transfixed into place.

"Oh, that," her mother said noticing Julia's expression. "That is a portrait of my daughter, Elizabeth that I painted on her twenty-first birthday. She was so beautiful and young. She had her whole life ahead of her then, but that was all taken away," she said continuing to arrange the tea set and glasses.

"Now, I'm finally going to pull it down and put it away. Frank has always insisted that it stay there because he knows his little girl is going to come home one of these days. It stabs me in the heart each time he says it and I can't bear to look at it anymore. He can't see, since he lost most of his sight several years ago, so he doesn't feel the pain I feel everyday that it continues to hang there and I have to look at it. I painted all my new work, the ones that you saw at the gallery, to try to purge my soul and to try to rid myself of the hurt. The only thing left for me to do is to take down this last reminder."

For a moment, Julia could not speak she was so overcome with grief for her mother. Then she walked up to the woman who had held her in her arms when she was a baby, the woman who was broken by the pain she was trying to exorcize, and folded her into her arms. "I'm sorry, so sorry," she said.

Julia held her mother for a long time while her mother cried. It was much later that Julia realized that she was crying too.

***

Nancy and Julia were laughing like young girls, thoroughly enjoying the sunset that was a vivid orange glow on the horizon. They talked about gardens and how much they loved horses and other subjects that were safe topics for two people who didn't know each other very well.

It was during a particularly funny story that Julia was telling of an adventure she had had on a horse while in Argentina, that they both heard a gasp and turned in unison. Julia's father was sitting in his wheelchair in the doorway of the living room and he was crying and moaning.

"My God, Frank, are you okay?" her mother said, jumping up from the couch. "Are you hurt? Tell me what's wrong!" she demanded.

"Elizabeth? Oh, honey, I knew you would come back. Come to Daddy, baby. Come touch me so I can feel that you're really alive. Oh, if I could only see you. I told you Nancy! Didn't I tell you? I told you she would come home! Elizabeth, come to me, come to me," he wailed.

Nancy was dumbstruck. What was he saying? "Frank, you old fool, it's not Elizabeth. It's the young lady from next door. Her name is Julia."

"Nancy," he bellowed. "Do not tell me that I don't know my own daughter's voice! I know it's Elizabeth and I demand that you bring her to me right now!"

Nancy spun around and looked at Julia and then looked back at her husband. "I'm so sorry," she started to say, but before the words were out of her mouth, Julia, who had been standing with the blood drained from her face, launched herself at Frank, fell at his feet in front of his chair, and started calling him Daddy, holding onto him for dear life as Frank cried out her name, "Elizabeth", over and over again.

Nancy looked at them both, trying to understand as the room started to spin, faster and faster. Then the mystery unraveled, hit her right in the center of her chest, and she fainted dead away.

***

Julia and her mother and father sat up talking until dawn was a pink blush on the horizon. Julia told them the story of her capture and all the years in between as they sat listening intently. The stories poured out into the room as the hours moved by.

Sometime before dawn, Julia said, "I know that I'm Elizabeth to both of you. But, I only know myself as Julia now. Elizabeth is gone. I will never be her again. I know that now."

They said nothing but sat taking everything in their daughter had told them, filled with wonder that she was still alive and that she had, through some trick of fate, been given back to them. Frank knew he could die peacefully now. He knew his baby was safe and now he knew what had happened to her all those years ago when she had vanished. It was a damned miracle, he thought, and he rejoiced just to sit by her side and listen to her beautiful voice.

Then Julia told them about Alex, and Brian everything that had happened since she returned to America – about her torment over whether she should tell them the truth – and then she told them almost everything about her and David.

"Honey," her Dad said, "you'll know the right thing to do when it's time. Don't rush yourself. I think Brian and Alex would be real happy to know their Mom is still alive."

"Oh, how I wish. But, it's more complicated than that," she sighed.

"It always is, baby," her mom replied. "It always is."

***

Julia stayed with her parents for two days after changing her flight and letting Joe McGuire know that she would arrive later than planned.

Her mother was in the kitchen drinking coffee, when Julia entered and sat down at the table.

"I'm going to leave tomorrow," she said as her mother sat a cup of coffee in front of her.

"How did you sleep last night," her mother asked ignoring her.

"Oh, I have slept like a baby for the last two days."

"Good. You want some breakfast?" she said while washing her hands in the sink.

"Mom, please sit down. We need to talk."

"Oh, okay, "she replied, wiping her hands on a kitchen towel.

"I know you want me to stay, but I have to go to Chicago to see Brian. After that, I need to go back to Washington and help Alex. I can't stay here with you," she said firmly.

"I know, honey. I just wish we could be together a little longer," she said sadly.

"I'll let you know my plans. We are not going to lose touch. I promise you that. I love you and Dad very much, but I have to get the rest of my life in some sort of order before I'll feel comfortable," she said hoping her mother would understand.

Nancy D'Amato studied her coffee for a few moments. Her heart, which had been squeezed dry from suffering, was finally pumping again, full of the sheer joy that her daughter was alive. She could let her go. She was healthy and she was alive. That's all she really needed to know. It would be okay now. She and Frank had a new lease on life – and excitedly looked forward to each day – something they hadn't felt for a very long time.

"I understand. When will you go?"

156

"Tomorrow. But I promise I will call every couple of days and let you know what mischief I'm up to," she smiled with a twinkle in her eye.

"Oh, so you haven't changed that much then, have you?"

"Nope."

"I remember some of the ways you challenged any kind of authority, and when you did, how you got yourself into a few scrapes back then," she smiled.

"Yep," she laughed, "and, Mom, I'm just getting started."

Chapter Thirty-One
Chicago, Illinois

Julia was sitting in the lobby of Hart & Newman, waiting for her son, Brian. She was going to help him out of the mess Joe had told her about. She didn't know how, but this was a good start. You see she had a plan.

Brian walked into the lobby and shook hands with Julia.

"It's good to see you again Julia. You look lovely as usual."

"Thank you, Brian. You look pretty spiffy yourself," she smiled looking at his beautiful navy suit, white shirt and red tie. "Mr. Corporate", she thought to herself.

"Let's go to my office. I haven't had a real chance to look at your portfolio yet. If you don't mind waiting a little, I'll do that and we can discuss your objectives. Then, we can talk about how my family is doing," he smiled.

***

Julia sat in Brian's office as he went over her portfolio.

Brian whistled. "Wow! What are you doing working as a nurse? My boss is going to be breaking out the Cristal champagne when he sees this."

"Really?"

"Yes, really. Have you looked at this? Do you know how much you're worth?"

"Why no. No, I haven't looked. I guess I never thought about it before now."

"Well, Julia," he paused for effect, "you're beautiful and you're loaded," he said smiling brightly.

Julia said nothing. She just smiled back at her son's delight.

"Are you sure you want Hart & Newman to handle this for you?" he questioned her.

"Are you guys good?" she asked.

"Oh, yeah. We're good. But, this is a lot of money for one firm to handle," he protested.

"Then, I'll do it but only if you handle my entire portfolio. You can get help if you need to, but I insist that you be the one to oversee it, every step of the way."

"Well, I don't know about that, Julia, Mr. Newman might not like it."

"It's non-negotiable," she said firmly.

"Okay. I'll talk to him and let you know."

"Great! Now what is going on with the IPO you were so worried about?"

Brian sat back. The he explained that the IPO had been delayed but they hoped to go public later this month. Then he told her about the fraud, how he had broached it with the head partner, what his boss's response had been, how he was struggling with the moral dilemma surrounding the issue, as well as how it might impact his career, and how they had no hard evidence to support any of it.

"What would you need to have in order to prove your claim," she asked.

"Well, some of the shipments, I guess."

"How would that help?"

"Any boxes shipped out that were empty or had something besides the eMicro product in them would prove that they were lying about their sales to inflate their profits. This would affect the IPO and would be a Securities Exchange violation."

Julia said nothing.

"Might as well wish for the moon," he sighed. "That guy you sent us, Joe McGuire, has been great, but we're all real stymied over how to expose it without putting our heads on the chopping block."

"Maybe I could help," Julia offered.

"That's very nice of you, Julia, but I'm not sure what you could do. Thanks anyway."

"Well, let me know if you can think of anything," she smiled.

Then they talked about Alex's recovery and what was going on up in Washington.

But Julia wasn't really listening.

She was working on her plan.

Chapter Thirty-Two
Milpitas, California

Julia had flown out on a red-eye flight, non-stop from Chicago, in order to attend a meeting at eMicro in Milpitas, California. She was sitting in the lobby of the building and it was beautifully furnished. The receptionist's desk was built of solid mahogany. It sat in the center of the reception area and had several halogen lights glowing down in bright beams above it. It was the size of a small ship. A beautiful young girl was typing on a computer behind the behemoth, while another woman answered the phones.

Julia was dressed in a black, silk blend, pant suit. She wore a beautiful, white silk blouse, her Mikimoto pearls, Via Spiga pumps and she carried a Chanel bag. She was so happy to be dressed in something besides her usual attire that she sighed with pleasure.

Joe McGuire has set up this meeting between Julia and Al Hansen, the owner of eMicro, indicating that he had a rich, eccentric investor who might be willing to invest several million dollars when their IPO hit. The result of that conversation was Julia sitting in the lobby of eMicro waiting for Hansen to escort her through his facility.

Julia had demanded a full tour of the California offices, fabrication facility, and warehouses, including a tour of the distribution warehouse in Chicago when she returned to the city. Hansen had told Joe, "No problem. We can comply with all her wishes." He wasn't a fool after all.

All she had been really been interested in were the warehouses and the layout of the plants and their surrounding buildings. Joe had explained what she should be looking for and that she should diagram the area at the Chicago facility, as best she could, immediately following her visit. She was scheduled to tour that warehouse two days from now.

Julia was ready to go. She had a photographic memory and had no doubt she could give Joe all he needed and more.

This place has all the trappings of the 'Rich and Famous' and appears to be on it's way to becoming a "Mega-Millionaire" company, she thought as she surveyed the room. But, because Julia knew the truth about the eMicro's finances, the excesses that she saw disgusted her. Oil paintings that looked like originals hung on the walls and antique oriental carpets covered the marble floors. The whole place screamed of money.

Julia was not impressed. She had seen bigger and better. "And to top it off, 'Mr. eMicro'," she said to herself, "you've been lying to the public and that's one thing that doesn't sit well with me. But now what you're doing is about to hurt my boy and that is not going to happen. I can promise you that!"

Hansen watched her from the top of the stairs, leading down to the lobby. He had known that she was rich, but Mr. McGuire did not tell him that she was also beautiful. He was anxious to meet her, but now he knew he was going to thoroughly enjoy their day together.

Skipping down the remaining stairs, he called out, "Mrs. Bertinelli?"

Julia stood and smiled her brightest smile, "Mr. Hansen, how nice to meet you."

Julia thought he looked like the old cat that had just swallowed a canary. Julia smiled inside; he didn't know that he was about to be her lunch.

Chapter Thirty-Three
Chicago, Illinois

Later, when Julia told Brian about her plan and her visit to eMicro's two facilities, he had erupted in anger.

"I'm not sneaking into the warehouse to steal boxes of inventory for our proof. I'll go to jail, or even worse, I'll be shot. I am not remotely interested in this dangerous scheme!" he shouted.

Julia smiled at her gorgeous son, walking back and forth, waving his hands in the air. He was like a sleek panther when he moved and he was so handsome she could not take her eyes away from the face of the man she had helped to create.

"And, how did you get into eMicro, Corporate to see Mr. Hansen? No," he said, stopping her from speaking, "don't tell me. I don't want to know. When I'm called to testify, I will be able to honestly say that I had no idea of what you were up to. Of course, that will be right before they cart me off to jail!"

Julia laughed.

"You're so cute when you're mad."

"What?"

"I said...."

"I heard what your said and this is not funny."

"Brian," Julia said calmly, "Joe will help us. We can do this. If you want to save your job, we have to get the evidence. Joe has arranged something with a newspaper reporter to do an expose and she has the Attorney General set to go, once we get what we need. You will be left out of it. No one will know about your involvement. Be honest, this is a great plan. It takes care of all contingencies that are in our way and we can pull this off."

"We, we are not doing anything," he challenged her. "If I agree to do this, and I haven't yet, you are not going with me!"

Julia smiled. So, he was thinking about it. Good for him.

"Okay," she said, meekly.

***

It was past midnight and Brian was still at his office. He cursed Julia, as he packed the documents into a brown leather satchel, for getting him to agree to this hair-brained scheme.

He was almost ready to leave the office on his way to pull a sneak attack on the eMicro warehouse. Thanks to Julia's drawings, he knew the exact layout and where he should focus his search. Joe had called earlier to say that he had made sure that the alarm systems were disabled. He went on to say that he had also cut a section of fence on the back side of the property so that Brian could access the interior grounds surrounding the warehouse and have at least some chance of making it in and back out of the building without notice.

For this part of the plan, Brian would be alone. He was damned nervous, too. Breaking and entering, and grand theft, were not accomplishments listed on his current resume, although he would be forced to add them, along with his jail time, if this all went south tonight. What was he thinking, he wondered again? This was total madness.

But, madness or not, he was going to do it, so he continued to pack up his papers.

Finally ready, he stepped to his office door as the phone began to ring. It was building security.

"Mr. Grant."

"Yes, Teddy. What is it?" he said recognizing the voice of the night security man.

"There's a lady here to see you, Sir and she's real insistent."

"A lady?"

"Yes, Sir."

"That's odd. I don't know of any lady who would want to see me at this time of night. Why don't you ask her to come back tomorrow during office hours?"

"I tried, Sir, several times," he said wearily.

"Did she give you her name?"

"Yes, Sir."

"And?"

"It's Mrs. Bertinelli, Sir."

Brian didn't speak. What the hell was Julia doing here?

"Sir?"

"Yes, Teddy. It's okay, you can send her up," he said resignedly, "I'll see her."

"Yes, Sir. Thank you, Sir," he said gratefully.

Several minutes later, Brian opened the door to his office. Julia was standing outside and he gasped when he saw her. She was dressed all in black. Black cat suit, tucked into black boots, black jacket, black gloves and she was carrying a black ski mask. She was as cute as hell and he couldn't help but smile at her.

"Julia, what are you dressed for? The 'Darth Vader' convention?" Before she could respond, he added, "And what are you doing here?"

"Well, thank you. I will come in," she said brushing past him.

"I'm here to help," she answered. "I can be your look-out or the getaway driver. I know the place better than you and I can move very quietly." She demonstrated by taking tiny, stealthy footsteps, moving slowly across his thick, padded carpet. "See?" she said smiling brightly, when she had taken about eight steps.

He laughed. He couldn't help it. Oh, yeah, Julia, you are a real cat burglar, he thought, thinking how funny she was when trying to make her case.

"Julia, you are not, hear me now, not going! Don't try to change my mind. This is too dangerous. You have done enough. Go home. This is my problem and you're not going!" he said firmly.

"I'm going, Brian. If you don't let me go with you, then I will follow you. You realize that if two cars are going in and out that it will probably draw attention to us. Then I might be coming into the building, while you're going out of the building, and the guards will probably hear us and then we'll be caught, and…."

"Julia," he said interrupting her diatribe, "stop it. You're as cute as a little black bunny and I'm sorry that you spent the day at Bergdorf Goodman picking up your little 'I Spy' outfit, but, I need to move quickly and I don't need to be worrying about you while I'm doing it."

"I can take care of myself," she said stiffly.

Oh sure, he thought. She was five feet, nine inches of pure, raw sexual wet-dream material and while that would have been a real comfort to him at any other time, it was not a comfort now – not when he was headed out to face his certain death. He knew that if he let her go with him, he was going to be really, really sorry.

But, as it turned out, Julia was the one who saved both of their lives.

***

167

On the ride over, to what Brian liked to refer to as the "future scene of the crime", Julia had insisted that they needed to work out hand signals.

"Julia, this is not 'Law and Order'. We don't need 'special-ops' training for a simple B&E."

But she had insisted. Well, so much for what he thought about anything, he mused. But he was willing to let her have her way. He was too nervous to argue.

They parked a block away and walked in the shadows along the street up to the fence surrounding the property. They didn't speak.

Walking a short way around the perimeter of the property, they found the gaping hole that Joe had cut out of the chain link. Giving Brian the thumbs up – she scooted through to the other side. Brian rolled his eyes. Would she never stop? Then, he followed her, his heart pounding.

Dressed in black, they could hardly see each other, so they weren't too concerned that they would be seen. No alarms had sounded yet, so they felt they were probably in the clear. Well, that is, they were in the clear unless the alarms were silent and the police were converging on them at this very moment, Brian thought nervously, glancing around, jumping at his own shadow. His heart was racing but Julia appeared to be enjoying the hell out of their little adventure.

They had agreed, after looking closely at the plans, that they would enter the warehouse through a door on the northeast end of the building. This door was usually left open, as it was the entrance used by the guards to enter and exit as they made their hourly surveillance of the perimeter of the property. Julia had asked Hansen, of eMicro specifically about security and how often the guards patrolled the grounds and he had eagerly given her the schedule that the guards followed each day for both the Chicago facility as well as Milpitas. Nice, she had thought at the time, wondering at his incredible stupidity.

The guard was not supposed to walk through another inspection for approximately one half hour. They needed to hurry if they intended to be out of the warehouse and back to their car before he began his next inspection.

Pushing the door open, they tiptoed into a very large room that had small bulbs hanging from the ceiling. The lights were placed irregularly up and down the aisles that were filled with shelving units containing boxes of equipment, stacked from floor to ceiling. The bulbs gave enough light to see so they wouldn't need flashlights. Julia noticed that the main florescent lights were not on, so she assumed that the low-watt lights were there strictly for security purposes.

Brian motioned that she should start her search on the left rows of shelving and he would search on the right. Julia gave him the "thumbs-up" sign and Brian returned the gesture, smiling at her. She was so cute, he thought. Turning away, he wished, not for the first time, that he could pull off his ski mask. It was itching like crazy.

It had been twenty minutes and Julia had not found anything that would prove their case. Each small box that she had opened and replaced back where she had found it, held nothing but electronics. Moving back to where Brian was searching, Julia tapped him on the shoulder. He jumped, and when she signaled him, he held his hands out with his palms up to indicate that he was having the same result. Then Julia remembered something from her earlier visit to the warehouse.

Leaning over, she whispered in Brian's ear. "Shipping. Follow me." Brian nodded.

But, it wasn't long before Julia realized that she was completely lost. She thought she remembered the direction they had taken when she had visited the shipping area, but something was obviously wrong. They had walked deeper and deeper into the cavernous building and still they had not found what they were searching for. Time was running out, and she could feel the sweat pouring down her back from her anxiety.

A short time later, she rounded a corner and, there it was, sitting about twenty feet in front of them.

Moving very quickly, they began their search with the boxes, labeled to be shipped to Taiwan. The found what they were looking for on the second row down on the pallet. The boxes were filled with rocks. This was it. This was the proof they needed.

Smiling, they hugged each other. Then they gave each other the "high five." They didn't celebrate long because when Brian looked down at his watch, Julia could see the panic in his eyes and she knew they had run out of time.

Grabbing as many boxes as they could carry, they started to walk quickly, moving toward the exit. Julia went first and thankfully, this time she took a direct route to the exit door. As she went, though, she would drop down on one knee and then she would peer around the corner at the end of each aisle, before she continued across to the next grouping of shelves filled with boxes of inventory.

They were almost there when Julia tripped and dropped most of her boxes. The noise they made shattered the silence. Brian and Julia stood perfectly still and held their breath, praying that no one had heard the commotion. After waiting a few minutes, they each blew out their breath while Julia loaded her arms again with the boxes littering the floor. She tried to do a "thumbs-up" gesture but it was not possible since her hands were full. Smiling, she stepped out from the cover of shelving and ran straight into the night guard.

"What the hell," he bellowed, leveling his gun at her and Brian.

He was a heavy set man, probably in his mid-fifties and looked as startled as they must have looked.

They stood perfectly still. All Brian could think of was that he had enjoyed his years of freedom and that he would hate being locked up in a cold cell with "Bubba".

His heart was thundering out of his chest as he stared at the gun, which had taken on the dimensions of a small cannon.

"Well, well, well," the guard chuckled. "What do we have here? Going somewhere boys?" he smirked, waving his gun around in the air, incorrectly making the assumption that Julia and Brian were both males.

"What you got there? Oh buddy, my boss is going to give me a raise when he sees what I found here tonight. Don't you move..."

Before he could finish, in a move of blinding speed, Julia spun, dropped her boxes, whirled in the air and kicked the gun out of the guard's hand. It went spinning across the concrete floor, discharging as it hit. The roar of gunfire was deafening.

The guard was stunned for a moment as he stared down at his hand where the gun had been just moments before.

"Why, you...." he cried out, grabbing Julia by her arm.

Julia reached back, grabbed his other arm, twisted, rolled down and screamed "Aaaiiiiaaahhh!" as she threw him over her back. Flying up in a high spiral, she spun, landed on the floor, one leg bent in front of the other, in a straight-armed position with her hands curled into fists. She screamed another "Aaaaaiiiaaahhh!" It was a horrible sound that reverberated in the room. Then she did a one-two punch into the now empty air.

It was a wasted effort, you see, since there was no one to hit left standing in front of her. The guard was lying on the ground unconscious. He had hit his head as he went down when she threw him.

Moving over to him, Julia placed her fingers on his neck. He was breathing. Thank God, she thought. Giving Brian another "thumbs-up" she began gathering her boxes, while Brian stared at her stupidly

What the hell had he just witnessed? It was like a movie had been played in slow motion in front of him. His heart was still hammering.

"Let's go," she commanded.

Brian followed her, but he didn't remember the journey back to the car, or how he got there.

***

Sometime later, Brian pulled over to the side of the road. They had been driving for quite a while and he felt they were probably safe for the time being. However, he was trembling so badly that he couldn't keep his hands on the wheel and thought it might be a good time to stop and get his bearings.

Turning to look over at Julia, who seemed to be perfectly composed, sitting quietly in the seat, he wondered, who in the hell she was. She seemed to have as many facets as a rare stone. What else could she do, he wondered? What other surprises resided under her smooth, lovely exterior. How old was she? He knew she must be in her late forties, or maybe more, but she acted much younger and she was in incredible shape as was just proved in their recent encounter.

"Where did you learn to do that?" he asked, his voice shaking.

"I told you that I could handle myself," she said smiling back at him with a twinkle in her eye.

"Right. But, that was a little more than the common everyday, 'I can handle myself', now wasn't it?"

"Well, yes, you're right. It is the result of over ten years of martial arts training. Roberto wanted me to be safe, so he enrolled me in a few classes. I enjoyed them so much that I continued."

"Really?"

"Yeah, really."

Brian thought about that for a moment. The he erupted, "Cool! I mean double cool! You know what? You just saved our butts!"

Then they started to laugh hysterically, shrieking crazily from the relief of not being caught and better yet, not being shot or killed.

"Brian," she said, still giggling as she tried to calm herself, "we better get going. It's getting late and we still have to make another stop."

***

Much later, they drove off the highway onto a dirt side road and into a grove of trees. Sandy, the reporter for the Chicago Tribune, was waiting for them. Brian and Julia waved hello and started loading the boxes they had just stolen into the trunk of her car. Then Brian gave her a large leather satchel that he said was filled with copies of the other paper records that would support his findings.

Sandy smiled as they told her the story of what had happened earlier that evening. She was laughing when they finished.

"Well, Julia, I must say that you don't look like a 'bad-ass' but I guess looks can be deceiving," she grinned at the woman in front of her who was dressed in skin tight black clothing. She looked like a Ninja Warrior, and based on the story they had just told her, that might be an appropriate description of the woman who had helped pull this caper off. Sandy wondered what her story was and what she was doing involved in something like this.

"Yeah," Julia smiled, "it was a lot of fun now that I think about it, but God in heaven, at the time, it was not a bit of fun. I thought I was going to faint when he showed up with that gun."

Brian put his arms around her and hugged her tightly.

"My hero," Brian said as Julia grinned at Sandy.

"It was all in a night's work," Julia responded. "Now we need to get the heck out of here before we all get caught."

"Yeah," Sandy said, shaking their hands, "I've got a lot of work to do if I'm going to make the front page headline on tomorrow's paper. And, don't you two worry. No one will ever hear from me that you were involved in any way. Now get out of here, or I'll never meet my deadline."

Waving goodbye and saying 'Thank you" all around, Brian threw his arms over Julia's shoulder and walked her back to the car. She had just saved his life and his job.

Julia was beaming.

Chapter Thirty-Four

The headline exploded off the front page of the Chicago Tribune the next morning.

eMicro Executives Indicted For Fraud!

Software firm, eMicro, located in Milpitas, California, was shut down today following a raid by the FBI, which was conducted before daybreak this morning. Warrants were sworn out, by the Attorney General, Jim Hammer, for the arrest of CEO, Albert Hansen, and other corporate executives, who are charged with fraud and Securities Exchange violations. Sources say the evidence is substantial and will probably result in jail time for all involved. CEO, Hansen, had no comment.

Much further down on the last page, on the bottom right was a small article, which read:

Guard Hurt in Robbery

William Melvin, guard at the distribution warehouse of eMicro, located in south Chicago, was found unconscious at the facility early this morning. Mr. Melvin stated that a gang of Asian men attacked him during his rounds last evening. "They overpowered me, took my gun, and knocked me unconscious. There was nothing I could do. There were too many of them," he stated from the emergency room at Rush Presbyterian, St. Luke's Medical Center where he was taken for treatment and released.

***

Robert Boland and Brian were sitting in Brian's office, laughing and discussing the indictment, when Newman burst into the office without knocking. He was waving the front page of the paper.

"Brian, have you seen this? There's a disaster at eMicro, and if I find out that you had anything to do with it, I will fire you and you won't get another job in this industry again. I'll have you blackballed!" he shouted.

"I'm sorry," Brian said calmly, "are you speaking to me, Mr. Newman?"

"Don't toy with me Brian," he said slamming the paper down on the desk, his face a bright purple, "you know I'm talking to you."

"Well, Sir, I'm not sure what you're talking about. You told me not to get involved with eMicro, so I didn't," he said very quietly.

If Newman had been aware, he would have felt the heat of Brian's anger pouring off of his body. But Newman missed all the signals and kept right on talking instead of shutting up.

"You're involved up to your eyeballs! I know it! How else would they have found out about what eMicro was doing? You were the only one who knew about this!" he shouted.

Robert Boland spoke, this time. "Sir, surely you're not telling us that you knew what eMicro was doing and you didn't report it. Are you?" he said sweetly.

Newman blustered for a few moments and then the implications of what he had just said hit him and he fell silent.

Brian stood up from his desk and walked over to him. "I wonder if that reporter from the Chicago Tribune would be interested in knowing that your investment banking firm was handling the IPO, that you were old buddies with the CEO, and that you knew about the fraud that was being perpetrated against the public and did not feel it necessary to report it to the Securities Exchange Commission," he said through clenched teeth. "Someone can always call her. Besides if I leave here, the ten million dollar trust fund that I just brought into Hart and Newman goes with me, but it's all up to you," he finished, smiling brightly.

"Why I, I... How dare you speak..." he muttered. Then, finally all his synapses clicked, and he recovered his bearings, and his mind that he had just lost a few moments ago. He was in deep trouble if he stayed on this course. Then there was the ten million. That was certainly an adequate exchange for the loss of the eMicro account. They couldn't afford to lose this new account, too.

Straightening his jacket, he smiled, "Good work men. Carry on!" As he left the room, he patted Brian on the back. "Good work, Brian. Good work indeed."

After Newman rounded the corner, Robert and Brian shook hands and burst into laughter.

Chapter Thirty-Five
New York City

They were both asleep when he slipped the hotel key into the lock and opened the door to the suite at the Marquis in Times Square. It had cost him a bundle to buy a copy from the front desk clerk. The guy probably wouldn't have sold it at any price if he had known what Luke had in mind to do tonight.

At least this hotel was a high class place and not one of the cheap motels, filled with hookers, pimps and rummies, where she usually spent her nights, he thought. But why should he care where it was, or in what neighborhood? It didn't help the constant pain he carried in his chest every day.

Rosita was naked, asleep on her stomach, with her arm thrown over the man's chest. Her mass of beautiful, black hair was tossed in mad disarray over her pillow, with tendrils hanging off the side of the bed almost touching the floor.

She was so damned beautiful, he thought as his eyes swept the room and his heart squeezed tight inside his chest.

Every light in the suite was ablaze. There were empty liquor bottles on every available surface and drug paraphernalia was tossed carelessly on the nightstand next to the bed. A stereo was playing softly, and he heard the plaintive voice of Etta James singing somewhere back behind the storm burning in his chest and the images in the room, in front of his eyes, that his mind refused to accept.

He rocked back on the heels of his cowboy boots and tried to both control his anger and to focus his vision - blurred with unshed tears- as he continued to survey the room.

The couple never stirred.

They never knew he was there.

They never knew that their lives were in his hands or that he was dangerous.

Walking softly to the bed, Luke pulled his gun from the back of his jeans and knelt down by Rosita, pushing the hair back from her face. She was so gorgeous, he thought. She was his life and the only woman he had ever loved.

And, she was killing him, one lover at a time.

Each time he learned she was with another man, he felt another part of himself break off and fly away, leaving him less and less grounded and less able to control the murderous rage that tormented him.

Night after night, he suffered, waiting for her to come home. More and more often now she never even tried to make it, didn't call to tell him some lie. She just acted like she didn't care or have the energy to keep up the act and the charade they called their marriage. He was losing her and it was more than he could bear.

She had told him she wanted a divorce and it had rocked him so hard he hadn't slept for a week. He had started drinking, trying to burn out the pain and his loneliness. That had been when he had started following her.

"Why?" he wondered? "Why doesn't she love me?" He had asked himself this question time and time again and still he didn't understand.

Leaning down, he kissed her on the cheek. God, her skin was so soft and he wanted her so badly. This was the only time he could remember, in a very long time, that she hadn't flinched away when he tried to kiss her. Suddenly, he smelled their sweat and their sex and his stomach reeled. He closed his eyes for a moment and tried to push back the bile in his mouth,

Luke opened his eyes and took his gun and rubbed it softly against Rosita's cheek. It would be so easy to kill them both, he thought, and oh, how he wanted to do it - end her life, right now, this minute. But, as much as he wanted to, he knew he wouldn't.

He cursed himself for being a weakling where she was concerned. He was in love and there was nothing he could do. He was doomed to a life of pain and heartache unless he killed her now, and he knew it.

"Not yet, not yet," he muttered as he stood up wearily and turned away to look at the man lying beside her. He didn't recognize this one, but he usually didn't anymore. Probably, just someone she had picked up for the night. That was her favorite trade these days, one-night stands with strangers. When he thought of how she gave herself to these men that she didn't know, but never to him, it caused his gut to squeeze with a pain so deep it took his breath away.

At first, after they were married, she had wanted him and they had made love two, sometimes three times a day. It was heaven and he couldn't get enough of her. He knew he was a good lover but something was never right between them from the very beginning, no matter how hard he tried. He knew now that it was all part of her plan and that she played the game to make sure he would fall for her lies.

She had laughed in his face when he had started asking her when they would be together again. "Don't you get it Luke?" she had hissed. "I don't love you. I never did. You were easy and you were there.

Don't ever touch me again. I can't stand it when you touch me!" Then she had turned and stalked away.

The words had destroyed him, but he had kept on hoping. Praying she would change her mind.

Trembling from the painful memories, he walked to the small armchair in the room and sat, hanging his head, pushing back his tears trying to get his breath. Then the tears pushed out of his eyes, against his will, and started to flow as he looked up at his beautiful, unfaithful wife and thought of the vows they had made.

"Till death do us part," he whispered. "Till death do us part," he said louder, "that's what you promised. You promised to forsake all others," he said his arm trembling as he aimed the gun at the sleeping couple. "You promised," he repeated. "Remember those words, Rosita?" He was shaking so hard, his hand was jumping, as he contemplated how to put an end to all his misery.

"Do it," he whispered, "do it now!" he commanded himself, but he couldn't. No matter what, he couldn't kill her.

Then his world spun out of control as he slowly lost his mind. No more, he thought, no more. "I can't take this anymore," he moaned, as the despair and all the long, lonely nights piled up like a heavy anchor pushing him down, drowning him in a huge wave of regret and hate.

Taking the gun in his two hands, Luke spun the chamber, loaded with three bullets, aimed the gun at the bed, then quickly turned the gun away from Rosita and placed it against his temple.

Then he pulled the trigger.

Chapter Thirty-Six

Victor was relaxing in front of his TV, sipping a drink and thinking about Julia. She was coming to New York for a few days and she had said that she needed to talk to him. He was dreading it, but he couldn't say no to her. She would be here in a few days and hopefully he could handle whatever she threw at him.

He had loved her since the first time he had seen her. But, she had been married to a man who was like a father to him, so he moved away, left the country of his birth and made a new life for himself. He dated many women and he slept with some of them, but each time he slowly dropped out of their lives. They were not for him. After a time, he stopped dating and he stopped looking. He wanted Julia and no one could extinguish the burning desire he felt for her in his heart, so he quit trying.

After Roberto died, and after they learned how he had betrayed his wife, Victor had been unable to leave her. She needed him. Then, one night, he lost his mind and he had given in to his hunger and spent a wild night with her, filled with passion and love. The problem was, that for Julia, it had only been a wild night of passion, nothing more. At the same time, that same wonderful night had left Victor feeling euphoric and secure in the knowledge that now, after all this time, all his dreams would be coming true. Well, yes, it had changed everything for him, but it had not fazed Julia. She had other plans to reunite with her true husband and the family that she had lost so long ago. Those plans did not include another man who loved her even if she thought he was a good lover. So, Victor was forced to stand aside as she rushed out of his life one more time.

The weekend he had just spent with her in Montana would have to be enough. If she chose to spend the rest of her life with her family, he would get through the pain. He loved her and he wanted her to be happy - no matter what that meant. His memories of her smile, playing with her in the snow, her clean scrubbed face standing in the kitchen with her "feety" pajamas, smiling up at him, and her beautiful body trembling under his as the moonlight spilled across the bed, would have to be enough to take him to the end of his days. It would be enough. If it had to be, it would be enough.

As he was contemplating the years he might spend without her, a news clip rolled across the television screen in front of him.

Victor gasped as what he was watching hit him. His glass dropped from his hands and hit the floor. The impact, when the glass hit, shattered it into a million tiny pieces and sounded like a gunshot going off in the room. Victor never noticed.

Jumping up, he rushed into his bedroom, pulled the drawer from his bedside table, and dumped its contents onto the bed. Pulling a brown manila envelope from the debris, he opened it and pulled out a photograph. Rushing back to the television he looked from the screen back to the picture.

"I'll be damned," he exploded. "I'll be damned. I'm going to kill her!"

Chapter Thirty-Seven

"Click".

The sound of the gun pressed against his temple, echoed in the room as sweat poured off Luke's face. He was staring at the bed where his wife lay with another man.

"She's not worth it," a voice said to him. "She's not worth your life", the voice continued somewhere inside his head. It was a voice only he could hear.

The music in the room penetrated into his mind just at the exact moment that he started to pull the trigger again, hoping to end his pain this time. Something made him reconsider. He pulled his shaking hand down and pushed the gun away.

The song playing, "You've Changed", was one of his favorites. When he was feeling down and drinking himself into oblivion, which was pretty much every day now, he would play it over and over again. The song said it all.

Listening to the words, he knew he was not alone in how he felt. Many others before him had suffered too. He knew he should hold on to that truth. They survived – he could too.

Luke knew he had to get himself together and to think rationally about what he was about to do. After all, there was someone else to think about, someone who couldn't protect himself. Luke was all that he had in the world. No, he couldn't be selfish and he couldn't afford to lose it. Not now.

He swore to himself as he stared at beautiful, deadly Rosita. His wife, he thought, as he sang the words to the song softly to himself.

"You've changed.
You're not the angel I once knew.
No need to tell me that we're through.
It's all over now, you've changed."

Luke stood and walked slowly away from the bed, while the words echoed sadly in the room. Looking back just once more, his heart, once tender, hardened against Rosita for what she had done to him, time and time again. All the tears he had shed, all the promises she had broken, and all the lies she had told, took their toll as his heart broke apart and turned to stone.

If Luke could have seen himself in a mirror at that exact moment, he would have seen a man with dead eyes staring back at him - a man who had lost it all.

Then he turned away from his pain, his wife and her lover, and left them safely sleeping.

They would never know how close they had come to dying.

Never looking back, with a strong step and his shoulders straightened for the first time in a long time, Luke walked out and closed the door gently behind him as he whispered softly, "Goodbye Rosita."

Chapter Thirty-Eight

Rosita was in her dressing room when the call was patched through to her.

"Rosita," Victor growled, "why didn't you tell me!"

"Why, Victor. How nice to hear from you. How have you been?" she purred.

"Cut the crap, Rosita. Why didn't you tell me? I had a right to know."

"Tell you what, Victor?" she asked innocently.

"That you and I have a son!" he yelled at her, his frustration boiling over.

"I don't have a clue what you're talking about, Victor. We," she said placing special emphasis on the word, "don't have a son. I have a son."

"Look Rosita, I saw you on TV. The news anchor said that the picture was of you, your husband and your young son," he said, trying to be calm.

"And?" she said calmly.

"And, that boy is mine! Not only does he look just like me when I was a baby, but the timing puts you and me together in Argentina," he said through clenched teeth.

"He does look like you, doesn't he?" she said so sweetly you could practically taste the sugar.

"I want to see him," he said in a voice that brooked no argument.

Rosita chuckled and said nothing.

"Rosita, I want to see him. I want to support him and I want him to have my name."

"Well, that may what you want, but it is not what I want. What I want is for you is to drop dead; you and your sweet Julia. You're never going to see my boy. He's mine so you can just forget it!"

"Rosita, I have rights. Legally, you can not stop me from seeing him."

"I can and I will, Victor," she said angrily. Then she added, "Hurts, doesn't it!" and slammed down the phone.

Chapter Thirty-Nine

Several days after the disastrous phone conversation with Rosita, Victor received a call from Luke.

"Hey, Victor. How are you doing, old man?"

"Luke, I'm fine, but who are you calling 'Old Man' bud?"

Luke laughed.

"Hey, Victor, I was wondering if you'd like to meet me for lunch today?"

"Today?"

"Yeah, today."

"Sure, it looks like my calendar is clear. That would be great. Where and when?" he replied, surprised that Luke had called him out of the blue.

"How about if I come up to your office? We can catch up and then walk out somewhere close for lunch."

"Good plan. How about 11:30? Would that work for you?"

"Sure would. See you then."

As Victor hung up the phone, he wondered what that was all about.

***

Luke arrived promptly at 11:30 A.M. When his secretary announced his arrival, Victor asked her to send him back. Then he stood and put on his suit jacket as the door opened.

Luke walked in ushering a small boy in front of him, into the office. The little boy had blond hair and huge blue eyes.

They stood side by side at the entrance to the room, and Victor suddenly felt dizzy. The child had his hand clutched firmly into Luke's as he stared around him in wonder. Victor was speechless.

"His name is Nicholas," Luke said solemnly. "He's fourteen months old."

Victor wavered on his feet.

"Daddy," Nicholas said looking up at Luke.

"Yes, sweetie. It's okay," he responded smiling down at the boy.

Victor stepped in front of his desk and sat down in a chair. He didn't think his legs would continue to hold him.

"He's beautiful," Victor whispered having lost his voice.

"Yes, he's a fine boy," Luke offered.

Nicholas dropped his father's hand and tottered across the huge expanse of rug between the door and the desk. As he approached Victor, he placed his tiny hands on Victor's knees and regarded him with a solemn gaze from large rounded eyes. Then he turned away, his attention caught by a toy metal soldier Victor kept on the corner of his desk.

The small toy was one of the few precious memories left from Victor's childhood. He had found it in the rubble after his home had been destroyed by fire. It never left his desk.

Pointing up to it, Nicholas indicated that he wanted to hold it. Taking the toy from his desk, Victor gently placed it into Nicholas's tiny hands.

Nicholas took it and turned it from side to side, studying it intently. Then he turned to Victor. A single toothed smiled crossed his face and he started to laugh happily.

Victor had to turn away he was so overcome with emotion, as he tried to control his shaking hands.

Luke moved over to a chair situated beside the one where Victor was seated, and sat down next to him. Picking Nicholas up, he placed him onto his lap. The boy was content to continue his perusal of the toy.

"I thought you might want to see your boy," he said sadly.

Silence hung in the room.

"You knew?" Victor choked, surprised by what Luke had just said.

"Yeah, I knew. I tried to pretend, but I knew."

More silence.

"I'm sorry Luke," Victor said ashamedly, since this man clearly loved Rosita, and was suffering over the knowledge that the boy was not his son."

"Yeah, well, I heard Rosita talking to you on the phone the other day and I knew she was going to use Nicholas as a weapon against you and I couldn't go for that. No sir, it's not right."

Victor said nothing.

"She's still in love with you," he finished in a voice so filled with pain that Victor wondered at the courage it must have taken to come here and to lay out his open wounds before Victor.

Victor tried to speak but his couldn't.

"It's not right," Luke continued. "A man needs to know his son," he finished softly.

Finally, Victor spoke, "I'm so sorry Luke. I didn't know she was pregnant and then she married you and..." he stopped unable to continue.

"Aw, it's okay. You don't owe me any apologies. It is what it is."

The room was quiet for a time; each man lost in his own thoughts.

"Now, here's the deal," Luke said breaking the stillness. "I'll bring Nicholas to you several times a week, when you're not traveling. He'll be my son the rest of the time and you'll make no claim on that time. Rosita must never know. You will be discreet. If you can live with that, we'll strike a deal."

Victor said nothing; he was not sure he had heard what Luke had said correctly.

"I know you want him and I know that he's your boy, but I love him even though he's not mine by blood. I've been getting up with him in the night, since he was first born and he feels like he's my son. I'm real attached to the boy, so I hope you understand and won't try to make me give him up to you," he said smiling warmly at the little boy playing in his lap.

Luke waited and said nothing more.

When Victor could speak, he said, "I'll agree to your conditions Luke and I'll thank you for it. You're a better man than I," he said, overcome for the moment. "Any time I can have with my boy, I'll take. I'll never betray you to Rosita and I will not try to take him away from you. I promise you that. I can see that you love him and even more, I can see that he loves you too. I know you'll take good care of him. I appreciate what you have done for me here today."

"Good. That's all settled then. Why don't we go to lunch? Rosita is on the set today, so she'll never know. Besides, she couldn't care less what I do," he said absently.

"Want to hold Nicholas?" he said changing the subject.

Victor nodded his head and took his little boy from Luke's arms. Nicholas looked up at Luke. His lip was trembling.

"It's okay son," he reassured him. Nicholas smiled and promptly laid his head on Victor's chest, the little soldier still held firmly in his grasp, and snuggled into Victor's arms.

Victor's heart flew up out of his chest and blew away.

Chapter Forty
Chicago, Illinois

Julia was sitting at a table in Yvette's Jazz Club and Restaurant on Rush Street, with her son Brian. They were about to have dinner together to celebrate the end to the mess at Hart & Newman and eMicro and how well it had turned out since Julia had become involved. Brian wanted to thank her for her help, thus the dinner.

She tried hard not to stare at her boy, but she couldn't help it as he spoke to the waiter and placed their orders for food and drink. He looked exactly like Keanu Reeves, and every girl in the place couldn't take their eyes off of him. She was so proud to be his mother.

He didn't know that he was her son, but she was about to tell him. She had pondered long and hard about her decision, but she wanted her family back. Her daughter, Alexandria, her son Brian and the husband she had been forced to leave behind. They belonged to her and she was taking them all back.

Julia's heart twisted for a moment as she thought about Lainie who loved David and both of Julia's children and who would be destroyed if Julia took them from her. Then she thought about Alex's words to her, "I would hate you if you tried to come between my mom and my dad".

But, Alex was young and she didn't understand, she thought excusing what she was about to do. She'll get over it, she thought. Then she hardened her heart and prepared to tell her son.

He would be the first to know.

Things were moving along nicely for her and David too. She felt certain that he was falling in love with her. This trip to Chicago, which made David miss her very much, based on the many phone calls he had placed to her hotel, only confirmed what she was thinking.

Damn anyone who thinks this is unfair, she thought angrily. I deserve to have my family back. Why shouldn't I have them back?

"Why are you staring at me?" Brian said softly; interrupting her thoughts as he looked into her eyes.

"Because you are so beautiful I can hardly stand it," she replied smiling brightly. "Gorgeous, smart, and oh, let's not forget, tall, dark and handsome. A man that some lucky girl is going to be crazy about," she continued, taking her hand and placing it on his face, touching him gently on his cheek.

"You make my heart sing," she said very softly. "If you could only know how proud I am of you." Then, without thinking, Julia blurted out, "I love you so much Brian," as she prepared to tell him her secret which would change their lives forever.

"Julia. Stop for a moment, please," he said gently taking her hand and kissing her palm. "I want to talk now, before you go on. I was going to wait a little longer, but you need to know that I feel the same. I am madly in love with you. No, please don't say anything yet. Let me finish first", he continued when Julia tried to speak, while pulling her hand from his grasp. He never noticed that all the color had left her face and she was trembling.

"Julia, I know there is a difference in our ages, but I feel a connection to you I have never felt before," he stumbled on, trying not to lose his nerve. "It's like I have known you all of my life. It is as if you have been away and I have been holding my breath waiting for you to return. I can see the love that you feel for me when I look into your eyes and my heart leaps with a joy I can't explain each time I see your face. God, I love you so much," he finished reaching out to try to take her hands back into his.

It was only then that Brian realized something was wrong. Julia was staring at him, her color ashen, and her eyes huge in her face. Her hands, which she had pressed against her mouth, were trembling and tears had started to trail down her cheeks.

"Julia, what is it?" Brian asked, alarmed, but Julia interrupted him before he could go on.

"Brian, my God….. No! No ….Don't….. Oh Brian, I am so sorry," she wailed. With that she jumped from her chair, whirled around and ran, staggering, almost falling, bumping into a waiter, barely missing dumping his tray onto the floor, and then pushed out the front entrance of the restaurant into the street.

A cab was idling at the curb waiting for its next fare when Julia yanked the door open and threw herself inside prostrate across the seat crying so hard she could hardly speak.

"I am so stupid. What in the hell was I thinking?" she cried bitterly, pounding her fists against the seat. "Why didn't I notice what was going on with him and what he was feeling? Oh my God, what am I going to do now? I have hurt my son and he will never forgive me. Oh no, no……" she wailed, crying hysterically.

The driver of the cab, a small Pakistani man, watched her in the mirror. Then he turned off the meter, looked back at his passenger and drove slowly away. He understood grief and pain very well having lived through so much before he left his country and came to America. He wasn't completely sure what she was saying, but he knew tears and he knew suffering when he saw it. So, he would just drive around in the area near the restaurant until she could tell him where she lived and where he should take her. Poor little thing, he thought as she cried and cried as if her heart were broken.

***

Julia was exhausted. She didn't know how long it had been since she had left the restaurant and made her grand exit, but she couldn't cry anymore so she had finally asked the cabbie to take her back to her hotel. He had refused to charge her for the fare and when she asked why, he just smiled softly and told her, in broken English, to take care of herself, and that he hoped whatever it was that had caused her heart to break would turn out okay. Then he drove away.

Turning away from the street, the doorman, who had waited silently during her exchange with the driver, opened the door to the lobby of the hotel and held it so she could enter. As she made her way slowly to the elevator, she was oblivious to the stares of the people milling around the lobby who were wondering what had happened to her. Her eyes were swollen and her face was streaked with tears. Her clothes were a mess, but she didn't realize the spectacle she created as she waited for the elevator to take her to the safety of her room.

Once she entered her suite, she threw her purse onto the bed, stepped out of her shoes and dialed the only person she felt she could talk to about the mess she had made of everything. She called Victor.

***

Brian sat at the table alone. The candles on the table were burnt almost to the end of the wick and the wax had pooled and spilled down the side of the silver candlestick holders. He was drinking and had been steadily tossing the alcohol down since Julia left the table in such a rush several hours before. The restaurant was almost completely deserted and the jazz band was about to call it a night as they started packing up their equipment.

"What went wrong?" he asked himself again. "I can tell she loves me so why did she get so upset when I told her how I felt? Did I say something wrong?"

Brian had been asking himself these questions over and over and still could not find any fault in what he had said or done. Obviously, the evening had ended before it had begun, and it had ended very badly. He wasn't sure what he should do or what it all meant. It sure hadn't turned out the beautiful way he had planned.

Pulling the ring out of his pocket - the ring he had planned to give to Julia tonight - he stared at the large diamond with the platinum band. It was the ring his father had given his mom when they were married. For some reason, his mother always took it off her finger and left the ring on the dresser when she went to the park in Paris. It was one of the few beautiful things that his mother had left behind. His dad had given Brian the ring the last time he was home, for that day, he said, when his son might find the woman that he loved as much as he had loved his mom. He knew he had found that woman; he was sure of it but something just wasn't right.

Brian tried to remember what he said as he continued asking himself the same questions over again; the same ones that he had been asking himself all night. Pushing his head down into his hands, he scrubbed his face, rubbed his neck, and called for another drink.

***

The next week was a blur for Julia as she wandered the streets of Chicago, seeing nothing, as she wrestled with what she was going to do. A storm front had moved in so it rained every day but still she walked blindly along, fighting with herself; the pros and the cons of her decision playing out in her mind, dancing in front of her, taunting her, as she walked, cried and prayed, then walked some more.

Julia was lying in the tub in her suite, with an entire box of soap bubbles surrounding her. The lights were dimmed, the candles were burning and an iced bottle of Pouilly Fuisse sat in a stand next to the tub. She was exhausted. She could not relax, though she kept trying.

She had walked, cried, tossed, turned and still she was tormented. She had spoken to Victor and he tried to help her, but she was still broken apart with the realization of what she was going to have to do. She didn't see anyway out of it.

"Julia, come to me," he had said. "Let me help you. Leave Chicago and come here and we can spend as much time as you want talking this over. Don't do anything rash right now. Take your time. We can figure something out together. Do you want me to fly there? I will, you know. All you have to do is ask and I'm on the next plane."

She remembered his voice and how caring he had sounded.

"No, Victor. I don't want you to come. I have to do something now. I can't wait. Brian is in love with me, and I don't want to hurt him."

"Well, you can't blame him. You are very beautiful," he had teased.

"Victor, this isn't funny. I'm desperate. If I tell him I'm his mother… well that's just too horrible to contemplate."

"Julia, he's a boy and he will get over it, either way. Try to remember, sometimes, things happen; you are placed on a road, many times one not of your own choosing, and you are forced to stay that course. There is an old saying, 'You can never go home again' and this could be one of those times. You have to look at the good and the bad that telling him the truth might mean. Who does it really help? If the answer is only you, then you might want to think about what impact his knowing the truth might mean to him as well as the rest of the family."

God, that's all she had needed to hear, she thought. True, oh so true, but she just didn't need to hear it.

Stepping from the tub and leaving the oasis of comfort she had tried to create to no avail, she wrapped herself in her robe, walked up to her desk, and broke her resolve not to call. She picked up the phone and dialed the one person she knew would have the answer, someone who would understand, –someone she should have already called and who Julia knew would be worried since she hadn't – she called her mom.

***

Brian was excited. Julia had called, after one of the longest weeks of his life, and they were meeting tonight for dinner. They were going back to Yvette's and he thought that this was an excellent sign. He didn't think someone would want to go back to the "scene of the crime", so to speak, if they were feeling badly about what had happened the last time they were there. At least he hoped not.

Julia had told him that she was sorry for the scene that she had caused and that he had just caught her off guard when he told her he loved her that night. She had gone on to say that she hoped he would forgive her and that they could meet again for dinner and to talk. Yes, he thought it was all going to work out.

Twirling around in a perfect dance spin, Brian straightened his tie, pulled the ring out of the velvet box in the top drawer of his dresser and slipped it into the pocket of his trousers.

***

Julia was already seated at the table when Brian entered the restaurant. She hadn't noticed him yet since her back was to him. His heart was pounding so hard he was afraid everyone could hear it.

She wore a beautiful, off-white suit with several strands of pearls and her skin was translucent in the soft light. She is so beautiful, he thought as he approached the table.

198

Julia looked up just as her son started toward the table. Their eyes met and she whispered to herself, "Give me the strength to do this, God. Help me, I need you," as he came to her side and kissed her cheek softly before sitting down across from her at the table.

"Brian, thank you for coming. I wasn't sure you would ever speak to me again after the horrible way I acted the last time we met. I hope you can forgive me," she finished as her heart hammered in her chest.

"How about us sharing a meal, having a few drinks and then you can tell me what it is that you have on your mind. Then we can both be fortified and able to handle whatever comes tonight," he said teasing her and smiling at the woman he loved.

"That sounds wonderful," Julia said relieved that she could put this off a little while longer.

***

Dinner was over and the waiter had cleared the table, when Julia reached over and took both of Brian's hands into her own. She needed to tell him now or she was going to lose her nerve.

Her son sat quietly, looking at her with a slight smile on his lips and Julia choked. The room started to spin and she went back to that day in Paris, the last day that she had seen him before she had been kidnapped. She saw his little face and how cute he was when he ran back and forth trying to kick the ball and she felt as if her heart was going to stop beating in her chest. This man, this wonderful man, sitting across from her was her son; her son, she repeated in her mind. My beautiful baby; all grown up, ready for love and I have to fix this. Somehow, I have to be strong and fix this.

Then she thought back to the day that changed all their lives forever.

We always make the mistake of thinking, she mused, that it is the big things that place you in the car that flips over on the highway when the drunk driver coming toward you swerves and crosses the median, or puts you in the bank when the robber starts to shoot, or makes the day so beautiful that you feel that it is the most perfect day to take your children to the park and play a game of soccer, never knowing that the decision you make that day will end in a terrible tragedy.

She knew now, after all was said and done, after all these years; that it was the little things; leaving your hair loose, flowing freely down your back, instead of pinning it up the way you always did, or that extra cup of coffee shared with your husband, that made you leave later than usual that morning, your diamond rings that you pulled off and placed on the dresser, or the picture of your family that you, for some reason, decided to slip into your dress pocket at the last minute as you walked out the door.

Julia wondered again as she traveled back in time, what if we would have left Paris that day, or if David would have been with us at the park, or if she would have known that Roberto was prepared to let her go the night that she flew at him in a rage and was severely injured from the fall that took away her memory? How would their lives have been and where would she be now? Obviously, she wouldn't be forced to have the heartbreaking conversation she was about to have with her only son.

Then she thought of the struggle this had been, trying to make a decision that would alter her life. Lying on her bed at the hotel, she would ask herself what to do and listen while the angels spoke back.

"You would give your life for him. Isn't that right?"

"Yes, you know I would."

"Then you must let him go. There is no way back; no way to reclaim what you have lost."

And as much as she argued with herself, night after night, she finally knew that destiny had decided the life she was to have and that it didn't include those she left behind. Fair or not, there it was.

Shaking herself, she brought her mind back to the task at hand.

"Brian, when I told you that I loved you the last time we met, I didn't mean a sexual kind of love," she started. She could feel Brian tense as his hands stiffened in hers. Looking him straight in the eyes, she fought her tears back behind her eyes and forced herself to go on.

"You don't know this, but I once had a son. He would be about your age now," she choked. "He was taken from me…" Julia struggled with the rage and the pain that she felt, knowing that she would have to let her son go again. I have to let him go. "Help me, help me," her heart cried out. "I have to leave him and go away, so that he can have the life he was intended to have," she admonished herself. Taking a deep breath, she struggled to compose herself and do what needed to be done.

Forcing back a sob, she said, "I would like to believe that he would have had a soul as pure and beautiful as yours and that he would hold a light inside him, like you do, and that this light would warm my heart the way you do each and every time I see your face. When I look into your eyes, I see him and how he might have been. That he might have been beautiful and full of grace and love, like you. My heart tears apart for the loss of him and you help me to heal each time I see you and share a piece of your life. You are all I ever wanted him to be, and I love you for allowing me into your life and letting me pretend that my son still lives and breathes and loves like you. You have given me back my boy, the son I lost and the hole I had inside me has been filled with the love I feel for you."

Brian was stunned into silence. Then he was embarrassed. What a complete idiot he was. Of course she didn't love him the way he loved her, and then he spoke, "Julia, I am so embarrassed. I am sorry, I didn't know," he stammered.

"Brian, please don't," Julia said so softly it was almost a whisper. "How could you ever have known? I am the one that should have told you from the start and I should have put my pain behind me and just told you."

"Oh Julia, please don't apologize," Brian said just as softly. "Let's forget this every happened."

"Brian, thank you for understanding. You are so sweet and kind. But, I would like to stay a part of your life, if you will let me. I could be your friend and I would love to see you from time to time and to know how you are doing," she paused to gather her strength again, because every bone in her body was screaming against what she was doing.

"I am going back to Argentina. Maybe you could come to visit me sometime," she stumbled on hurriedly wanting to get this over with. "I want you to forgive me. I never meant to hurt you. I didn't know how you felt," she finished as the tears she had tried to contain coursed down her cheeks.

Brian sat quietly, letting all she had said sink into his mind and trying to control the pain in his heart. He did love her, but he understood. Who was this beautiful, incredible woman who could touch him the way she did? He could handle his feelings for her, he thought as he started to relax. It was foolish on his part to think that she could ever love him the way he had imagined. It hurt him, but he knew in time he would be okay.

"Julia, you honor me by telling me this and I am so sorry for your pain. I know how hard it must be for you to speak about your son. I don't talk to anyone about this, but I lost my mother a long time ago and it still haunts me sometimes, although, I have to say that since I met you, the bad dreams have stopped and I have been at peace."

"Can you tell me about her, your Mom? Would it help you to talk about her to me? What do you remember," she asked, as her heart trembled inside her chest.

Brian thought for a moment then he said. "She was very beautiful. She had long, black hair, at least from what I can remember and the pictures that we have. Her face, it's odd, but you sometimes remind me of her even though your hair and eye color are different.

That connection I feel when you look at me a certain way, makes me think of my Mom. Isn't that odd? But, in the dream, there is a bad man and he is hurting her and I feel so lost and I can't seem to help and then I wake up screaming for her. For years, it has haunted me."

Julia sat frozen, afraid to move. Her breath was gone and she could not find any air in the room. Brian continued to speak.

"There's this feeling that she is here sometimes. I seem to feel her spirit and suddenly I am sleeping better and the dreams have stopped. There's an air or something magical in my room now when I wake up each day and I feel sheltered by her somehow. It's weird after all these years, but maybe I have finally forgiven myself for not being able to help her."

There was a deafening roar in Julia's head and she had to wait a moment to speak. "You were just a child. There was nothing you could have done and it would have been dangerous for you to have tried to help."

"How did you know that I was a child and that it was dangerous?" Brian questioned her.

Julia stopped, trying to think of something to say. Say something, she demanded of herself. Then she took a deep breath and said casually, "Oh, I think maybe your Dad may have mentioned the way your mother died," hoping that would stop his questions.

After a time when neither one of them spoke, Brian said, "Maybe, we are really good for each other and by being friends we can both heal from what we each have lost," he said speaking very softly. Julia was slowly breaking apart but she fought to shut her mouth and not say the words that she wanted to say.

"Argentina, huh? Are you sure?" he said thinking how much he would miss her when she went away.

"Yes, Brian. There is a man. A man that I love very much," Julia said as Victor's handsome face swam before her eyes. At that moment, Julia realized that it was true and that she did love Victor. She had intended to use Victor as an excuse so Brian would let her go and so he would know there was absolutely no hope that she would change her mind. My God, she thought, it's incredible. I do love him.

"But," she continued, "I don't want to lose our friendship. Can you promise me this won't change that?"

"We'll be the Lone Ranger and Tonto," Brian said laughing and squeezing her hands. "Look what we did at Hart & Newman."

"Or Lucy and Dezi," she joined in remembering how she had screwed up when she dropped all her boxes, and to be really honest, almost gotten them captured or killed before they had finally pulled it off.

Then they both stood and she went to him and embraced her son, her little baby, her only boy and Julia's heart raged inside her while her mind screamed that it wasn't fair and that she couldn't do this; but finally she let him go.

"I need to leave you now. I have a trip planned that will take me back to Washington to say goodbye to your sister and David and Lainie. I will call and let you know when I arrive back in Argentina. Remember that I do love you and if you ever need me for any reason, I will be on the next plane. If you will let this old woman, I will have my son again whenever I am with you."

Brian took Julia into his arms again. "Goodbye Julia, I will miss you." Then he pulled back and looked into her eyes, "Friends forever," he said softly.

"Friends forever," she said with a sad smile. Then Julia turned and walked away from her only son, tears blinding her eyes, leaving him behind with the people he knew and loved and the life he had made with them.

Chapter Forty-One
Washington, D.C.

Lainie Grant, studied the letter in front of her, sipping the coffee at the desk that she used at the newspaper office. She had read the letter several times and it broke her heart each time she picked it up, read the words and tried to imagine what would make a woman do what her friend had done.

It was a letter from a girlfriend that she had grown up with in St. Louis. How she had found Lainie after all these years was a mystery, and why she had chosen to write this letter was another.

They had both grown up poor, knowing that getting out of their poverty was going to be a real challenge. They were fast friends all through high school and had started to drift apart when Lainie went on to college and Brenda found she didn't have the drive or desire to go any further with her education. They both loved to dance and loved music so, many nights, when Lainie wasn't studying; they would head out to East St. Louis to listen to one of the wonderful Blues bands playing in the late night clubs.

Lainie knew that Brenda had fallen in love and married a black musician named Leroy. At the time, Lainie had warned her about the difference in their cultures and that a white woman with a black husband in East St. Louis was going to have a hard road ahead. But, Brenda was crazy about him and she was determined that it would work out and she would be able to make a life with the man she loved. Lainie had moved to New York after graduating and had lost contact with Brenda.

Opening the letter again. Lainie read,

"Dear Lainie,

I know you must be surprised to hear from me after all these years. It must be at least twenty years or more since we last saw each other, but I thought you might like to hear how my life turned out. I read about you when you got that big job with that paper in New York and I was very proud of you.

I am living in the West and have a wonderful husband. I studied hard and got my nursing degree and now I work in a very large hospital out here. We have a cute little house and are very happy. Are you surprised? I just bet you are. Things have really turned out great for me just like they did for you.

I guess you can tell that things didn't go so well for me and Leroy and I thought I would write and tell you my story so you would know that I am just fine and that, in the end, it did work out all right.

To start my story, I'll try to tell it from the beginning after you left St. Louis.

Within nine months and fifteen days of my marriage to Leroy, I had our first daughter. She was named Dinah, for Dinah Washington. Leroy liked that and said that she should be named after one of the greatest black singers of all time. I, of course, had no say in the matter.

Then the beatings started. I was his woman, was I seeing someone else, where was I when he called that afternoon, did I think he would put up with me fooling around? "You said you was gonna take a shower when I called, why isn't the shower wet? Was someone here, there's an extra plate on the table? You, b----, you're foolin around on me, ain't yuh?" and then the beating would begin.

Except for an occasional trip to the corner store, I was never allowed to leave the house unless he was with me.

Within a year, our second daughter, Sarah, this time named for Sarah Vaughn, was born.

After her birth, I slipped out and saw a doctor. I didn't want any more babies and I told him so. He gave me a diaphragm and taught me what I had to do. When Leroy found out, he beat me so badly that I could not leave my bed for over three days. The lady upstairs, a real sweet, old black woman named Esther, would come down and take care of the babies and nurse me. I can still hear her saying, "You pore li'l thing. Bless yore heart. Why that man gotta go on an beat you an treat you this way and you the mama of his li'l babies?" Then she would tsk, tsk, tsk, straighten my covers, tell me not to cry, then leave my tiny apartment and wait for the next time. There was always a next time.

I started saving the change from the soda bottles and cans that I would hide and then when I could slip away, take back to the store for a refund. Every time I slipped out, my heart would pound so hard I thought it would stop beating; worrying that if he would catch me and what he would do if he did. Esther would keep the girls for a few minutes those days and tell me to please hurry. She knew what I was up to and she knew I was desperate. Whenever Leroy let me walk to the corner store, I would hide a few cents out of the change when I bought a loaf of bread or some milk.

Slowly my money started to grow. I kept it all hidden in a can, under a pile of leaves, old bottles and bricks out in the back yard. I told Leroy that I saw a snake out there one day around that pile of rubbish. Leroy was deathly afraid of snakes, so he never, ever went near that pile, so I knew I was safe. Sometimes, when he was real, real drunk and passed out on the bed, I would slip one or two dollars out of his wallet, never enough that he would notice, and sneak it into my "going away can".

One time he caught me lying about the change from the store and broke my arm. I lied to the doctor when Leroy took me to the hospital and told him that I fell. He knew, of course, that Leroy was beating me since my eyes were swollen shut and my lips were broken and bleeding. I think he felt like I deserved it; a blonde woman with a very dark, black man. He had no pity for me and made sure I knew that he thought I had made my own bed and I could just lie in it.

About one and a half years later, Aretha was born. Yes, you guessed it. She was named for Aretha Franklin. Still, the beatings continued. I was his b----, and I'd better get used to it. "Ain't no man gonna have my woman but me," he would say as he hammered away at me day after day. My babies would stand around the bed afterwards and cry as Esther tried to help me recuperate but it got harder and harder to leave that bed and many times I thought of killing myself.

Leroy always told the girls that he was "Big Daddy" and when they asked what their names were, he would say Dinah Washington, Sarah Vaughn and Aretha Franklin. As it turned out, this was a real advantage to me, but I did not know this yet.

Leroy finally allowed me to start taking the girls to church. What kind of trouble could I get into there, particularly with my three daughters by my side? He was wrong.

Each Sunday, we would walk the three blocks to the little Church of God and they would attend Sunday school while I went to the Church services. Then we would walk back. I never stayed an extra minute; I made sure Leroy would have no reason to beat me. It was all part of my plan.

One Sunday, several months after starting the routine; following the services at Church and after a particularly bad beating, Sister Crenshaw, asked me if I needed any help and, if I ever did, I should call her and she would come. She gave me her phone number on a small

208

piece of paper. I slit a tiny hole on the inside hem of my Sunday dress and slipped the paper inside the hem. Leroy never knew.

I waited and prayed for the right day. I read newspapers and looked for information in other cities. I asked Sister Crenshaw for a listing of all Churches in and around Chicago. I lied and told her I had a sister there and that I wanted to leave Leroy and move to Chicago with my little girls and live with her. She believed me. She told me to call when I was ready and she would make sure that I made it to Chicago. I told her I didn't have any money. She said not to worry she would take care of it.

Sister Crenshaw picked me and the girls up one Saturday when Leroy had an event his band was playing that would take up most of the afternoon. She drove me to a bus station in Belleville, Illinois, so Leroy couldn't trace me. She paid for one-way tickets to Chicago and I cried and thanked her, telling her I would never contact her again but I would never be able to thank her or repay her and that she should know that we would be fine now thanks to her. She said she understood, kissed me, hugged each one of the girls, and told us to go with God, before driving away.

In Chicago, near the bus terminal was a Church that had services starting at 10:00 A.M. that morning. I spent a long time in the restrooms at the terminal getting my daughters into their very best dresses and making sure their hair was braided just so. And I must say, they were surely a pretty picture. With their beautiful mulatto skin, ash blond hair and gray to green eyes, I was very proud. Dinah was four, Sarah was three and Aretha was one and a half and they were as cute as they could be.

I walked them to the church about 8:00 A.M. and told them to wait at the church door; that I had forgotten something, and I would be right back. I left them there crying and trembling, but knowing this was best thing for them and that they would be just fine now. Then I

209

went back to the bus station and bought a one-way ticket out west with my "Going away money".

Sometime they will cross my mind and I wonder what happened to those little girls. The picture of them standing there at the door of the church, with their great big eyes, wakes me up at night sometimes and it makes me hurt down deep in my stomach, but, I know I did the right thing. There was no way I could take them with me and ever make anything of my life. Anyway, I'm sure they turned out just fine. Don't you think I did the right thing and that they probably had really good lives?

So, I just wanted to write you this letter and let you know not to worry about me. Things have worked out just great and I have never been happier. I hope all is well with you and that things are really good for you too.

Love Brenda

There was no return address on the envelope.

Lainie had tears in her eyes when she finished the letter that she had read for the third time. How could Brenda leave her children behind? What had happened to those poor little girls who didn't even know their names? Both the blacks and the whites, because of their mulatto skin, probably shunned them, Lainie guessed. Their lives must have been very difficult and they had no mom or dad to turn to. God, this was awful. Maybe she should try to find out what happened to them?

Then Lainie thought about her beautiful stepchildren, Alex and Brian. Oh, how she loved them both. She had never been able to have children of her own and David's son and daughter were like her own flesh and blood.

And Julia was going to take them away from her if she didn't do something to stop her.

Yes, she was about to lose them all, she thought in panic.

Julia had called Lainie earlier that day and asked if they could meet later that evening for dinner. Lainie knew what was coming. She had seen David and the way he looked at Julia. He was falling in love with her and Lainie was terrified. What was she going to do? How could she fight this woman? Then she knew.

She had never done it before and she never thought she would, but she was going to beg. If she had to, she would do it on hands and knees. She was going to beg and plead with Julia to go back to Argentina and leave her family alone.

Her girlfriend Brenda might have denied her children, never fought to keep them in her life, never kept struggling against all the odds. She just gave up the fight and threw her little girls away, Lainie thought, but I'm not going to go down that path. "I'm strong and back there somewhere, deep down in his heart, David still loves me," she said out loud, preparing for battle. "I'm not giving them up to anyone," she promised herself as she straightened her suit, patted her hair and headed out of the office, determined to take her family back

Chapter Forty-Two
Washington, D.C.

Julia was back in Washington, seated in Robert Walker's office.

"Julia, what a surprise," he said as he entered his office. "My secretary told me you were waiting. I'm sorry to have left you in my office alone, but I was in meeting and I wasn't expecting you."

"I should have called first but I decided I should be spontaneous and just show up. I also thought our first meeting might be better if it were held in your office rather than at a public restaurant, " she smiled sweetly.

"Well, okay. You're probably right. Would you like something to drink?"

"No, thank you."

Robert Walker rubbed at the pain in his leg and sat down.

"It hurts me sometime, even though I don't have a leg there anymore," he said when he noticed Julia's interest.

"I've heard of that. When I was working with Alex during her rehab, there were others who were really suffering from pain they said they felt in an arm or leg when there was no arm or leg to hurt anymore. The doctors called it something but I can't remember the name."

"Yeah. 'Phantom pain' is the term. I know what they say but it hurts and sometimes it hurts damned bad."

"I'm sorry."

"Thank you, Julia, but I'm getting used to it now and there's not much anyone can do."

They were silent for a time.

Finally, Robert spoke, "I know, Julia."

Julia said nothing.

"I know that you are Elizabeth Grant," he said.

Julia thought she had prepared herself for this possibility – that he might know - but still she gasped when he said the words.

"I know that you are the wife of David Grant. The wife who was kidnapped from Paris over twenty years ago," he continued.

"How," she squeaked.

"I read your husband's file. I missed it before, but I noticed that he had married, several months after Elizabeth's disappearance. Last week, I had pictures of Roberto's wife sent to me by a friend of mine at the Argentina Embassy. Your hair is different and you must be wearing contacts but it was easy to see that Roberto's wife was Elizabeth Grant."

"Oh," she said quietly.

"My question is this? Why did you stay with him? Why didn't you try to get away? Why did you stay until he died? And what are you doing here, messing with David Grant and his family?"

Julia said nothing.

"Your boyfriend's dead and now you want your old husband back?" he said with a look of disapproval on his face. "David's been looking for you for over twenty years. He never gave up. Everyone else gave up, but he never did. And the whole time you're living the high life in Argentina. God, it makes me sick when I think about what you did to your husband and your children. When David told me about this new woman he had met and how wonderful you were, I got worried so I thought I'd better look you up. What a surprise it was when I found out that you were Elizabeth Grant and that you had been playing house with your supposed abductor for over twenty years!"

Julia had tears in her eyes.

Then those tears were replaced with fire.

"You were in Anzio when you suffered the wound that would eventually cause you to lose your foot," she said quietly. "You were a young lieutenant and you watched two soldiers rape and kill a young Italian girl, a day or so after you landed on the beach. They slit her throat. You killed the soldier who caused her death," she continued as the color left his face. "You followed the boy when he carried the girl back home. Your soldiers carried you in a sling they made of their jackets."

Robert Walker felt the room spin. It's too warm in here, he thought, pulling his handkerchief from his pocket and wiping at his face, which was sweating profusely.

"How did you...?" he whispered.

"The girl looked a lot like I looked when I was younger. The girl that was killed resembled me, didn't she?" she questioned.

Robert had never thought about this connection. "Why, yes she did, now that I think of it."

"That boy, the one from Anzio?" she continued harshly. "The one who carried the girl all those miles in the snow? Do you remember him?"

"Yes," he said dazed by her words.

"Well, that boy was Roberto Bertinelli."

Then she stopped speaking and the room grew very still.

"I don't understand," he said finally, as he looked into her face. "What are you saying?"

"I have something for you," she said, instead of answering him. Then she reached into a bag at her side. Turning back to Robert, she handed him a box. "These are the tapes that Roberto left me when he died. I want you to listen to them and call me when you have finished. Then I want to meet with you again. I think you will find them very enlightening. After you've had a chance to digest what you have heard, then I want you to tell me that you have the right to ever judge or condemn me! You self righteous, old bastard!"

Then she stormed out of his office, leaving him holding a box of old tapes.

Chapter Forty-Three

He stood in the shadows of the building, holding a cigarette in his fingers, and watched her as she left the FBI office. He had been watching her since she arrived back in Washington.

Ummm, Ummm, he thought as she walked down the street. She was a real looker.

Then he wondered why they wanted this woman killed? Most of his hits were men. Men who had cheated their bookie, stolen from the mob, a guy who was cheating with another guy's wife, but he had never killed a woman. She must have really pissed somebody off. He was the best in the business and she must have really done something to get him called in for the hit.

Taking another drag from his cigarette, he studied her as she stood for a moment looking at her watch. Yes, she was a real beauty. It was too bad, but a job was a job and he was being paid handsomely to take her out.

As he took another pull on his cigarette and continued to watch his quarry, he saw a car pull up and a large man get out, wrapping a coat around her shoulders.

"What's this?" he muttered out loud. This could put a wrinkle in his plans, and he didn't like wrinkles. He thought she was here alone, that's what he had been told, and he could follow her back to her hotel, scope out the place, and get ready to do it, maybe later tonight.

"Damn," he said softly.

As he watched, Julia was helped into the passenger side of the car and the driver went around and got into the driver's side and drove away.

As the taillights got smaller, and still smaller still, he threw down his cigarette, stomped out the tip, flipped out his cell phone and said.

"We got ourselves a problem, Houston."

Chapter Forty-Four

Julia sat in the car still flushed and still stewing over her meeting with Walker.

"I gather it didn't go well?" Joe said.

"Like going to a funeral for your best friend," she snapped.

"Oh, so he knew."

"Yes, he knew and he was happy to tell me that he basically thought I was a whore for staying with Roberto."

"Julia, it's only natural that he would wonder. I did, remember?"

Julia said nothing.

"Look, what I'm trying to say is that once he listens to the tapes, he will totally understand that you were the real victim of Roberto's crime against you and your family. You must try to remember that you are not to blame."

"Then why do I feel so dirty and ashamed?" she said as she started to cry.

"Julia, they don't know who you are. They don't know how you suffered. And, because they don't know, they jump to conclusions. I'm ashamed to say that I jumped to those same conclusions and you forgave me, didn't you?"

"Yes, yes I did."

"Well, Robert Walker will be sorry as hell he spoke to you that way once he understands what really happened. Try not to blame him. It will be all right. I promise," he said softly taking her hand in his.

Julia smiled at him through her tears. "Do you have to go?"

"No, but I think it is about time for me to take some time off, to lie in the sun and drink Mai Tai's on a warm beach," he said.

"Well, you do deserve your moment in the sun, but I will miss you very much."

"And I will miss you, Julia. You are a very impressive woman, Miss 'Kung Foo Fighter'." They laughed together and tried not to think about his flight that would leave soon.

"I don't know anyone who could have carried themselves with so much grace and love through the hell you have had to face," he continued. "Your decision to never tell you family was a hard fought, soul-wrenching decision. I know. I watched you suffer through it. Now you have made the biggest sacrifice of your life. I could never do what you are doing, but I applaud you for the immense love you must have in your heart for those you left behind so long ago. I'm sorry for your loneliness and the sadness you must be feeling. I would do anything for you. I hope you know that."

"I do know it, Joe," she said, smiling up at him. "You have been a great friend to me during the past year and I will never forget you. Please promise me that you will stay in touch."

"Julia, you don't need my professional services now, but all you have to do is call me and I'll be there."

Julia paused before answering and seemed to ponder something. Then she spoke, "Joe, do you remember how you used to take pictures of my children and David for Roberto?"

"Yes."

"I would like you to do that for me, now. I don't want them to know, but I think I can face this if I can have pictures of their life to help me through."

"Sure, Julia," he smiled. He had already decided he would keep up his surveillance. "I'll start when I return from my vacation."

As they pulled up to her hotel, Julia shook his hand and pulled him into her arms. "I will certainly miss you, Joe," she said through her tears.

Watching him drive away to the Washington Dulles airport, she trembled, blinded by her tears.

It was another loss for her - another good-bye.

***

Joe McGuire was not leaving town; Julia just thought he was. He pulled into another hotel; he had already checked out of his last one, earlier that morning, signed his fictitious name, and went to his room and unpacked.

Julia was in trouble. He had planned to leave today and he didn't want Julia to know that he had changed his plans. His sources had warned him that a hit man was in town and that his target was Julia Bertinelli. Joe had tried to find out who had hired the guy, but no one could tell him. He wasn't worried, he had someone working on it and he would know soon enough.

What he did know was that Billy Randolph Hale was called "The Shooter". He was a hit man; a very expensive hit man, so good at what he did that he was in constant demand by people all over the country, when they wanted someone to disappear.

Billy had grown up in Atlanta, spent several years in the military where he learned how to be a first class marksman, then mustered out to a career built on killing. He was good and he was paid handsomely for it.

He was an attractive man, square jawed, tall and thin with a muscular frame. He looked like a Texas cowboy – a look that he enhanced by walking with a swagger, wearing cowboy boots, jeans and a cowboy hat. Women loved him and sometimes, from what Joe had read, he may have loved them back, but he still left them, never staying in one place very long. He had never married, had no children, and lived a nomadic life style, moving from one place to another, putting down no roots, and it seemed to suit him. It also made it real hard to keep track of him. They were always a day late whenever they found the body because each time he had already moved on.

Usually, he went after men who had skipped out on their debts or who had taken an inappropriate liking to another man's wife. Sometimes it was a man who was set to testify and, the person he was going to testify against hired Billy because he didn't want that man to make it to court. The real problem was that the hits were always men. Not women. Julia just didn't fit his profile. So why was he here?

Joe was worried. Julia was unpredictable and keeping track of her movements was going to be difficult.

Picking up the phone, he dialed Victor Salvatore. He was going to need his help.

Chapter Forty-Five

Billy Hale was a good hit man. He didn't particularly like the work, but he was good at it, it gave him a great deal of cash, and he had expensive tastes, so it worked for him, most of the time.

He wasn't happy about this job and wasn't sure he should have accepted it. He didn't like killing women. He would probably do it because the money was really good, but he felt bad vibes from it. Something didn't feel right.

He had done his usual research on the target and he couldn't find anything that would cause someone to want her dead. Also, a private investigator, Joe McGuire, had been keeping a close watch on her. Joe could be dangerous, based on his file, so this had upped the ante on this assignment and added another chink in the plan. Joe was supposed to leave town today, but Billy knew he had just moved to another hotel and was still guarding Julia.

Billy was sitting in his hotel suite speaking on the phone to his boss, explaining how getting next to Julia was turning out to be a little more difficult than he had planned. And, since she was being guarded by a private investigator, did they want him to kill her when someone else was around or did they care? Should he kill both targets?

The voice on the other end of the phone chuckled, "Having a hard time Billy?"

"What do you mean?"

"You having a hard time taking out a woman?" the voice said.

"I'm not real comfortable with it, but you want it done, it will get done."

"Good. I wouldn't want you getting all mushy on me."

Billy said nothing, but he was thinking that he still didn't like this one. He liked it when the hit was a creep. He couldn't figure out what Julia Bertinelli had done and that bothered him. In fact, it bothered him a lot.

As they continued to talk, they agreed that it would be preferable to find a time and place when Julia would be alone because the hit was only for the woman. They didn't want any collateral damage. After speaking a few more moments, Billy hung up.

This is a mistake, something told him. This is a mistake and you'd better walk away from it, his inner voice told him. But, he pushed those thoughts away, and made a decision. If he was going to do it, he was going to use a gun. That way it would be quick and painless.

She would never know what hit her.

She wouldn't suffer.

Chapter Forty-Six
New York City

Julia paced her hotel room. Lainie was in New York for a couple of days and she was scheduled to meet her at "Windows on the World", a restaurant and bar on the one hundred and seventh floor of the north tower of the World Trade Center, at 6:30 P.M. It was almost time to go.

She wasn't sure how Lainie felt about her but if she were Lainie she didn't think she would like her very much. So, the meeting with her could be trouble and the anxiety of worry about it was killing her.

Julia wondered what unlucky star she had been born under. Why did it have to end this way? Then she choked back her pain and told herself to stop feeling sorry for something that could not be changed. It was time to face Lainie and to try to fix the damage she had done to her and her family. She had to do it if she wanted Alex to forgive her.

Julia picked up her purse, prayed that they wouldn't run into Victor, since he worked in the South Tower and sometimes ate his dinner there, took the elevator down and walked out to a cab waiting at the curb.

***

Lainie was late arriving at the restaurant, so Julia's anxiety kept her from speaking when Lainie sat down across from her.

"Julia," she said arranging herself in the chair, "you look lovely as usual," she said sarcastically.

Touché, Julia thought. I do look awful but it is so nice of you to mention it, is what she really wanted to say, but she bit her tongue. Lainie was declaring war and she wasn't going to play nice about it. That's okay, she thought, I would do the same if I were in her shoes.

"I wasn't sure if you were coming back to Washington. Are you?" she continued, not waiting for any reply. "Don't you have other people you need to visit?" she said sweetly.

Oh, she was on a roll, Julia grinned. She was proud of Lainie for being strong enough to fight for those she thought were hers.

Lainie bristled when she saw the smile that covered Julia's face.

"Lainie," Julia said, "let's not beat around the bush, shall we? Maybe it would be best if we just laid our cards on the table."

"Oh, I'm all ready to do that, but I'm just so surprised that you had any evenings free to meet with me. Before you left on your trip you were almost as busy as David. He was out most nights of the week then. It's strange, but that all stopped while you were away this time. I wonder why that would be?" she finished angrily.

So, the gauntlet has been thrown. I'd better start talking before she self-destructs or punches me in the nose, she thought nervously.

"Lainie, I am leaving again."

"Really," she said. But what she was thinking was, 'I hope you do leave and that you never come back.'

"Yes, I'm going back to Argentina."

Lainie didn't speak. She had been shocked into silence.

"Alone?" she finally squeaked out.

225

"Yes, alone. I'll be leaving soon. The reason I asked you to dinner was so that I could say goodbye."

"You're really leaving?"

"Yes. I think Alex is well on the road to recovery and my work here is mostly done."

"I don't know what to say," Lainie choked.

"You have been great Lainie. You're a wonderful Mom and you and David are a wonderful couple. I hope you never worried about any of the dinners that David and I shared, they were just dinners between friends, nothing more."

"Why, no. I wasn't worried," she lied.

"Good. Well, I want you to know what a joy it was to meet you and your family and to help with Alex's recovery. She's very dear to me."

"Yes, I know she likes you too. I worried about it because she seemed so attached to you," Lainie said wistfully.

"Yes, well she does like me but she's a wonderful girl who loves you very much."

Lainie said nothing.

"I'm still a fairly new widow, so working has helped me get past some of my grief."

"I heard that your husband died. I'm sorry, Julia. I don't know what I would do if something happened to David."

Julia's heart sank. Lainie loved him. She had known this of course, but it still hurt to hear her speak so sweetly about him.

"Your family has helped me to get my feet back on the ground and I will never forget any of you. Why don't we have a drink to toast my going back home?"

"That would be great, Julia," she said softly.

They ordered drinks and toasted 'Bon Voyage'. One of them had tears in her eyes, while the other celebrated and smiled she was so filled with joy.

***

Julia was leaving the north tower of the World Trade Center with Lainie by her side. They were laughing like old friends. Now that the pressure was off, they'd had their talk and cleared the air; they both had relaxed into an easy intimacy. The drinks they had shared were certainly showing as they laughed uncontrollably and staggered and weaved toward the taxi stand.

That was when Julia heard a shout that sounded like Joe McGuire's voice.

"Go back, Julia!" he screamed. "Run!"

But Julia didn't run. She stopped and turned toward his voice. It was then that the bullet ripped through her, lifting her up, off of her feet and slammed her into the pavement behind her. Blood flew everywhere and covered Lainie, who was down now, crawling away, screaming for help.

Footsteps pounded, people screamed, and general pandemonium broke out as everyone tried to seek cover.

Joe was suddenly there leaning down over Julia, while Lainie held her hand, tears streaming down her bloody face.

"Hold on, Julia. You've been shot," he said his voice shaking and his hands trembling.

"Damn it! Where's the ambulance? She's bleeding bad!" he shouted to the people standing behind him.

"Julia, don't move honey. Don't move," he said as she tried to lift her head. "Their coming now, so hang on baby. Hang on. Do you hear me Julia? Keep breathing, sweetie," he choked as her breathing faltered and she struggled to get air.

"God, this is my fault. Damn it! I should have been here sooner," he said struggling not to break down. Lainie shook him and

227

said, "Don't lose sight of what is important right now, mister. Get it together! Save her!" she yelled, snapping him back into the moment.

"Oh, Julia. Don't die honey," he moaned.

Julia tried to speak, but nothing seemed to work.

Ambulance sirens split the air and the sounds surrounding her all started to mix into one great roar.

"Victor, did you get the guy?" Joe yelled.

"We got him. How is she, Joe?"

"She's bad. She's real bad. God, where are the paramedics?"

"Get your guys over here to take this piece of shit," Victor shouted, "or I'm going to beat him to death, damn it! Joe, I don't give a shit about him, I'd just as soon see him dead, so if you want to take him in, you'd better get somebody over here, now!" he yelled.

"Brady," he said indicating a uniformed police office, "go take over and give Victor a break. Watch the bastard and make sure that the son of a bitch doesn't move a muscle. If he does just shoot him!" he commanded.

"Julia, Victor's coming. We got the guy. He'll never hurt you again, honey. Hang on. Please keep breathing baby. Take a breath now," he begged as he applied more pressure to her wound and screamed orders at the paramedics who were just then unloading their equipment from the ambulance.

Lainie was cradling Julia's head in her lap and she was crying. She had felt Julia's pulse and it was very weak. She wasn't sure she would make it if they didn't hurry. Her breathing was harsh and sporadic and her face was ashen.

Victor ran over and fell to his knees by Julia's side.

"Oh my God. Why didn't you tell me it was this bad, Joe?" he said grabbing her hand which was ice cold. "Oh God, oh God," he cried, "Julia you can do this, honey. Hang on for me, sweetie," he groaned. She moved her lips but no sound came from her mouth.

Then they came for her and pushed everyone away. Working feverishly, the team tried to staunch her bleeding. They tried to get a response from her, but she couldn't answer.

It had all faded away and Julia wasn't listening anymore.

Chapter Forty-Seven

Billy Hale was screwed. His long life of freedom was about to come to a screeching halt. God, he knew he shouldn't have taken on this hit, but his greed had overcome his common sense. Now the woman was probably dead and they had him in the cross hairs.

Lieutenant Charles Edwards was watching Billy through the two-way mirror. He was in leg irons that were bolted to the floor and they had cuffed his hands behind his back in the most uncomfortable position they could place him in.

"Sure don't look like a killer, does he?" Edwards said to Joe McGuire who was standing beside him.

"No, he doesn't. You have to wonder what makes a man like him go bad."

"Yeah. I've seen them come and I've seen them go, but they don't usually look like this guy."

"It's hard to believe that we brought down the guy they called the 'Shooter'," Joe said staring through the window at Billy.

"Yeah. My boss is real excited. Thinks he might be in line for a promotion, thanks to you guys," Edwards chuckled.

"I wish I could have gotten to him before he shot Julia," he said, pain in his voice. "It's going to tear me up if she dies. It's going be my fault."

"Waste of time man."

"What is?"

"Taking any of this personally and letting your feelings get in the way. Good way to break a man."

Joe thought about that for a moment.

"What are you prepared to offer him?" he said changing the subject.

"They're working on it. They should get back to me pretty soon."

"Good. I need to know who hired him and I need to know as soon as I can. We have to get a handle on how much danger Julia is still in, if she lives through this," he said his voice strained with anger.

"How's she doing?" the lieutenant asked.

"I'm not sure. She's lost a lot of blood and she's still in surgery. They have her listed as critical. I was surprised she made it to the hospital. I almost lost it when she stopped breathing back there. I thought she was dead. They finally revived her but it took a lot to convince me that she was still breathing. I was pretty much out of control until Victor slapped the hell out of me," he said rubbing at his sore jaw.

The lieutenant chuckled. "Yeah, Victor's pretty scary when he's upset. I had to go up against him one time in court. It was a real experience, I'll say that."

"You two still friends?"

"Oh, yeah. He's a great guy and we crack a beer together once in a while and tell each other lies," he said smiling, still watching Billy Hale.

"Well, this one's pretty special to him."

"How's that?"

"I think he's in love with the victim."

"Really. Are you sure? He's been pretty much a loner for all the years I've known him. She must really be something."

"Well, it seems he's known Julia since his early days in Argentina. Her husband died over a year ago, and he seems to be pretty crazy about her."

"Good for him. I've been a little worried that he was never going to find anyone and settle down. Man needs a good woman. I hope she makes it."

A young sergeant approached them with a stack of papers in his hand, interrupting their conversation.

"Sir, the captain said to give you these," he said.

"Thanks, Tom. I appreciate you double-timing them over to me."

"You're welcome, sir," he replied then walked away.

Edwards looked over the papers and then he grinned.

"Hot damn! They went for it. Let's go see our boy."

Chapter Forty-Eight

They worked on her for several hours before they decided they had done all they could do. Blood plasma was ordered to replace the blood she had lost and she was admitted to Critical Care ICU. Victor had almost paced a hole into the floor outside the surgery suite waiting for the doctor to come out and tell him Julia's condition.

"The bullet went clear through her body. Her shoulder was shattered, but we were able to place a plate and pin the pieces back into position. We found the bleeders so she shouldn't lose any more blood. Her condition is very grave. She was in shock and her blood pressure was practically non-existent when we got to her. I'm sorry but only time will tell if she can pull out of this or not."

The doctor left him dazed, standing alone in the room.

***

Victor was sitting by Julia's bed holding her hand, speaking to her very softly, when Lainie walked in. She looked terrible. She was still dressed in the clothes she wore to dinner and her clothes, hair and face were covered with splatters of blood that had dried to rust colored stains.

"Are you Lainie?"

"Yes. It's not a great way to meet, is it Victor? Julia told me a lot about you," she sniffed.

"How are you doing?" Victor asked. She looked dead on her feet.

"I'm okay. I had to make some phone calls and reassure David that I was all right. Then I had to talk to the police. I can hardly remember anything, it all happened so fast," she paused remembering the horror that had unfolded in front of her just a few hours before.

"How did you get in here past old nurse 'Ratchet'. She made it clear only one visitor at a time."

"I snuck in, what else?"

Victor smiled. Lainie Grant was David Grant's wife and Julia had been trying to make David fall back in love with her. Victor ground his teeth as he thought about it. Now Lainie and Julia appeared to be old, fast friends. He was totally confused. Apparently, Lainie still didn't know Julia was Elizabeth Grant. So, what was going on? When Julia was better, he was going to demand some answers.

Tonight had made it very clear. This had been too close of a call and he needed Julia to know how he really felt about her and nothing was going to stop him from telling her once she regained some of her strength.

"David and Alex are on the way here now. She's done a lot for our family. They want to see her. How is she?" she said interrupting her thoughts. She had tears in her eyes.

"They don't know, or at least they're not saying. I guess she's pretty bad right now. We can only pray that she'll pull through."

"Who did this, Victor? I don't understand. Was she the target?"

"Yeah. We heard he was in town and that he was gunning for her. We just don't know why. I've racked my brain, but it doesn't make any sense."

"Well, she a very nice woman, very gentle, very caring. I can't imagine that anyone would want her dead."

Victor suddenly felt a sense of dread creep up his spine and spread a chill throughout his body while Lainie was still speaking.

He might know someone who might want her dead.

Chapter Forty-Nine

Billy listened quietly to the deal they were proposing. They would take death by injection off the table if he cooperated. He would still get life in prison with no possibility of parole, but he would live.

They had his prints. They could place him at the other murders. Yeah, he was screwed all right. There was no way out. Not this time. He would be stupid not to take the offer. The problem was that he had to give up his source in return for the deal.

She wasn't going to like it.

Chapter Fifty

Julia woke and found Lainie sitting next to her bed.

"Lainie?"

"Yes, sweetie. How are you?"

"I'm not sure," she croaked. "What are they saying?"

"Well, they're saying that you are one damned lucky woman because the bullet just missed one of your main arteries," she smiled.

"Well, that's good, I guess. But what happened? The last thing I remember is laughing with you over something really silly and then hearing something that sounded like a gunshot. Ooooh. I sure don't feel like laughing now. I feel like hell."

"Yeah, you probably will for a while. Your shoulder has had extensive repair. They inserted a plate and had to pin most of it back together."

"So, I was shot."

"Yes. It was a thirty-eight bullet and because you turned away at the last minute, right when the shot was fired, you probably saved your life."

"Joe?"

"You mean Joe, your private investigator, who was also protecting you, which by the way raises lots of questions about why you need a private investigator or someone to protect you - which I will be happy to ask you once you are back on your feet - is at the police station," she said teasing Julia. "They booked the guy who shot you and they're interrogating him right now."

"Why me? I don't understand. I don't really know anybody here," she said softly, her voice growing weaker.

"That's what they're trying to find out, Julia. Don't worry. No one knows the answer and they're hoping this guy can tell them."

"Victor? Was he there? I remember hearing his voice, I think," she whispered very softly.

"Yes, it's a long story which he can tell you later, but right now you should probably rest. He'll be here soon. He had to go with the police. They had a lot of questions for him. It seems this guy they caught was a big time hit man."

"A hit man? Why in the world would anybody hire a hit man to kill me? He must have shot the wrong person."

Julia eyes started to close.

"I'm sorry, Lainie," she whispered. "I'm so tired and I can't seem to keep my eyes open."

"Sleep Julia. I'll be here when you wake up."

Chapter Fifty-One

Billy Hale was being fitted with a wire that would transmit a conversation he would soon have with his employer, the one who had hired him to kill Julia Bertinelli. He had agreed to do this because he didn't want to die. The deal he'd made called for him to wear a wire and to get his employer to make incriminating statements regarding the shooting.

The police would be a short distance away sitting in a van outside the building. They had both agreed on a verbal signal that Billy would use if things went wrong during the meeting. If all went well, they would be charging his accomplice with attempted murder and locking them both away for a very long time.

Earlier, Lieutenant Edwards had spent some time with Victor listening as he gave his theory about a possible suspect in Julia's shooting. He hadn't told Victor, but that was where they were heading right now.

Chapter Fifty-Two

Billy swaggered into NBC studio, 8H in the Rockefeller Plaza, and headed to her dressing room. Whenever security stepped over to him, he walked right past. No one was going to bother him; he looked like he belonged here and he looked too dangerous. He wasn't nervous. It was his life that was now hanging in the balance. She would talk. Oh, she would talk, even if he had to force her to.

"Billy," she cried, when he walked into her room without knocking, "what a surprise. Did you kill her? Is she dead? Tell me man, don't keep me waiting."

So much for making her talk, he thought as the little machine whirled away on his chest.

"Yes, she's dead. I shot her just like we talked about."

"Did she suffer," she said her voice trembling with emotion.

"No. One shot through the heart and she was down. It was quick and painless. She never knew what hit her."

"Good, that's good. Did you leave the evidence?"

"Yeah. I left the letter in her room and I managed to get one into her coat pocket while it was hanging in the hat check."

"Great. Now she's out of the way and Victor is free. Good. This is good."

Suddenly her elation at learning that Julia was dead vanished and she realized that Billy was in her dressing room and that someone might put two and two together.

"What are you doing here?" she hissed. "I told you to never come here. Someone might put us together and figure out that I hired you."

"Well, I had to come. You see we have ourselves a little problem."

"I don't understand..." she said confusedly, looking up at his face.

He was smiling at her when the police burst into the room.

Looking from one face to another, she erupted.

"You bastard. You set me up!" she screamed. "You've ruined everything. You fool."

"Sorry, little lady," he answered. Then he tipped his hat as they carried the screaming woman away.

***

Victor was waiting at the police headquarters. Lieutenant Edwards had called and asked that he come by. He had said he had a few more questions for him.

When Victor was led into an interrogation room, he wondered why and if he was being considered a suspect. But instead, as he entered the room, he stood slack jawed staring at the person who was cuffed and sitting quietly behind the table. This couldn't be the woman who did this, he thought as he sat down in a chair that they indicated.

Lauren Prescott was sitting across the table from him, surrounded by her attorney and several policemen, who were guarding her as well as Billy Hale who sat directly across from her, and next to seat indicated for Victor.

She was still beautiful, in an older woman way, Victor thought. He knew she was the star of "Another Day" and he couldn't begin to imagine what she was doing here and how she was involved. She was dressed in a beige tailored jacket and navy slacks and showed no nervousness, even though she obviously was in a world of trouble, as evidenced by the handcuffs, armed escort and her ankles that were shackled to the floor.

Lauren sat perfectly still, never blinking. Her eyes followed him into the room and rested on his face. She was totally composed as she waited for the process to begin.

"She wanted to talk to you before we finished processing her," Lieutenant Edwards said.

"But, I thought Rosita…" he said lamely staring at her.

"Yes," Lauren said wearily, "that was the way it was supposed to work out, but as you can see it didn't."

"What are you saying?" Victor was confused.

"I'm saying that I'm the one who hired Billy to kill Julia Bertinelli."

"But why. You don't even know Julia, do you?"

"No, but Rosita did," she said.

Victor just stared at her. He didn't know what to say.

"Let me try to explain. Rosita hated Julia. I hated Rosita. She wanted Julia dead. I wanted Rosita dead. Not literally dead, but out of the way. It's simple really. But, the little bitch wasn't going to do anything about it, so I decided to help her along."

"She was in on this with you?" he asked shocked.

"No. No. As much as I'd like to take her down and incriminate her in this, she had nothing to do with it. I figured if I had Julia killed, we could plant some evidence and place the blame on Rosita. Almost worked too. Problem is, I didn't expect our world renowned, star hit man to get himself caught," she said bitterly looking over at Billy.

Billy smiled at her and said nothing.

"But Julia never hurt you and you were just going to have her killed because Rosita didn't like her?" Victor asked incredulously.

"Yep. That was the plan. Rosita was in my way at the studio and I wanted her gone. I heard her on the phone with you when she told you how much she hated Julia and I got the idea."

"Why didn't you just have Billy over there kill Rosita for you?" he said pointing a finger at the man. "Seems to me that would have been simpler than killing an innocent woman."

"Well, you would think that wouldn't you? But, it wasn't that simple. Everyone knew I hated Rosita so if she died by an act of violence, I would have been the primary suspect. This was better. This way no one would have ever suspected me since I didn't even know Julia."

"My God," was all Victor could say, falling back into his chair.

"You have to realize that I was a star until she came. My work was my whole life and she was taking that all away from me. I had to stop her," she whined.

"But, what about Julia?" Victor shouted. "How can your hatred for your co-star be your defense for what you've done?"

"Well, I'm sorry she's dead, now," she said as if that would absolve her of what she had done. Then she unfortunately had to keep talking and add something else. "Of course, if I have to be truthful, I wouldn't be so sorry, if I hadn't gotten caught," she admitted sadly.

The room was stunned into silence.

Billy's face had slowly grown darker and his scowl had deepened as Lauren continued to ramble. So, this is what he had thrown his career and his freedom away for. A stupid, self-absorbed, old woman, crazy jealous over some younger woman - an old, has-been actress who was willing to kill an innocent person for revenge and a job! What was he thinking when he decided to do this? He was so stupid, especially when everything inside him had screamed that he was making a mistake.

"She's not dead, Lauren," he drawled breaking the silence.

"What," she said clearly stunned, "I thought you said you shot her."

"I did. But, I didn't kill her."

"You're telling me that you missed? You never miss."

"No, I didn't miss. At the last moment, I couldn't do it. I had thoroughly investigated her and I couldn't find anything that would make you want to kill her. It didn't set right with me, so I decided to put a bullet through her shoulder, instead. She would be hurt, but if the emergency teams did their job, she wouldn't die. I figured I'd have your money and be out of town before you caught on," he smiled at her, but his eyes were dead and cold.

"Oh, God," she groaned. "You mean I've been blabbing my guts out, and she isn't even dead?"

"That's right, you idiot. But then, you haven't ever been very smart have you?" he said smiling more coldly this time.

"This meeting's over!" Lauren's attorney shouted, slamming his hand down on the table. "Lauren, you are not to say another word. As your attorney I advise you not to speak again."

"Little late for that isn't it, Einstein?" she said sarcastically.

"I told you to be still, but you insisted on unloading. You wanted your conscience cleared. You were going to tell them everything. There was no reason to hold back. 'The woman is dead and they know I killed her.' That's what you said. Remember?" he said angrily.

"I know. I know," she sighed loudly, placing her head down into her hands.

Edwards stood. "Book her, guys, and don't forget to do a really thorough body cavity search. You never know what she might be hiding," he said smiling. Then he added, "I think we're done here." Walking over he shook hands with his men and Victor.

Lauren Prescott whimpered. Then she blanched and started to shake as she was pulled up from her chair.

Billy Hale threw back his head and laughed.

Chapter Fifty-Three

Julia slipped in and out of consciousness during the next several days, but slowly she made the turn back and the doctors agreed that she would live.

During that time, as she drifted, Julia thought about letting go. She had long talks with Roberto while she hovered between life and death. Finally, she knew, like before, that it wasn't her time yet and that she would have to go back. The fear of leaving her family again, had almost broken her heart this time. It was a tremendous struggle to fight through the pain in order to come back to a world that was only filled with tears and heartache for her. The one bright light was Victor. She loved him and she wanted a life with him. The angels smiled at her when she told them.

Three days after the shooting, Julia awoke and found David sitting in a chair by the bed.

"David," she groaned.

"Well, hello there, sleepy head. How do you feel? Do you want anything?" he said smiling at her.

"No. I'm fine. But, what are you doing here?" she said looking around at the room.

"I flew up two days ago with Alex. We wanted to be here for you when you woke up. Alex was determined that she would be here for you the way you were there for her."

Tears stung her eyes. "That was sweet of you. How is Alex?"

"Well, she's outside waiting for her ten minutes with you. I almost had to fight her to get into the room this time. Actually, you have quite a fan club out there rooting for you. You had us all very worried. How are you feeling, really," he asked concerned when he saw her grimace.

"Like I've been shot with a cannon ball," she laughed.

David laughed too. "Right. Well, would you like me to sneak Alex in here so she'll stop worrying?"

Julia reached out and touched his hand.

"We need to talk when I'm better," she said softly.

"Yeah, Lainie told me you were leaving," he said looking down at her small hand covering his.

"David, I'm sorry," she whispered. "I meant to tell you, but..." she trailed off.

"Julia," he smiled a little too brightly, "it's okay. We'll talk but right now Alex is going to kill me if I don't tell her that you're awake. And what in the world have you done to Lainie? She won't eat. She won't sleep. She hasn't left your side since your accident."

"Well, we talked. We laughed. Then we drank a lot of something, cleared the air and drank some more. You know that 'girl stuff' you read about? Well, that's what we did, and, oh yeah, then we bonded," she laughed happily.

David smiled. "Yeah I heard you two were bombed out of your minds. Since neither you nor Alex ever drink, I'll expect to hear all about it when we talk," he teased her. "Now, I'll go and see if I can slip Alex in," he said squeezing her hand.

Julia smiled as he walked away. He was a wonderful man and a wonderful father. Maybe it could have worked out for them if they would have found her sooner, before he had forged another life, but not now. There could be nothing between them now. She didn't love David anymore. He belonged to someone else and so did she.

Brushing away her tears, she tried to compose herself, so she could say goodbye to her daughter, her little girl that she loved with all her heart. This would be much harder because she did still love Brian and Alex. That had not changed and it never would.

"Help me God. Get me through a few more days. Help me to be strong so I can let them go," she prayed.

***

As the door opened, Julia saw Alex struggling as she limped across the room. The pain on her baby's face ripped at her heart.

"Alex," she whispered so overcome with joy at seeing her again.

When Alex reached the bed, she dropped her cane and threw herself into Julia's arms.

"Ooompphh!" exploded from Julia as pain seared through her body.

Pulling away, Alex tried not to cry.

"Oh, Julia, Julia, I'm sorry I hurt you," then she dissolved into a fit of tears.

Julia wanted to hold her, but her arm was in a cast and restrained in some contraption that held it in the air, leaving her incapacitated. So she cursed silently and patted her daughter gently on the back and hoped she could hold back her tears and keep from joining her little girl. If she didn't hold on, she might start wailing herself.

"I thought you might die," Alex hiccupped. "I was so mean to you the last time we talked, and I was so scared, and you looked so pale, and you had that ugly thing on your arm and I didn't want you to die, and they wouldn't tell me anything, then they wouldn't let me see you, and…"

"Alex," Julia interrupted, "do I look like I'm dying?"

"No. Not now," she choked as the tears poured down her face.

"Sweetie, do you remember when you were so sick?"

"Yes," she said blowing her nose softly.

"Well, I faked all of this just to get your attention. I thought it was my turn. Besides, I always wondered what the view was when you were flat on your back," she grinned.

"Julia, that is not in the least bit funny," she said firmly. "You could have died!"

"Yes, I could have, Alex, but I didn't. Now let's talk about something else," she said brightly. "How are you doing? You're walking really well now."

"I am, aren't I," she beamed through her tears. "Thanks to you pushing me like a chain gang boss, and working me until I was almost dead, I'm probably going to eventually walk without a limp," she teased.

"Chain gang boss is it? From your perspective, it must have felt like that, I guess," she laughed.

"No, it was much worse, but I've been told not to use that kind of language."

They both laughed at each other.

"Mom told me that you two talked," she said softly, changing the subject.

"Yes, I made a promise to you, Alex and I meant to keep it. I would never hurt you. I know you love your mother very much," Julia managed to say as her heart spilled over.

"So, you're really leaving and going back to Argentina. I mean you're really leaving," she said sadly.

"Have you ever been there?"

"Where?" she asked confused.

"Argentina."

"No. I always wanted to go though."

"Well, consider it done. Whenever, you're ready, you just give me a call and I'll arrange it. I can show you the country. We'll have so much fun. You'll love where I live."

"You mean it?" she said excitedly. "I can come and see you!"

"Absolutely. Just because I'm going home doesn't mean we have to say goodbye forever," she choked.

"That would be so great. Gosh, wait until I tell Mom and Dad. This way I won't miss you so much when you're gone. I'll know I'll be able to see you again."

"I already told Brian the same thing. I want all of us to remain friends."

"Oh Julia. Forgive me so being so mean. I love you so. Please forgive me," she said starting to cry again.

"Baby. It's already done," she smiled and choked back her tears.

**

Victor came to the hospital every day. They avoided talking about how they felt about each other, but they talked for hours about everything else. Once Julia was listed as stable, she was moved to another room where the restrictions on the hours she could have visitors was lifted. After that, her room was always filled with chatter and she had many long emotional talks with Alex and Lainie, never mentioning whom she really was.

Victor told her the story about the shooting and all about his involvement. Then he told her about Lauren's hatred for Rosita and how that had caused her to hire Billy Hale to kill Julia. She listened intently, asking questions to help her understand how she became the target for a bullet.

"I can't believe that this whole thing revolved around Rosita. Why would she hate me so much?"

Victor wanted to tell her why, but he figured this was probably not a good time, when she was so weak and trying to recover from her wound. He wanted to tell her about his boy, his beautiful boy, and how he wanted to marry her and how the three of them could be a family. It wouldn't give Julia back her children, but together they could help to raise Nicholas and maybe over time it would heal some of the cracks in her heart.

As it turned out later, he would regret not telling her. But, he didn't know that yet.

"Rosita's not the girl we used to know anymore. Luke tells me that she is drinking heavily and that she has turned to drugs. It seems she is her own worst enemy these days. The reasons she has for hating you are complex, and complicated by her drug and alcohol problems," he said hoping to steer her away from the reasons Rosita hated Julia

"I didn't know," she said stunned that Rosita would take up these habits. "Rosita was always so beautiful and smart. I wish I knew what had happened to make her want to destroy herself this way. It's so sad."

She probably wouldn't feel the same way about Rosita, once she knew the whole story, he thought as he looked at her. She was pale, and dark circles were under her eyes. He gritted his teeth together. He should have killed the guy who shot her, he thought again for the thousandth time. She looked so frail and the thing on her arm was horrible looking. I'm going to take good care of you, Julia. When you are better, I'm going to convince you to marry me and go back to Argentina. Nobody's going to ever hurt you again. I promise, he told her without words.

"Why are you staring at me?" she said self-consciously moving her free hand through her hair.

He smiled. "It's a secret. I'll tell you when you're better and don't try to weasel it out of me," he teased.

Julia laughed. "You're crazy, you know that?"

Crazy, crazy about you – that's what I am – crazy, mad in love with you and you don't even know it. How you can't know, when it's written all over my face, is beyond me, he thought winking at her and not speaking.

"Well, with Lauren out of the way, the road should be cleared for Rosita to take over the top position at 'Another Day'. If she's smart, she'll get herself clean and grab this opportunity, " he said changing the subject.

Julia looked at the man she loved and wondered how she was going to tell him how she felt.

Victor looked at Julia and wondered the same.

Chapter Fifty-Four

The headline in the New York Times exploded off the page.

Soap Opera Star Charged with Attempted Murder

"Lauren Prescott, star of the soap opera, 'Another Day' was charged earlier today with the attempted murder of an unknown woman. Ms. Prescott has held the starring role in the syndicated soap for over the last twenty years and had no previous criminal record. The producers of the show stated to reporters that they were shocked, but that they had no further comment at this time. The crime involved a murder-for-hire plot that failed; but did result in the life-threatening injury of the woman who was the target. The victim's condition is still critical at this time. The potential assassin, Billy Hale, a notorious hit man, known in law enforcement circles as "The Shooter", was charged with several felony counts of murder and attempted murder. The Chief of Police, Vincent Carreno, gave a statement several hours ago and said; "The capture of Billy Hale is a real coup for us..."

Rosita set the paper down and picked up her coffee. Sipping it, she tried to understand what had made Lauren go after Julia and what this meant for the show.

Then the phone rang and Victor explained it all to her in glaring detail.

Chapter Fifty-Five

David was waiting for Julia in the hospital lounge when the nurse wheeled her in. They had removed the traction unit from her shoulder and arm, making her more mobile. She was still too weak to walk on her own, but she was getting stronger everyday.

David saw the pain etched on her face as she tried to move her arm, which was covered from the shoulder down to her wrist in a massive cast. It would be several more weeks before it would be removed. She was very beautiful and David felt such love for her, he almost cried out.

Julia's release was scheduled for tomorrow so she had asked David to come to see her so they could talk.

"David, thank you for coming," she said smiling at him. David felt the pain in his chest grow stronger. He knew what she was going to say and he was going to miss her very much. It was truly amazing how much she looked like Elizabeth. The way the light struck her face when she turned a certain way. Her laugh, which he remembered being exactly like Elizabeth's. Their ages appeared to match if he was guessing correctly; so much time had passed since her disappearance. He knew now that no matter what, she did not belong to him. He could anticipate her next sigh, and smile and it left him dizzy with a sense of déjà vu as he flew back in time.

After she was gone, he would have a great deal to make up to Lainie. He had hurt her terribly during the last few months.

"David," she started, "you know that we will always be friends, don't you?"

David groaned. Uh, oh. The "friends kiss-off" talk was the way she was going to handle this. Looking up, he smiled at Julia.

"Sweetie. Let's not waste time with all of that. You're going. I'm staying. It's that simple. I will miss you and I hope that you will miss me."

"David," she said trying not to cry. "If I had met you a long time ago, before life took us off on different paths, before you met your beautiful Lainie, it might have been different for us."

David said nothing.

"I'm sorry," she continued, "if I led you to believe that there could have ever been anything between us."

"Just wishful thinking," he said teasing her. "Kind of a school boy's crush by an old man. It's strange, I love Lainie, and in all this time I've never once considered that I could feel anything for another woman; that is until I met you. And so it seems that you have taken the hearts of all the men in the Grant family," he said, unexpectedly.

Julia blushed. "You've talked to Brian?" she asked hesitantly, afraid of what he was going to say.

"No. Actually Brian talked to me, so stop blushing. He's okay. I'm okay. So, we don't need to talk about it anymore. Lainie and I need to work out a few things, but we'll be okay, too."

"I'm glad David," she said sighing with relief, "I would never forgive myself if I hurt any of you. You're a wonderful family."

"You actually have made us all stronger and Alex would certainly not be where she is now if it weren't for you. We will never be able to repay you for what you have done for us. By the way, I know she gave you hell over me, and I'm sorry."

"Well," Julia huffed, "did your whole family get together and discuss me?" she said offended.

David laughed loudly. "By God, Julia, you are getting better. But, no, we didn't get together. Alex and I had a private conversation when you were so sick. She was distraught that you would die and she wouldn't be able to tell you how much you meant to her."

Julia said nothing.

"We're leaving later tonight."

"Yes, Lainie told me," she said softly.

"We will miss you very much, Julia," he paused. "Now I must go."

Standing up, David came to her then and laid his cheek against her cheek and whispered something in her ear.

Julia almost fainted at his words.

"I know who you are, my little one. Robert told me everything."

Julia said nothing as the tears fell from her eyes.

"Thank you for what you are doing."

Julia sobbed.

"Goodbye, my beautiful Elizabeth. Goodbye my lost love," he said kissing her gently on the cheek. His tears dripped down her face.

Then he turned and walked away. He never looked back.

Chapter Fifty-Six

In the weeks following Lauren Prescott's arrest, Rosita went a little crazy. Her drinking and drugging increased to such a proportion that Luke worried that she might accidentally overdose. The producers of her show had brought her in several times and warned her, but she persisted.

Rosita was tormented. She had pushed the old woman too far and she couldn't handle the guilt she felt. Sure, she would have loved to have Julia out of the way, but she didn't want her killed. Rosita had made Lauren's life hell and she had been so desperate that she had thrown her life and her career away. If Julia had died, Lauren would be facing a death penalty and Rosita would have had Julia and Lauren's death on her conscience. It was all Rosita's fault.

Rosita had tried going to the jail where Lauren was being held, to meet with her. Lauren had repeatedly said no when she got Rosita's request, always saying, "Tell her I don't want to see her. She'll understand why." Finally, one day, to her surprise she had agreed. Looking back, Rosita didn't know what she thought she might accomplish by going, but she needed to see Lauren to try to explain.

The day they met, it was wet and raining. The jailer led her to a small, dark room where he asked Rosita to wait. A short time later, Lauren was brought into the room, escorted by two guards, one on each side of her, who took her to a table, sat her down in a chair, un-cuffed her wrists and re-cuffed them to the chair. Then they placed leg irons on her ankles. She was dressed in a bright orange jumpsuit. Rosita was devastated by her appearance. Her skin was yellow and sagged with wrinkles, her hair stood out in all directions and her gray roots were showing. She had lost a great deal of weight and her eyes were dead in her face.

Rosita burst into tears when she saw her.

Lauren waited and said nothing while she cried.

When she could finally speak, Rosita said, "Lauren, I am so sorry," she stopped, choking on her words. "I never meant for this to happen. I didn't know you were listening when I was talking about Julia and how I wanted her out of the way."

The room was silent. Finally, Lauren spoke in a raspy voice, "Rosita, except for the fact that Julia is still alive and you're never going to get Victor back, you should be very happy. I'm out of the way now and you can be the star."

"But, that's what I'm trying to tell you. I'm not happy. I didn't want you to end up here. I can't stand it!"

Lauren just smiled hatefully.

"I know I was really mean to you, but I never thought that you would hate me so much that you would get involved in something like this."

"I still hate you Rosita. I hate you when I get up in the morning. I hate you when I lay down my head on the flea-ridden pillow here at night. I hate you with my skin, my bones, and my soul. Only when one of us is dead will I stop hating you," she said sweetly.

"Oh, Lauren. Please don't say that. I'm telling you, I didn't want this to happen. Why did you do it? It can't be because you hate me. Tell me it's not because you hate me?"

"Poor, poor Rosita. It's eating away at you isn't it? I can see what is going on here. You want me to absolve you of what happened, it's destroying you and you want me to take the pain away. But I can't. You're as guilty as if you pulled the trigger yourself. You stomped me into the ground. You told me I was ugly and old and then you pushed me out of the studio. You were taking away the only thing I had ever known. You were killing me. You did this, Rosita. You caused it all. You're to blame," she said viciously. Having found Rosita's weak spot, she pushed in her knife and twisted it.

"None of this would have happened, if you would have played fair. But, you wanted it all. There was no room for anyone else. Now you have it and I hope it chokes you," she finished, spitting out the last words she said.

Rosita couldn't speak as the old woman's hatred hit her in the face and tore at her heart. Her pulse was racing. She needed a drink. The room started to spin.

"Now get out of here and don't ever come back. Go be the big star," Lauren hissed.

"I don't want it," she stammered.

"Sure you do. You wanted it so bad that you were willing to kill me for it." Pausing, she leaned her face across the table as close as she could get.

"Mission accomplished, bitch!" she hissed and it was so evil that Rosita fell back into her chair.

"Guard!" Lauren screamed.

She never spoke to, or looked at Rosita ever again. She died of stab wounds inflicted by two other prisoners, who caught her in the shower, three weeks after their visit.

Rosita fell apart.

She drank, she drugged and she screwed. She had black outs where she couldn't remember where she had been. She would wake up and not know how she had gotten there and wouldn't recognize the guy she was with. She could barely get up in the morning and she started to miss work

Luke hovered and made her crazy.

She couldn't stand that she might have been responsible for Lauren's death and the only thing that took the pain away was when she was unconscious.

The producers tried to work around her; the public still loved her. They kept hoping she could turn her behavior around. When Rosita had been pregnant with Nicholas, they had spent months photographing her from the neck up, so the audience wouldn't know that she was pregnant. Now they used diffused lenses and tried to photograph her at her best angle so that the dark circles and lines wouldn't show under her eyes. It was taking more and more time to make her up each day as her lifestyle took its toll on her face. Still they kept hoping. With Lauren gone, Rosita was all they had to keep the show going. She knew it, so she gave them hell.

Victor had talked to her at length and made it very clear that he was in love with Julia. He was disgusted with her complicity in the shooting and blamed her for a great deal of what had happened both to Julia and to Lauren. He had begged her to get help and to stop drinking. She had laughed and told him she didn't have a problem and could lay it down anytime she wanted. He insisted, reminding her that she had a son to raise, and telling her that she was a beautiful, gorgeous woman and asking her why she wanted to throw it all away. When he brought up Luke, it was too much for her and she had hung up on him.

The problem was he was right about everything. Of course, that just made her hate herself more than ever.

Then one day, she snapped out of it. This was not her fault. Stupid old cow had made her own choices. She was not to blame.

Victor was an idiot and couldn't see she was the right woman for him. She was beautiful, desirable and she was a star!

She still drank. She still drugged. And she still screwed, but she didn't have any more black outs and she made it to work everyday.

She thought she had it all licked. She could have her cake and eat it too, but she had forgotten something important.

She had forgotten Luke.

Chapter Fifty-Seven

Julia cried and she would not be comforted. Victor took her from the hospital the next morning and drove her back to her hotel and took a room that adjoined hers. She made only one phone call. It was to Brian. Victor heard her speaking very softly explaining that she was fine and that she would be leaving for Argentina soon. After they spoke, she locked herself in her room. He could hear her crying and he spent night after night sleeping on the floor outside her door.

On the third day, Julia opened the door and smiled weakly at Victor.

"I'm hungry," she said, "maybe we should order something to eat."

Victor ordered pizza up to their room and they ate it sitting on the floor in front of the fireplace.

"Robert told David about me. He gave him the tapes and now he knows everything," she said very calmly.

Victor sat silently staring at the fire. "So that's why you were so upset?"

"Yes."

"I'm sorry, Julia."

"David kissed me goodbye and told me that he knew that I was Elizabeth, and my world spun out of control. I couldn't feel anything but sadness and such loss that I couldn't stand it."

"Julia, I wish I could help. I've had to stand by and watch you put yourself through torture trying to be with your family, but not telling your family who you are, then telling some of your family and not others, crying one time and laughing others, and it's worn you down until the light you carry inside you is almost burned out. You're too thin, there's a haunted look in your eyes, and damn it all to hell," he erupted, "I'm not going to stand by and let anyone else hurt you and I'm not letting you continue this hair-brained scheme for another minute!"

Julia burst out laughing. "Victor, you're so funny."

"Funny?" he shouted. "Listen to me Julia. This is done. I want you to stop all of this. You are not a mountain. You are not made of steel. You can be broken. You're a woman who has limits of what she can take. The human body and the human mind cannot take all this abuse."

"Victor, sit down and come here," she said patting the place beside her on the floor.

He came and she took his hand. "You are the best friend anybody could ever have. You keep saving me. If I try to dig up a grave, throw myself off a cliff, turn into an aging hooker, dress up like a nurse, run away with another man, almost get arrested..."

"Wait!" he said. "I don't know about that one!".

"Really? Well, I'll have to tell you some time. It's kind of a cute story."

"Oh, I just bet it is," he groaned.

"As I was saying, before I was so rudely interrupted, when I'm getting shot down in the streets," she laughed, "somehow you are always there for me."

She stopped and looked at him closely.

Silence hung in the air.

"I'm beginning to think that you're following me, Mister!"

Victor just stared at her.

Then they both burst out laughing.

"Victor, Victor. What would I ever do without you," she said, hugging him to her body. Victor didn't want to let her go but he did. Her arm was still immobile and he was sure it still hurt.

"So you're done crying?"

"Yes."

"You were sobbing your heart out."

"Yes, I was."

"Your ready to move on now?"

"Yes, I am."

"You're really all right?" he asked.

"Yes," she beamed. "I made all my choices and I have to believe it's all going to be okay. I have to trust that there is someone up there," she said pointing upward, "who has a plan for me. Everyone is healthy. Everyone is happy. Mom and Dad are thrilled that I'm back. I can see them from time to time. My children have both promised to visit me in Argentina and I'm through feeling sorry for myself," she declared, still smiling.

"It's not goodbyes. It's all hellos now. Can't you see it?" she said softly.

"You're something, you know that?"

Julia just smiled. She was loved by all of those she had left behind. It didn't matter who she was; they loved her for her alone. Her real identity wouldn't change that. She knew that now. Being on the sidelines of their lives would be more than enough.

"Sure, you're okay?" he asked again.

"Yes, sir! I am," she said, saluting him with her uninjured arm.

"Good. Now how about sharing some of that pizza you're hogging." Julia laughed.

Chapter Fifty-Eight
Washington, D.C

Three weeks later, Julia was back in Washington, sitting in the office of Robert Walker for the second time. He had called her this time and he had been waiting for her when she entered the room. Her arm was in a sling now and it was still painful, but it was healing, unlike her heart. She was still working on that.

They spoke of pleasant things for a while; the weather, how the trial was going, how her shoulder was healing, until they settled down to the real reason for her visit.

"Julia, I don't know how to start. I don't know what to say," he said.

Julia said nothing. She was damned if she was going to help him in any way.

After a long pause, he started again, "Can you ever forgive me Julia? You were right. I am a self-righteous old bastard."

Julia smiled. He had remembered her exact words from her last visit.

"I had no idea what had happened to you. I made assumptions, wrong assumptions, about you, and I am very ashamed. Please forgive me," he pleaded.

Julia didn't respond.

"The tapes were heartbreaking. It's strange, but I could actually understand what Roberto did and what drove him to kidnap you. His love for you drove him to take many things into his own hands. You were helpless. I know that now. Your story was very tragic and I had to stop many times before I could continue listening. I was so wrong about you and why you came here to America. How you kept from telling all of your family the truth, when your first arrived, is a real question for me. I don't think I could have held back. You are the epitome of someone who truly loves someone else – completely selfless with no regard for yourself. I am broken by how I treated you and the words that came out of my mouth. Can you ever forgive me?" he finished choking on his words.

Julia said nothing. Then she erupted, "Why in the hell did you tell David? You had absolutely no right. I shared those tapes with you in complete secrecy. How dare you!" she said raising her voice in indignation.

"Yes, you're right, of course," he said, sitting back in his chair. "But he was suffering so badly that I felt he needed to know how great your sacrifice had been so he could understand that, he too would be asked to make a great sacrifice as well."

"That should have been my choice. Not yours. There was no need for him to make any sacrifice. I was leaving and he didn't need to know the rest," she said fiercely.

"You're wrong of course."

"What?" she asked incredulously.

"You're wrong. David was not taking no for an answer. You would not have been able to persuade him. He would have followed you to Argentina."

Julia was stunned into silence.

"He had made all the plans. Lainie was going to be told that he was leaving her. A dinner had been scheduled for Alex and Brian so he could tell them - notice I said, tell them, not ask them for their opinion about anything - that he was leaving Lainie and that he was going to ask you to marry him. He was going to throw everything away. I couldn't let him do that, not after you had worked so hard to keep the secret from them. I tried to talk to him. He refused to listen."

"What are you saying? Are you telling me that David was going to leave Lainie? And, he was going to tell our children? My God!"

"Yes, well desperate times call for desperate measures. So, I did the most desperate thing I have ever done. I betrayed you and your secret, but I did it because I didn't know what else to do," he said sadly.

Julia said nothing as the words he had just spoken swirled in the room and rang in her ears.

"He told me he was in love with you. That was the hardest part. I knew that you didn't feel the same way. I knew that you were no longer in love with him," he continued. "Too many years had gone by, and there was your love for Roberto when your memory of David was gone, and now there was this other man, Victor. I knew when I saw you and David together, that he was a stranger to you now - that you were trying him back on for size, so to speak, and that he didn't fit you anymore. I knew that you loved the other man. I could see it in your eyes. Tell me I was wrong," he said.

Julia thought for a moment. "No, you were right," she said starting to cry.

"I had to tell David so he would understand the gift you were leaving him. I had to let him listen to the tapes."

"Yes," she said simply, because now she understood.

"We talked for hours after he finished them. He was devastated. Learning what had happened to you all those long years ago, brought him to his knees. After a time though, he understood your pain and the courage it must have taken for you to spend all these many months with your family and never tell them your true identity. Also, Brian's confession that he was physically in love with you decided it for him."

"Oh, God," Julia said thinking about her son, Brian .

"Yes, David was pretty worked up about it all, but he knew that to keep the family together, he would have to let you go."

"Why does this have to hurt so badly?" she sobbed. "Why couldn't he have kept loving Lainie?"

"Oh, he loves Lainie. He knows that now. It's just that he was falling in love with his past. He was trying to reclaim something he had lost and didn't want to lose again. After he heard the tapes though, he knew that the only woman he loved now and owed his allegiance to, was Lainie. He knew then that you were making the right decision."

Julia cried softly.

"Julia, I am so sorry," he said placing his arms around her shoulders. "I know that you made a choice and that you are going to go back to Argentina so that your family can go on with their lives, loving each other. You are so strong and courageous and wonderful that you take this old man's breath away."

"The children must never know," she choked. "Promise me that they will never know."

"David and I discussed Alex and Brian. They will never know and neither will Lainie," he said softly, oh so softly, as he rocked her back and forth in his arms.

When she could speak again, they talked about all those years she had spent in Argentina. They laughed sometimes and grew pensive in others as she walked him through the years, from the time Roberto kidnapped her up until his death. They talked about Roberto's years spent growing up, about the war and what it had done to his family, and finally, the part Robert had unknowingly played in Roberto's grown-up psyche.

Later, Julia left his office. It was dark and the streetlights were burning as he helped her into a cab. He kissed her cheek, shut the door and watched, long after the car had turned the corner and moved out of sight.

Chapter Fifty-Nine
New York City

Julia sat in Victor's office staring out the window at the beautiful view of the Hudson River while he spoke to someone on the phone. His offices were in the south tower of the World Trade Center in lower Manhattan on the 85th floor.

Designed by architect Minoru Yamasaki, it was a modern skyscraper with two commercial office towers and had stunning views. 110 floors, each, sitting on 16 acres, 12 million square feet of floor area housing approximately 50,000 people; they were an architectural miracle. Reaching a quarter of a mile into the air, they were staggering to behold.

On February 26, 1993, a terrorist group had bombed the garage in the lower level of the north tower killing six and injuring one thousand more. Victor was head legal counsel and Senior Partner for World Wide, an international import/export company. There was a great deal of discussion about moving their offices from the twin towers at the time of the attack. They had made the decision to stay. They would not allow the terrorists to force them out.

Victor's offices were lavish and filled with beautiful paintings and antiques he had collected while traveling the world for World Wide.

Staring out the window, Julia smiled. It was a glorious day with clear skies and beautiful white clouds that billowed across the horizon like large puffs of white cotton candy. She focused on the ships moving lazily across the water on their way to a final destination that Julia could only guess at. Maybe they're adrift just like me, she mused. No, she thought again, they have a place to go, a place where someone was waiting for them, anxious to unload their cargo. She had no place to go and no one waiting for her to arrive anywhere, she thought gloomily.

Victor watched Julia as she sat in his office and wondered again at her beauty. She was stunning in a Chinese red sheath that fit her body beautifully. He laughed as he remembered the clothes she had worn over the past year, during her visit to the America. She had probably burned it all, he thought chuckling to himself. Now that she would not be seeing anyone from her family, with the exception of her hair that was still blond, she was back to the old Julia wearing beautiful, classy ensembles that fit her like a glove.

She seemed composed as her eyes wandered around the office and out at the river. Where she got all of her strength was something he could not comprehend. He wanted to take it all away, all the pain, all the loneliness, all the heartbreak of losing her family again, and the grief of leaving them behind one more time. He wanted to give her a life and the love that she was missing so terribly right now. He wanted to fill her up with happiness. He wanted her to know that she was loved. He wanted a family with her. Now that he had a son, if he had Julia, his world would be complete.

He had already resigned his position. During the past fifteen months he had built a beautiful home on the land where he had grown up in Argentina. His property adjoined Julia's so she would always feel at home. He would go back and he hoped Julia would marry him and live with him there. Money was no object. He could afford to retire and spend the rest of his life living with the woman he loved. Nicholas would come from time to time when Luke could get away.

She was troubled. He could see it in her face. Once this call was completed and he re-worked his brief, he would be finished for the day.

Victor's voice murmured softly in the room as he finalized his call and Julia looked up and noticed him watching her. He smiled and his eyes twinkled with some kind of mischief, before he winked at her. Her heart thumped in her chest and she blushed. My God, she thought, I'm acting like a schoolgirl with her first crush on a boy in her class. She averted her eyes away from him, back to the view from the window and tried to still her hammering heart.

She knew now that she loved him. She loved him madly and completely, she thought, breathing deeply and trying to calm her pulse, but it was complicated. Putting aside that he might not feel the same way since they never spoke about it, he also had a life in New York and a prestigious practice with clients who depended on him. She couldn't stay in New York or anywhere else in this country. She knew that now. She was going back to Argentina where she belonged, and try to start her life over. He would probably choose to stay and that hurt so much.

She tried to remember. Did he ever tell her he loved her? She didn't think so. He had told her many times that she belonged to him but was that the same as saying he loved her? Probably not, she sighed sadly. But to tell the truth she had not told Victor how she felt either. Well, it was time, she would tell him tonight at dinner, she thought.

The decision to leave her family had been soul wrenching and it had taken everything she had to pull it off and make herself accept the finality of it. Now, her mother and father would be her only connection to her past life. She would fly several times a year and visit with them. But to the others in her family, she would always be just a friend, an outsider, or, in Lainie's case an unwanted intruder and possible competition. Yes, they had forged a friendship, but it had tight boundaries. Her children would come to visit, but they would never know that she was their mother. The pain of that knowledge was still raw and hurt her deeply. She couldn't stay here and see her family and pretend any longer. Her pain was too new and it was too unbearable. She knew it would surely destroy her if she didn't get away.

Julia was suddenly glad that she had made the decision to accept the dinner invitation Victor had extended earlier today. Tonight she would take the opportunity that the dinner offered, to tell him that she was going back home to Argentina. She might even tell him that she loved him, she thought. Then she laughed gaily which caused Victor to look up from the phone and smile.

Julia smiled back. "You're about to get lucky tonight, big boy," she said under her breath.

***

Joe McGuire was standing at La Guardia Airport, saying goodbye to Julia.

"Joe, be sure you call me after you get settled. I want to stay in touch with you. You never know when I might need to break into a warehouse and steal something, or get shot at and need your assistance."

Joe laughed. "And I also might need you to scare me to death."

Julia smiled. "Yeah, that too."

Grabbing her close, he pulled her into his arms.

"You sure you can get through this? Are you strong enough?"

"Yes, Joe. I'm okay now. My arm still hurts, but I'm fine," she joked.

Jumping back, Joe grew red in the face. "I'm sorry. That probably hurt."

"Yes, but I wouldn't have missed that hug for the world," she said, taking him back into her arms.

"Call me, kid. Whenever you need me," he whispered into her ear.

"I will. Now get going or I'll start crying and have to make a scene."

"God forbid," he chuckled. "I'm on my way."

Julia waved as he walked away, turning back once to salute her. Then hitching up his shoulder strap on the bag he carried, he laughed loudly and said, "Bye, Elizabeth!"

Julia smiled with tears in her eyes.

***

Victor received the phone call just as he was finishing his brief on the Lyman project. Scribbling his name at the bottom of the paper, he scrubbed his face with both hands and contemplated letting the phone ring.

He had dinner plans tonight with Julia. They were very special dinner plans and he wanted to make one stop before he arrived at the restaurant. This phone call might mess up those plans. With a sigh, he realized he probably should answer.

Grabbing the phone and his jacket at the same time, he growled, "Make it quick, I'm heading toward the door as we speak" he said walking around the desk while trying to jam his arms into his jacket sleeves.

"Victor, it's me," Luke's excited voice came over the phone.

"Hey, Luke," Victor said as he stopped walking. "How are you doing? It's good to hear from you. What's up?" Victor said surprised to hear from his friend on a day he normally would not be seeing Nicholas.

"Well, Victor, how would you like to have your son? You know like have him permanently. I don't have much time. If you want him, you'd better get your butt in gear and get on out here to the Teeterboro Airport before we take off!" Luke stammered out.

Stunned, Victor said, "What do you mean, Luke, 'If I want him? Where are you going? Where is Rosita? Has she agreed to let me have him? What the hell are you talking about?"

"Whoa," Luke laughed nervously, "slow down old man. You'll give yourself a heart attack. Yep, Rosita and me, we're outta here. We're takin' off and never coming back. She wants you to have Nicholas. She doesn't want him anymore. So get on down here and get him. We're leaving in less than an hour and then we're off into the wild blue yonder. So if you really want the boy," Luke choked, "then you better get going. You'll never have another chance after today. Times a wasting, old buddy. And Victor," he stammered, "don't let me down, man. Don't be late. I need you to get here pronto!" With those final words he hung up the telephone.

Victor was surprised and shocked. Had Luke been crying or was he drunk? He sure sounded strange; excited and sad at the same time. He stood there trying to understand what Luke had just said and then he decided it didn't matter why.

Jumping up, he erupted in a loud shout! "Yes!" he bellowed. Realizing he still had the phone in his hand, he slammed it down and grabbed his keys.

He was going to have everything he ever wanted, his boy, his love and finally happiness after years of waiting. Julia would understand when he told her if he was late. She would understand and agree that this was the right thing to do.

Racing to the elevator, he glanced at his watch and swore to himself. It was going to be very difficult to get there on time. He would have to break all the speed limits.

"Let the God's be with me," he prayed.

Chapter Sixty
New York City

Luke was sitting in the pilot seat of the cockpit of the Cessna Citation II jet when Rosita came aboard.

"Hey, Hank," she laughed, "you ready to get this thing off the ground, so we can start partying?" Hank was one of her favorite pilots and he was also a fairly good time in the old sack. She had lots of plans for him and his coke. She only had a small amount left and she had used the last she had this morning. Giggling, she weaved up the steps into the plane.

Getting no reply, Rosita opened the cockpit door to see Luke sitting in the pilot's chair with a huge grin on his face. "Hello, darlin'," he said. "Surprised?"

"What the hell are you doing here," Rosita erupted, thrown off balance by the appearance of her husband. "Where is my pilot?"

"Well, it seems old Hank couldn't make it today, so I'm takin his place for this trip," Luke replied still smiling. Listening, he heard the door to the plane slam shut. Never missing a beat, he said, "Well, we better get going, if you're going to make that appointment in L.A."

"God, Luke, what are you doing? This doesn't change anything for us. I still want out and I'm getting out. Why do you keep doing this to yourself? Why do you still want to hang on to something that's dead?" Rosita said softly, feeling just a little sorry for her poor, stupid husband. God he made her sick and he made her tired, so tired. He was always clinging, asking her when she was coming home and looking at her with those big, sad eyes. It was finally getting to her. She was doing this for him, but he was too stupid to know it.

She wasn't happy. No matter how much she drank, screwed, or doped, she couldn't make the terrible feelings go away. She couldn't stand hurting him anymore but he wouldn't leave. She had tried every form of abuse, but he just kept on loving her and staring at her with those big, terrible, broken-hearted eyes.

Where had she gone wrong? Fucking Victor, she thought. It had all started with him and that sure hadn't worked out the way she wanted. He was still in love with that bitch, Julia, and it was as if little Rosita didn't even exist. She thought his son, Nicholas, would make him come to her, but that hadn't worked either. Damn him to hell!

Everything was spiraling out of control now. Her career was taking a terrible downturn and they were all were plotting against her. When she looked in the mirror, she saw the damage that her wild nights were taking. She was forgetting her lines and the make-up just didn't cover her fatigue and tiny wrinkles anymore. She was going to leave Luke so that she wouldn't have to continue to carry that burden around anymore and then she was going to get into rehab and get straightened out.

"Rosita," Luke said, interrupting her thoughts, "I get it. I agree this isn't working for us, but I thought we would make this last trip together, laugh a little, and then go our separate ways. I'm ready to let go now, so don't worry," he finished, looking down at the controls.

"Great," she said, thinking he could screw up a wet dream. Why did he have to come along this time? She needed some coke desperately and now she was going to have to cold turkey it to L.A.! Forgetting all her good intentions, Rosita started mumbling to herself. "Why am I feeling so miserable? Screw them all! I'm beautiful, I'm a star and I need a drink to stop my skin from crawling off my body," she finished suddenly feeling angry with everyone. Then she thought of her son and yelled out to Luke, "By the way, where's the brat?"

Luke cringed and wondered how any woman could not love their child. He loved Nicholas as if he were his own, but Rosita detested the cute, little boy who adored her.

"He's in the back sleeping, sweetie. He was ready for his nap," he said loudly so she could hear.

"Good, I don't want to have to deal with him trying to climb on me and messing up my clothes and hanging all over me with that Mama crap. You brought him, so you take care of him because I don't intend to," she shouted back.

"I always do," Luke whispered under his breath.

Rosita appeared at the cabin door and said, "I'm going to make myself a big drink".

Luke looked at her; he had just started down the runway and said, "Hey, you need to be in a seatbelt. Why don't you strap in up here with me and we can both have a drink as soon as we're airborne? It's a beautiful day and the sky is so clear you can see for miles. It is really breathtaking," he said trying to buy time.

"Luke, go to hell. Don't tell me what to do and when to do it. I want a drink and I'm damned well going to have one whether you like it or not," Rosita said loudly, abruptly turning away.

Luke knew she wouldn't listen, she never did, but he had hoped he would have the plane farther off the ground before Rosita started to drink. Oh well, it would have to do, he thought as he left the controls.

"Till death do us part baby, till death do us part," he yelled over the jets.

"What did you say, Luke," Rosita yelled back as she opened the door to the liquor cabinet. As the hinge unlatched, there was a loud click and in that split second she somehow realized what it meant. She twisted her head in time to see her husband standing in the doorway with a huge smile on his face. "Till death....." he said, and then the ripping explosion blew all other thoughts, words and second chances away.

Chapter Sixty-One

The End

Julia was sitting at Reo's in Spanish Harlem waiting for Victor, when she felt a wave of coldness spread through her body. Something was wrong. A sense of dread swept over her body. Jumping from her chair, she stumbled up and signaled the maitre d' that she needed to use a phone. She had to talk to Victor. Please, she prayed, let this be nothing, let Victor be okay.

***

Victorino Nico Salvatore, or Victor, as everyone called him – though most of them felt his name was too much of a mouthful and wondered what in the world his parents were thinking to put this kind of burden on a tiny newborn baby, smiled at the thought of what his full name had brought him when he was a small boy in school. A very small, shy boy, with big eyes and a bright smile - that was who he was as a child. Those traits had given the other larger and tougher boys the excuse they needed to tease, chase, and brutalize him at every opportunity. But the little, shy child had grown up to be a big, muscle bound, handsome boy by his mid-teens and all of the years of abuse had come to an abrupt stop. Some of those boys, ones who had made him freeze in fear when he came upon them on his way home, were now his best friends today and had been for many years. Of course those friendships were forged much later after he had taught each of them that he was not that little boy anymore. Yes, he was Victorino Nico Salvatore, a big man with a big name, and it suited him. Now everyone called him Victor and that suited him equally well.

Glancing down at the clock on his dash, he grimaced and pushed the Mercedes he was driving to go faster. "Damn", he cursed slapping his hand on the steering wheel. The traffic had held him up and he was running late. Although Luke had promised that he would hold the plane until he got there, he still worried that he would take off before he arrived.

When he received the call from Luke telling him that he should come and this would be his only chance, he knew Luke was asking the impossible. "They better not leave without me," he muttered as he pushed his car a little faster, hoping he wouldn't pick up the police since he was doing over eighty at every opportunity that the traffic afforded him; which wasn't often enough.

As he raced through the Lincoln Tunnel toward Teeterboro Airport, he thought again of how his life was going to change after this day. His son, his son he sang. The love he felt for his boy was a love he had never expected, one that had hit him hard and taken his breath away when he first looked at his little face and held his tiny hand. He was damned if anything or anyone was going to take Nicholas away from him now

Teeterboro Airport was a general aviation facility built to relieve the airport traffic created by small aircraft. The traffic could now be diverted from the larger New York airports, like JFK and LaGuardia, over to Teeterboro. With only two runways, one running northeast to southwest and the other running north to south, the airport only allowed planes weighing less than 100,000 pounds access. Victor knew he was meeting a small jet so this explained Teeterboro as his destination.

.   Victor had never been so excited and he felt very blessed. His heart was soaring. He was in love. He was so in love he was almost sick from it. He knew that the next couple of hours were going to complete his life and give it the purpose he had searched for. He was going to wrap this up, take his son, get his life in order and then finish one last piece of business. And, he was not taking "no" for an answer from Julia this time. Chuckling to himself, he thought about how much fun that was going to be, getting her to agree. Just thinking of her made his stomach turn flips

"That's later," he cautioned himself out loud, pulling his thoughts back to his current mission, "let's get this finished first. I'm coming Nicholas," he shouted. "Daddy's coming, baby!"

Finally, after what seemed an eternity of freeways and off ramps, with signs that promised he would be there soon; he left the road and saw the airport tower and the runway where the small planes were allowed to fly out of New Jersey. A small jet, with its engines running, had started to taxi from the far left end of the runway toward the airport tower. There were no other jets in site, so Victor assumed this was probably the one Luke had told him to meet.

Slamming his car to a stop outside the small gate that led to the private planes and the runway, he spun the car sideways, rocketing gravel up in a violent storm of flying debris. Struggling with his seatbelt, he pulled the keys out of the ignition jumped out of the car, slammed the door, and started racing toward the runway where a small jet was approaching the tower as it gathered speed for take-off.

"Stop," he yelled, as if anyone could hear him. "Come back! Stop, damn you. I'm here like I promised. Luke, it's me, I'm here".

Sprinting toward the runway and the now moving jet, Victor saw the start of the lift-off and he tried to run faster, all the while waving his arms frantically, hoping Luke would see him. "I'm here," he shouted above the roar of the jets, "give me my son!"

At that exact moment, when Victor thought he could have it all if they would only stop the plane, when his whole future hung in the balance, when life was so damned good, a tremendous explosion ripped through the sky, turning the plane into a huge, red-orange ball of fire. The percussion of the blast, like a wall of burning steel slammed into Victor and lifted him off his feet, hurtling him through the air where he was tossed and turned like a rag doll in the powerful fury of the plane's destruction. Finally, there was only the sound of crunching, burning metal bounding and scraping across the runway and the smell of burning fuel.

It was an inferno; devastatingly beautiful from the airport tower - devastatingly destructive, if you were one of the unlucky passengers on the plane.

Victor knew only the fire and pain and the stench of his burning flesh as he fell his final time and surrendered to the darkness that swept down on him.

Then he was back in Argentina and happiness flowed through his body. He saw his mother and father standing near the stream that ran through his family home. They were waving and smiling, and he wondered at how beautiful his mother was after all the years since her death. His father did not look a day older. He moved toward his parents and the bright light that surrounded them. He was filled with happiness so strong it filled his heart to overflowing. He had missed them so much and now the aching in his heart that he had carried since they had been taken away from him eased. "I'm coming," he said. "I'm coming."

Next, Victor saw Roberto standing with his arms outstretched. Roberto, his friend and the man who had been like a father to him when his parents had both died from the fever that swept his country, was beckoning him to come.

Wait, he thought, these people that I love are all dead. Then he realized, that he must be dead too and it didn't seem to matter. Nothing did anymore.

Then he heard her crying and Victor turned back to see her running toward him, begging him not to go. He saw her face, his love, his life, all he had ever wanted in a woman, a lover and a friend.

And as he closed his eyes in peace, he whispered her name one last time…. "Julia".